# FELIX AND THE PRINCE

## A FOREVER WILDE NOVEL

## LUCY LENNOX

Cover Designer: Angstyg - www.AngstyG.com

Cover Photography: Wander Aguiar Photography - www.wanderaguiar.com

Editor: One Love Editing - www.OneLoveEditing.com

Professional Beta Reading: Leslie Copeland (lcopelandwrites@gmail.com)

Sign up for Lucy's newsletter for exclusive content and to learn more about her latest books at www.LucyLennox.com!

❀ Created with Vellum

# CONTENTS

# SERIES NOTE

The Forever Wilde series is set in the same world as the Made Marian series but will feature a different family and locations. It is not at all necessary to read the Made Marian novels to enjoy the Forever Wilde novels.

Felix and the Prince, Forever Wilde book two, can be read as a complete standalone, but if you'd like more Wilde adventures, check out Facing West, Forever Wilde book one, which introduces the very large Wilde family from tiny, fictional Hobie, Texas.

Each Forever Wilde novel tells the story of a different Wilde child finding true love.

Happy reading!

ACKNOWLEDGMENTS

(IT SERIOUSLY TAKES A VILLAGE.)

Chad Williams. For making my dreams come true by sending me a photo of my books in print on the shelf in an actual bookstore and for providing invaluable feedback on Felix's story and making me laugh in the process.

My sister, Bear. For reading, cutting, laughing, slashing, and ultimately helping make Felix a better story as usual. If not for you, I wouldn't have even thought to write a royal romance in the first place.

Andrew and Wander for creating the gorgeous cover image.

AngstyG for making the image into a stunning cover.

Sandra at OneLove Editing for being incredibly flexible, thorough, and sweet.

Sloane Kennedy for being patient with me and not bragging TOO much about having finished four books while I finished just the one.

My family for supporting me even when I said "I'm almost done" ten thousand times and never meant it once.

THE WILDE FAMILY

**Grandpa** (Weston) and **Doc** (William) Wilde (book #6)

Their children:

**Bill, Gina, Brenda, and Jaqueline**

Bill married Shelby. Their children are:

**Hudson** (book #4)

**West** (book #1)

**MJ** (subplot in book #5)

**Saint** (book #5)

**Otto** (book #3)

**King** (book #7)

**Hallie**

**Winnie**

**Cal** (book #8)

**Sassy**

Gina married Carmen. Their children are:

**Quinn**

**Max**

**Jason**

Brenda married Hollis. Their children are:

**Kathryn-Anne (Katie)**

**William-Weston (Web)**

**Jackson-Wyatt (Jack)**

Jacqueline's child:

**Felix** (book #2)

For the sake of being able to write a fictional story about a king, I had to create an imaginary monarchy or borrow an existing one. I did a little of both. Apologies to my readers familiar with Monaco who know my prince isn't actually part of the royal family there. Thank you for suspending your disbelief enough for me to write this tale.

While I have, indeed, traveled to Monaco twice, go ahead and assume most details about the country, especially the government and royal family, are made up. In my Wilde world, Monaco's monarchy includes the expected Monte Carlo area near Nice on the Mediterranean Sea as well as a large swath of land between the Netherlands and Denmark (my apologies to you Germans living there), and several islands in the North Sea. This entirety is known as Liorland the way England, Scotland, Wales, etc. is known as Great Britain.

In actuality, there is no "king" of Monaco. There is a prince because Monaco is a principality. All apologies to Albert Alexandre Louis Pierre Grimaldi, His Serene Highness, Prince Albert II of Monaco.

# CHAPTER 1

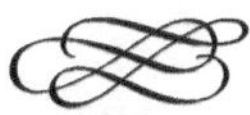

## WILLIAM TRIANNON FREDERIK HARALD CHRISTIEN GRIMALDI OF LIORLAND

"Huh?" I asked, turning over and bumping into a familiar, hairy chest.

The groggy voice behind me spoke again. "It's almost four in the morning. You need to get the hell out of here."

"Shit." I sat up and looked around, orienting myself. I was in my friend Iggy's flat again. We'd been out clubbing the night before. As had become our habit too often lately, we'd ditched the women we'd been dancing with and gone back to his place for a quick fuck.

"Yeah," he mumbled, turning over and presenting his bare ass to me. "I should have booted you out hours ago. If I find the paps on my stoop in the morning, I'll kick your ass. Plus, I have a date tomorrow night with that guy I told you about, so I need my beauty sleep."

I stood up and found my clothes in a rumpled pile by the bed. My phone and wallet were still in the pockets, and I quickly texted my driver to come pick me up by the side entrance to the building and made my way to the door.

As soon as I opened it, a pair of royally pissed-off eyes glared back at me.

*Fuck.*

"Sorry, mate," I muttered to my bodyguard, Jon. "Let's go. Hans is outside waiting."

"Feel better now?" Jon smirked once we were safely behind the tinted glass of the sedan. "All nice and relaxed?"

"Fuck off." I leaned back in the seat and closed my eyes. "You're just jealous you didn't get any tonight."

"Who said I didn't get any?" he joked, quirking his eyebrow and tilting his head toward my sixty-something-year-old driver.

I couldn't help but bark out a laugh. "Right. Hey, Hans, when was the last time you got lucky?"

"Nineteen eighty-seven, I believe," Hans replied wistfully. "Her name was Marbelle."

Jon snickered at me in the back seat while Hans continued. "Way better tits than you've ever had, Jonathan. And the woman could suck—"

"No!" I sputtered. "Please. You've been with me since I was twelve. Jesus, Hans. You're like my grandpa."

"Then maybe don't ask, sir," he replied with a sniff. "And may your beloved grandfather rest in peace."

I thought about my grandfather. Hans referred to him often. Grandpa, King Lior VII, had been one of the greats. An all-around good man and benevolent leader. Smart as a whip and savvy in European diplomacy. I missed him like crazy.

"He's probably not resting at all, and you know it. More than likely he's chasing Grande around heaven," I suggested.

"Your grandmother was a beautiful woman, Lior. I wouldn't blame the king at all for not letting her get any peace up there," Hans chuckled.

The car pulled through the service gates onto the palace grounds and parked in a hidden spot behind a short wall. Jon and I got out and made our way into the royal residential wing.

"Sorry about this," I said again to my favorite guard. "I didn't mean to fall asleep over there—truly."

"One of these days your cock is going to fall off from skank rot." He sniffed and looked down his nose at me as if he was the royal one.

"I'm safe," I said. "And more often than not, I only fuck Iggy as you well know." I was talking to myself more than anything. "I've known him since we were fourteen. I trust him with the *royal scepter*."

Jon ignored the stupid joke and continued his lecture. "Maybe you should stop this hooking up bullshit and find someone. A nice man or woman you can build a life with."

I stared at him like he was insane. "Yeah, right. A man. As if."

He shrugged. "Sir, the prime minister of Luxem—"

"Save it," I interrupted. "I know all about Xavier and Gauthier. That's not the same thing as hereditary royalty, and we both know it. If the next heir to the throne married a man instead of a woman, my grandfather would roll over in his grave along with every monarch before him for a thousand years."

"So, what are you going to do? Continue to sneak to Ignatius's flat when you're a fifty-year-old king?"

I felt my head begin to pound near my temple. It was a subject I'd considered ad nauseam for years. "No. I plan on finding a good woman to settle down with. Someone worthy of being the queen when the time comes. But right now, I'm going to sleep and hopefully not think about it for a few long years since my father is healthier than most men half his age. Good night."

"See you in the morning, sir," he said, holding open the door to the wing holding my private quarters.

Once in my apartment in the palace, I saw my valet sitting at the kitchen table in his button-up pajamas and bathrobe.

"Sir," he sighed. "Don't even tell me. I can smell the club smoke from here."

"Arthur, what are you doing up? I hope you weren't waiting for me. It's late."

"You don't want to hear about what happens to your body when you get older," he grumbled. His hands were wrapped around a mug I knew contained chamomile tea.

"You're forty for god's sake."

"When I see you drag your scraggly ass in from a romp in the Ignatius hay, I feel ten times older."

I kicked off my shoes and reached into the refrigerator for some water. "You're just jealous. He asked about you again, you know."

Arthur's eyes shot up. "Who did?"

"Iggy."

Despite his formal posture, Arthur blushed from his collar up to his hairline. "Dear god, you must be insane."

I shrugged. "He's had a crush on you since we were at Hotchkiss, and you know it."

"Pfft. I wouldn't go near that disease-ridden play—"

"He's one of my closest friends," I warned. "And he's never had sex without a condom in all these years. You know I wouldn't go there otherwise."

His nostrils flared before lifting into the air. "And you think I need your sloppy seconds? I may not be a royal, but I can pull as well as the next guy."

In almost fifteen years of being in service to me, I'd never once seen Arthur with a man. I'd heard rumors, of course. He'd dated a man named Paul for a few years, and when it ended, he hadn't been able to hide his sadness. It had happened not long after Grandpa passed away, and the two of us had bonded over our respective grief: Arthur for the loss of his love and me for the loss of my beloved role model. Arthur had been more than a valet ever since. He was almost a substitute for the warm, easy relationship I'd had with Grandpa.

I bid Arthur goodnight and retreated to my bedroom where I collapsed on my bed and fell into a deep sleep. Two hours later he was back, shaking me out of my dreams.

Before I could protest he said, "It's your father."

I bolted upright, alarm bells ringing in my head. Immediately I remembered a similar morning fifteen years ago when I'd woken to the news of my Grandpa's death. I grabbed Arthur's arm.

"He's okay," Arthur quickly reassured me. "He was experiencing chest pains but the doctor examined him thoroughly and is certain it was merely a panic attack."

I placed a hand over my thundering heart. "Thank goodness."

"He'd like to see you."

"The doctor?"

"Your father. He's summoned you to his room, and you know better than to keep the king waiting."

My head started to pound again.

❧

HALF AN HOUR later I made my way through the bowels of the palace to a specially designed medical bay in the basement. My father had it built years before so the royal family could get treatment without tipping off the paparazzi.

When I arrived, I found my father arguing with his doctor.

"I can't do this anymore," my father mumbled down toward the front of his thin examination gown. "I won't."

"You're fine, Father. You'll be back on your feet tomorrow with meds that'll fix you right up," I suggested. "Maybe you're just too stressed."

Truth be told, inside I felt nothing but a giant sigh of relief at the situation. Thank god it wasn't something more serious. As selfish as it may have been, I was grateful I didn't have to take his place so soon. I wasn't sure who had been scared worse by the situation—my father or me.

As I caught my mother's eyes across the bed, I noticed a slight shake of her head. She didn't look scared so much as… disappointed.

"Maybe it's time, Lior," she murmured to my father. "Tell him."

"This is neither the time nor place, Catherine," he asserted, taking on the persona of strength I was more used to seeing.

My mother looked at me with a kind of sympathetic sadness. "It's time you prepare yourself to take the throne, darling."

I stared at her in disbelief. "It was just a panic attack," I protested. "Lots of people get them."

"He's going to step down," she said quietly. We were the only people in the room, but even so, the news was shocking coming from her mouth. I glanced toward the hallway to make sure no one could have overheard.

"No," I said.

"Son," my father began, "she's right."

"No," I repeated, feeling my heart begin to stutter in my chest. "No. You're fine. It was just a—"

My mother shook her head. "He had a panic attack when he told me he was divorcing me. He's in love with someone else."

The words, spoken by my strong and beautiful mother, almost shattered me.

I stared at them both in stunned silence as my brain struggled to process this information. "You can't." This time it was a childish sound. A plea—a whine even. I wasn't a prince worried about his father stepping down from the throne, but a son blindsided by the news of his parents divorcing. "Please." A whisper.

Neither of them seemed moved by my protest. Their minds were made up. I spun on my father. "Who?" I demanded. As if it mattered. "Who the fuck is worth losing my mother for? Who is worth throwing away the monarchy for? A thousand years of your family on that throne and you walk away for a side piece of ass?" Anger heated and popped beneath my skin, leaving me restless and itchy. It was selfish, I knew. Every single bit of my reaction came from a desperate, almost manic, desire to keep my life from changing so drastically.

My father answered in a monotone. "Eleanor Wu. And I'll not have you speak of her that way."

My mouth hung open as I stared between my parents to see if he could possibly be telling me the truth. Mother's eyes closed with a wince, confirming it.

Eleanor Wu was my age. The grown daughter of my mother's best friend.

My father, the king of Liorland, cheating on his wife with a twenty-nine-year-old flight attendant. For fuck's sake, how did something like that even come about?

But it didn't much matter now. The result was the same regardless of who he was fucking. My father would be forced to abdicate the throne in disgrace once word got out. And word always got out. There was nothing to be done about it.

Then I would take his place. Become the true monarch of Liorland along with all of the duties and expectations therein. As well as the scrutiny. The press would be all over me, poking into every aspect of my life. Any small amount of freedom I'd enjoyed as prince would be over.

I would be the new king.

I staggered back and collapsed in a chair by the door. I was twenty-nine—mature enough to realize my Iggy-fucking days were over. Hell, my days even *thinking* about sex with men were over. There was no way in hell the monarchy could survive two such scandals. Suddenly I was being forced to make the tough decisions I'd been punting all my life. My parents had been pressuring me to choose a wife and settle down, to prepare for the stable life I'd need to have when it was my turn on the throne.

But I'd resisted, still in denial about the conflict between my sexuality and being heir to the throne. If only I had a brother to pass the crown to, but I didn't. I had a younger sister, who'd known from birth that Monaco's Liorland crown passed only to the male heir. As archaic as it was, the rule had been around for a thousand years. Not that it mattered. Henriette was twenty-six and single. She had no more stability than I did.

"And you're willing to throw everything away for her?" I asked my father. "She's forty years younger than you!" I felt my voice rising and clamped my lips tight.

"What's done is done," my mother said stiffly. I noticed she'd barely glanced at my father once during the entire discussion. I hadn't even thought about what this change would mean for her. How much this would upend her life as well. She'd been queen for more than a decade.

"Mom—" I started to say.

She cut me off with a tight shake of her head. "You should get some rest. I'm sure the next few days will be busy for you."

I wanted to protest but I could tell by the rigidity of her shoulders that now wasn't the time. I stood and kissed her cheek. I had no idea what to say to either of them so I just left, saying nothing.

Later that evening, after my mother had reassured the council officials awaiting word about my father's health, she found me sipping a lukewarm cup of tea in the kitchen of their residence. My father was back in his own bed, sleeping soundly while my mother and I were left reeling from the day's revelations. My father seemed to have abdicated not only the throne but any respective repercussions from the decision.

"You all right, darling?" she asked, walking up and cupping her small hand against my stubbled jaw. It was an uncharacteristic maternal move, and I felt myself leaning into her touch.

"No, of course not," I muttered. "It's shit."

"Language, dear," she said out of habit. She sat down on the love seat next to me and let her shoulders slump just a bit. Despite the awful, middle-of-the-night wake-up call she'd had, her suit was still pressed and fresh as if she'd had hours to primp.

"What happens now?" I whispered into the quiet room. "What the hell? How are you even handling this?"

"Does it matter? It's done. She's pregnant. He wants to announce within the month."

*Holy fuck.*

"No," I breathed. "You're kidding. Say this is all a joke."

She shook her head with a small laugh. "I wish."

I clenched my hand into a fist. "That fucking bastard."

Usually she would admonish me for speaking about my king in that way but she remained silent. Which was pretty much confirmation she agreed with me.

I let out a long sigh. "I'm not ready for this," I admitted.

She turned to gaze into my eyes. "It's time for you to grow up and take his place, Lior."

I felt a thick lump form in my throat at the sound of my name. My mother had only ever called me LJ. To her, Lior was a name reserved for the king. My mother, with her American ways, had jokingly referred to me as Lior Junior from early on, while my father and everyone else called me Lio.

"I don't know if I can," I said.

She shifted on the edge of the love seat next to me and sat up straight again, all signs of fatigue slipping away with a clearing of her throat. This was the queen of Liorland in all her glory.

"Whether you can or not remains to be seen, Lior. The fact of the matter is... you *will*."

# CHAPTER 2

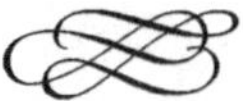

## FELIX

When I woke up, I was pretty sure a band of malicious teens was slamming my head in a door. I heard snickering and giggling, which only made it worse. *Way* worse.

"Fuck," I mumbled. Someone's nasty breath just about knocked me out until I realized I was shoved face-first under a pillow, alone. Which meant it was my own noxious breath, and clearly my head wasn't being slammed in a door. It was a hangover, something I wasn't overly familiar with.

"Fuck." This time it was more of a whimper.

"Open up, buttercup." It was a voice as familiar as a sibling's would be if I had one. My older cousin Hudson was a pain in the ass.

"Go 'way," I croaked. "Dead. Dead and dying."

The door next to me opened more fully. I recognized the furnishings of Doc and Grandpa's bunkhouse and I blinked, trying to remember how I'd ended up here, especially since I had a permanent bedroom in their house as well as my own small cabin on the property. The night before had been the big annual holiday party with all my family and half the town in attendance. I'd probably decided to stay near my cousins by taking one of the beds in the bunkhouse.

I regretted the decision the minute the pillow was snatched from my grip by an overeager morning person.

"Wake up, sleepyhead!" Hudson's smiling face needed to be shot point-blank.

"Fuck."

"Damn. Here I thought maybe you had a man in bed with you. Didn't get lucky last night?"

"Last time I got lucky was three years ago in grad school," I mumbled. "And that shitty Grindr hookup you and West arranged last year doesn't count."

"You said the guy sucked you off," Hudson said with a laugh. "How does that not count?"

"I was too worried about disease to enjoy it. I'd been studying glass disease that day, and all I could think about was the chemical process of crizzling and how it was described as glass syphilis. So I made the guy use a condom, which… just ugh."

Hudson's laugh was way too loud for me, and I groaned.

"Thanks for that mental image. I'm going to try to pretend you didn't say that. Felix, it's after ten. If you stay in bed any longer, you're going to miss breakfast before it's time to drive into Dallas to catch your flight." Hudson sat on the side of my bed and put his hand on my shoulder. "We're going to miss you, you know."

I peeked at him through the tiny slit of one eye. His face was sincere, and his eyes were kind as usual.

"Yeah," I admitted. "It's gonna be weird spending Christmas and New Year's without you guys."

"Grandpa was telling us all about your trip this morning. It sounds amazing. Are you excited?"

I closed my eyes and imagined the two weeks ahead of me. It was time to finish my doctoral dissertation, and I wanted to do it surrounded by the subject I'd spent years researching. In the process of studying art history and the fine art of stained glass during my undergraduate and master's education, I'd become obsessed with discovering the real identity of one of the most mysterious, intriguing glass artists in medieval history.

The unidentified stained glass master of Gadleigh.

Gadleigh Castle was an old historic keep located on a tiny island in the North Sea off the coast of Scotland. Known only for its boutique line of specialty glass, the castle was primarily a summer tourist destination. People came from all over to visit the castle and enjoy the unique colors found in the glass made from the special sand of the island's nearby beaches. The combination of mineral deposits on the island couldn't be found anywhere else on earth, and the glass colors created with it were exquisite.

While the middle of winter was probably the worst time of year to visit Gadleigh, I had personal reasons for going there over the holidays.

Namely, my infamous mother, the award-winning actress Jacqueline Wilde and her looming blockbuster release. Every time she had a film come out, the media descended upon her estranged son, and my life as I knew it disappeared until the press got bored or distracted with another target.

Because of this impending media frenzy, Doc and Grandpa had agreed to fund the final step in the research needed for my doctoral dissertation: an on-site study of the famous stained glass at Gadleigh. It was like a dream come true, regardless of my original reasons for wanting to skip town.

I sat up and rubbed my eyes with the heels of my palms. "Yes, for sure. Very excited. But first, I might need to puke or something," I said in a rough voice.

Hudson put his arm around my shoulders and began pulling me to a standing position.

"Come on, Felix. Up you go. Let's get some pancakes in you, and then I'll help you finish packing. I offered to drive you to the airport, but Doc and Grandpa refused. Apparently they're sending you off themselves even if it means four hours of needless driving back and forth."

I made a quick pit stop in the bathroom before pulling my clothes back on from the night before and following Hudson to the house.

Most of the giant Wilde family was still lounging around the kitchen when I came stumbling in.

"There he is!" Doc handed baby Pippa off to my cousin West before approaching me for a big hug. "Today's the day, huh? Oh Jesus, what did you eat last night?" He pinched his nose in disgust and backed away.

"Chili," I muttered, shooting daggers at Grandpa, who stood behind him making pancakes on a huge griddle. "And like… a million shots of Jager."

"Oh god," my cousin Hallie groaned from somewhere in the sitting area. "Don't even say the word."

I saw a pair of socked feet propped up on the arm of the sofa and assumed they were hers. "You too?" I asked. "Who the hell even brought that crap?"

"Grandpa made the chili. And can we not talk about it please," she whined. "As for the shots, blame my damned sister."

I spied Winnie sitting at the breakfast bar and shot her an accusatory glare. She shrugged and went back to tapping her short fingernails against the screen of her phone.

The television mounted above the fireplace was showing some kind of tabloid news show when Hallie suddenly sat up and reached for the remote.

"Ooooh! There he is. That prince guy," she squealed. "So fucking hot."

I looked up to see who she was referring to, but the video showed only a pair of panda bear cubs.

"What prince?" I asked, grabbing the glass of ice water Hudson had poured for me.

"You know, that hot guy from Monaco who's always in the magazines. The one whose sex life they love to speculate about. He always has some A-list celebrity chick on his arm whenever he's spotted at red-carpet shit. Hey, didn't he go to Georgetown or something? Wish he'd come back to the States. Let us Americans have a chance at him."

Hallie loved pop culture and celebrity gossip. The kind of thing I avoided like the plague.

I ignored her ramblings and turned to my aunt Gina. "What do I have to do to get some of Grandpa's pancakes?"

Doc fussed over me until I had a plate piled high with food. Apparently, most everyone else had already eaten. Aunt Gina sat next to me sipping her coffee, but every once in a while, I caught her peering at me in my peripheral vision.

"What?" I finally asked.

"I'm worried about you," she admitted in a soft voice. "Have you talked to your mom lately?"

"No."

Her arm came around my shoulders and squeezed gently. "Honey, don't you think you ought to let her know where you'll be over the holidays?"

"Why? So she can manipulate me into going on a publicity tour with her? No way."

I noticed Grandpa reach out for Doc's hand as they both looked at me with worried faces. I let out a sigh. "Guys, stop. I'm fine, okay? This is my usual thing. Just let me disappear for the movie release. Otherwise, you know how it'll be. Paparazzi in town, photographers on your front porch, people dogging me for my opinion of her movie, digging into my life. I just... No. Not going to do it this time."

"Is it because of Chris Corbin?" This question was from my aunt again.

"Not really. But that just gives me even more reason to want to duck out, you know?"

Chris Corbin was a notoriously outspoken conservative TV news host who ranted and raved against anything remotely connected to Hollywood. For the past few months, he'd apparently been seen in public with a certain actress on his arm. Why my mother thought dating that egotistical rabble-rouser would help her career was beyond me. And the fact that she was now intimately connected to someone who actively sought to damage the LGBT community pissed me off to no end.

But Jackie Wilde was like that. She did what was best for *her*. She didn't give a rat's ass what it meant to anyone else, including her very gay son and gay fathers.

Doc reached out and squeezed my shoulder with a large, warm hand. "We worry about you, Felix. You sure you don't want us to come with you? I'm a pretty good note-taker."

I snorted. "You have typical doctor's handwriting."

Grandpa let out a laugh. "He's good at rubbing tired feet."

I put my finger to my chin as if contemplating it. "Hmm, now that bears consideration." I winked at my aunt before continuing. "Thanks for your concern, but I'm actually excited to be by myself. I'm going to a place I've only ever dreamed about to study my absolute favorite topic. I promise I won't spend time wallowing in bed. I'll be sketching and photographing as many of the windows and glass pieces as they'll let me, and taking copious notes. If anyone came with me, they'd be bored out of their minds. Not to mention frozen solid."

"Promise me you'll let yourself experience new things, Felix," Doc said. His face was kind and full of affection.

"I will," I promised.

"Sex things," Grandpa added in a teasing voice. "Don't be afraid to live a little, Fee."

I felt my face heat up. "Jesus, Grandpa. I'm going to an island in the North Sea in the middle of winter to study stained glass. It's hardly a club in Amsterdam."

Doc put his arm around my shoulders and leaned his head in as if imparting critical wisdom.

"What happens in Gadleigh stays in Gadleigh. Go have an adventure. You deserve it."

"Okay. I'll think about it," I said, mostly to get them off my back about it. The topic of my love life was one I studiously avoided, primarily because it consisted of a big fat goose egg.

Once my family dropped the subject, I realized I must have done a better job faking confidence than I truly felt. To be honest, I was terrified.

I'd never been so far from home, much less by myself.

As a child, I'd been toted around Hollywood by my young, unmarried mother. Always sitting in waiting rooms or lobbies while she auditioned until she finally got her big break and decided having a kid was crimping her style.

I was nine when I came to live with Grandpa and Doc in little Hobie, Texas. By then, I'd visited a few times and was familiar enough with my grandfathers and their ranch to know I'd enjoy living with them a million times more than in the tiny one-room apartment in Los Angeles with my mom.

It wasn't until much later I learned some of those lobbies I'd sat in were for porn production companies, and my mom hadn't brought me to Hobie voluntarily. Doc and Grandpa had found out what was going on and demanded custody of me.

Since then, the only time I'd been out of Texas was when my mom had tried to lure me back to California as a teenager. After only three months in LA, I'd discovered she only wanted me with her because the man she was dating at the time was casting the next big teen film. My mother had mistakenly assumed that my DNA and looks would be enough to get me the part. Once the callback hadn't materialized, she'd thrown a massive fit and shipped me right back to Hobie.

So that was it. The sum total of my travel adventures. Los Angeles; my hometown of Hobie; Austin, where I'd gotten my undergrad and master's degrees at the University of Texas; and Denton, where I'd begun my doctorate program at the University of North Texas two years ago. Now I was preparing to fly to Europe.

Alone.

# CHAPTER 3

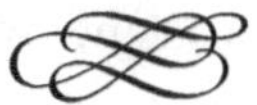

## LIO

Once my father had woken up later in the day, he immediately began voicing his opinions and bossing the rest of us around. When my mom insisted on sending me away for some time to reflect on my upcoming reign, my father suggested heading to the hunting cottage a few hours away.

I shuddered at the reminder of how little he knew about me. My father hadn't exactly been the parental type. He'd been old-school, leaving the raising of the children to my mother and a team of professional nannies and tutors. I'd never really blamed him for being hands-off. I'd assumed it came from long-standing tradition rather than a lack of love on his part, and part of me had known he loved me just fine in his own way.

So when he suggested his favorite hideaway, I tried to see it as a gift.

"You'll love it there," my father said. "Fresh air will clear your head. Prepare you to come back strong and ready to lead."

Instead of correcting him about my chosen location for a hideaway, I simply nodded before meeting my mother's eyes across the room.

"Tell Mari hello for me," she murmured with a nod, acknowledging that at least one of my parents knew the place of my heart.

It wasn't the hunting cottage in the French countryside. It was Gadleigh Castle, far away in the North Sea.

THE GREEN GRASS around the island was patchy with snow as the small jet came to a wobbly landing on the small runway. A sport utility vehicle sat ready to transport my small crew of guards and luggage to the castle itself.

Stepping onto the island was like exhaling for the first time in months. The bite of the salty air, the gray-green chop of the North Sea all around us, the whip of the wind against my clothes, and the crumbly stone outline of the keep in the distance all came together to make me feel like I'd finally arrived home.

*Thank fuck*, I thought to myself as my shoulders relaxed. Since Gadleigh sat on an island, there were no paparazzi, no hidden media cameras, and no meddling family members popping in without prior notice.

It was heaven on earth, and I planned to make the most of it for the next couple of weeks. Too bad I hadn't been able to sneak Iggy away for a last hurrah. But this was a time for coming to terms with a life that would never be mine— having the throne while still being able to enjoy a man in my bed.

I was at Gadleigh to let go of the daydream. It was a shame I didn't have a warm body to sink into while doing it.

"Good afternoon, sir." A familiar face came into view, stepping out of the shelter of the vehicle and approaching me with a hand outstretched.

"Bert, great to see you. How is your family?" I asked with a grin.

"Mari has all but ignored me in favor of you, sir, as well you know. I've gone half-starved these few days since word of your arrival hit her ears. Now that you're here, maybe she'll allow me some scraps from your table."

I couldn't hold back the laugh that bubbled up from my chest, and we shared more barbs back and forth as the luggage was loaded. Arthur scurried around, making sure I had my coat and scarf, making sure the luggage was treated with proper respect, and making sure to scowl at the wind coming off the sea as if it was downright offensive. He fussed at Bert as if the man had never picked me up from the tiny airport before. I caught Bert's eye and winked at him.

Gadleigh's house manager had been with our family since he'd been an under butler in the central palace. Once he was experienced enough to take charge of a royal estate, he'd requested consideration for Gadleigh. Since then, he and his wife, Mari, had made a home here and had cared for the island and its people as if they were their own.

Once we made our way through the small village and onto the estate grounds, Mari was waiting outside one of the castle's side doors with a comforting squeeze.

"Och, my Lior," she tutted. "You're a sight for sore eyes. Come to the kitchens, and I'll make you some chocolate by the fire. Arthur, stop fussing and sit your arse down."

I followed her through the stone entry, noting with relief that absolutely nothing had changed since I'd last been there a couple of summers before. Once we were in the huge open space of the main kitchen, I gravitated toward the set of rocking chairs bracketing the massive fireplace.

"It's good to be home," I told her holding out my hands for warmth from the flames. "But I forgot how cold it is here in December."

"Pfft," she scoffed. "Nothing but a fact to get yourself used to."

"Mother said to tell you hello," I told her over my shoulder. "She knew right away where I was running off to after... everything." So far, the official story of why the king had cancelled some public events, was his suffering from exhaustion. No doubt his publicist was hoping that story would imply what a hardworking ruler he was, always looking out for the people of Liorland.

Just the thought made me want to roll my eyes. Selfish fucking prick.

"Of course she did. A mother knows her son." I heard her gathering the ingredients for the warm chocolate drink she always made me, and I wasn't surprised when a plate of homemade stroopwafels appeared in front of me.

"Oh god," I groaned, grabbing one and biting into it. "You're the best." The caramel-flavored sugar wafer was light and crisp on my tongue. I settled into the seat by the fire, enjoying the hot drink and sweets. When I was done, I peered over at Mari, who'd taken the other chair beside me.

"How are Calum and the glassworks?"

Her face softened. I knew she treated the island's master glass-blower as a son the same way she did me.

"He's fine, yeah. Been working hard on the ornaments line, but that's all slowed down now this close to Christmas. I expect it'll be nice for him to take it easy for a couple of weeks now. Maybe he can show you a thing or two if you're here for a while, but you'll have to ask him. He's got a man here now."

I thought of the forty-five-year-old artisan who was as gruff and impenetrable as the north wind. "A man? What kind of *man*?"

She chuckled and turned to me with a look of slight embarrassment. "No, Lior. Not that kind of man. Holy hell, boy. I only meant a student of sorts. Someone studying the glass. The man is here for a couple of weeks, and Calum has taken him on. A cute one, that. Name of Felix. He's American, like your mother."

"Where's he staying?" I asked. Unease began to swirl in my gut as I thought about an unknown person on the island during my holiday from real life.

"Shh, calm yourself. The kid is as quiet and timid as a mouse, you'll see. Nothing to fear there. He's staying in the carriage house apartment, only comes into the main house to study the glass, you know? And to share a meal if there's one to be had."

I let out a breath. "Okay, good."

Later, as I made my way through the quiet hall toward the royal wing of the house where my bedroom lay, I thought about how much I wished I could simply hide away at Gadleigh forever. I couldn't, of course, but the idea of hiding took root, reminding me of my favorite nook in the castle.

After accompanying Arthur to my room and leaving him to unpack, I stepped to a panel in the side of the wide archway leading to my bathroom. The bathroom had originally been an antechamber of sorts, but when my great-grandfather had visited Gadleigh on a tour of his royal estates in the early twentieth century, he had demanded the royal apartments all be outfitted with the most modern water facilities of the time. The result was fewer rooms in the royal wings but grandiose washrooms for each bedroom. There wasn't a visit I made to Gadleigh Castle when I didn't thank my ancestor for his thoughtful upgrades.

I pushed the panel sideways until the open space was wide enough for me to fit through. Once in the space between the walls, I slid the panel back in place. It wasn't necessary to sneak to my hidden study, of course. But it was a habit born of years of trying to avoid nannies and tutors.

I made my way carefully through the cobwebbed corridors, down a simple and overly narrow spiral staircase, and into a cozy secret room I'd always referred to as the treasury. The space was clean, and wood for a fire was set and ready for me in the small fireplace. Once I started the kindling with a box of long matches on the mantel, I settled back in the overstuffed chair tucked in the corner nearest the warmth of the early flames. As the fire grew higher, the light began to catch the colored glass around the room as hundreds of years of Gadleigh glass baubles spun and sparkled from where they hung along the low, wooden-paneled ceiling.

If Gadleigh Castle was, in some way, the love of my life, the treasury room was its very heart.

# CHAPTER 4

## FELIX

I'd scheduled my trip to include a few days in Edinburgh to explore the St. Giles Cathedral. I thought the famous Burne-Jones window was impressive, but it was nothing like what awaited me at Gadleigh.

In a word, the glass at Gadleigh was breathtaking. Even after three days on the island my head was still spinning. I just couldn't believe I was actually here, surrounded by the infamous stained glass I'd been studying for years. It was both wonderful and overwhelming.

The caretaker, Mari, had taken pity on me the day before and taken me under her wing, feeding me breakfast while indulging my questions about the castle and its history.

I learned that the castle had a total of four hundred and forty-four rooms, and starting today I intended to explore them all.

It was harder than I expected, especially given how many rooms contained glassworks that I couldn't resist taking my time to examine. There were hidden gems among the antique furnishings in almost every room I came across. I'd barely even scratched the surface by the time the sun began to sink into the sea hours later.

Warm bands of orange and yellow light filtered through the large, clear leaded glass panes of the room I was in. It was a small formal salon, with red textured wallpaper on all four walls and gilt-edged furniture organized in a central social cluster. Red and gold curtains hung heavy from large dowels, and thick, silky ropes held them back with long tassels.

I watched the sun drag its stripes across the wooden floor and noticed the inlaid design in the center of the room beneath a dainty coffee table. As I edged carefully around it, I realized it was a crest of sorts. A lion with a large mane featured prominently in the center, and it wore a crown. The jewels of the crown were bits of colored glass, and I heard my own gasp escape as I noticed the colors sparkling in the fading sun.

This was why I'd come. Gadleigh Castle was a treasure trove of hidden stained glass. It was everywhere. A master artisan had spent decades lovingly adding glass flourishes all over the estate back in the sixteenth century.

Up till now, the identity of the glassmaker had been unknown, but I had my suspicions. This was the subject of my dissertation and why I was here. To find the proof I needed to unmask the master artisan to the world.

After several minutes of exploring the small room with my eyes, I knelt down on my hands and knees and ran my fingers over the glass jewels embedded in the floor. There wasn't a speck of dust to be found on them, and I marveled at how lovingly the glass on the estate was cared for. It was Gadleigh's treasure, and someone recognized how special it was.

As I studied the inlaid baubles, my knee slipped on the waxed floor, causing me to lean too heavily on my outstretched hand. The stained glass jewel under my fingers depressed farther into the floor, and I gasped, terrified I'd caused some sort of damage.

I sat back on my heels immediately and stared at the glass piece as it remained a full inch lower in the floor than it had been originally.

*Jesus Christ.* I had just wrecked a five-hundred-year-old masterpiece.

I felt my entire body begin to tremble in shame. How the hell was I going to make this right? Would Calum, the resident glass master, be able to fix it somehow? Would it require work underneath the elaborate wooden flooring? Would it demand some special team of art history preservation experts?

My heart hammered in my chest as I scooted back to get some distance from the elaborate inlaid design before fucking things up even more.

"Fuck. Fuck. Fuck," I stammered under my breath as I tried to calm myself down. I reached behind to steady myself against the wall, only to feel it move under my touch. Good god, was I going mad? Had I just destroyed another part of this historic room?

I turned to see what the hell was going on and noticed a six-inch-wide gap in the red-papered wall. Through the gap, I could see the hint of a soft warm glow of light.

I'd spent enough time in the room to know there hadn't been a door there before. All four walls had been solid with the exception of the door I'd entered through. I glanced back at the glass button on the floor. Could it have been some sort of hidden button?

I carefully slid the panel in the wall closed again, hearing the faintest click as it settled back in place, becoming invisible again as the edges of the panel disappeared in the texture of the wallpaper's natural lines and creases.

After gathering up my courage, I peered back at the stained glass in the lion's crown. All of the glass pieces were level with the floor once more.

*Woah.*

I crawled forward to touch the glass again, pressing down as gently as I could until I felt the button give.

Sure enough, the panel in the wall slid open a few inches.

A hidden room in Gadleigh Castle. Hot fucking damn.

I stood and approached the narrow opening, careful to ease it farther open as gently and quietly as I could. I wondered idly if I was doing something illegal or off-limits. Mari had told me I had the run of the house excluding the royal wing of bedrooms, but did that include hidden passages and rooms?

God, I hoped so.

I glanced through the opening and saw colored bands of light fading in and out across a simple set of bookshelves. Before I knew it, I'd taken a few steps into the room to investigate what was making the light reflect in those familiar colors. I'd only walked partway into the little hidden study when I noticed them.

Hundreds of colorful glass balls hung from the low ceiling. They twisted slowly in the glow from the setting sun coming in through the clear, leaded-glass windows. What hidden room had windows to the outside, and how was it possible I'd never seen these particular ones from the gardens surrounding the house? They were uniquely round and set in elaborate wooden frames with decorative carvings.

The room was magnificent. A hideaway rich with moving glass in every imaginable color. I sucked in a breath and stared in awe at the pieces I'd never in a million years expected to find.

It wasn't until I noticed some of the light in the room was coming from a crackling fire in a stone fireplace that I realized I wasn't alone.

# CHAPTER 5

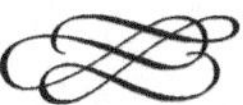

## LIO

I'd been dozing in the comfortable chair by the fire when a slight draft brushed across my neck. I opened my eyes just wide enough to confirm the windows were closed before letting myself drift off again. Not a moment later, the draft grew stronger.

It was the doorway to the State Salon letting in the cooler air of the castle, and I didn't need to wonder how it had opened.

A man stood just inside the open panel and stared in wonder at the treasury glass.

He was slender and young—possibly midtwenties at the most—dark-haired with round tortoiseshell glasses, and cute as hell. Whoever he was, the man was clearly mesmerized by the Gadleigh glass on display in the room. His sudden intake of breath, the pink flush of his cheeks, and the slow rise of his fingers to his lips all came together to make my heart thump. There was something about him that stopped me from calling out to tell him I was there.

I wanted to watch him for another moment before he realized he wasn't alone. Once he saw who I was, he was bound to get all weird around me, and I hoped to put that off as long as possible.

He took another tentative step into the room and glanced across the small space to the round windows beyond. His eyes seemed to take in the craftsmanship of the carvings on the lintel, and his hand came out as if to run fingers over the wood. Something must have alerted him to my presence in the room, however, because he turned and noticed the fire in the fireplace and me sitting in a chair next to it.

"Oh god!" he cried, jumping back and knocking over a small side table behind him. "Oh fuck!" He scrambled to right the table and began babbling apologies.

"I'm so sorry. Oh god, I'm so, so sorry. I didn't mean… I, uh, I was startled by your… and… *oh shit.*" His anguished tone made me want to either laugh or wrap him up in my arms and reassure him it was okay.

His hands seemed to shake, and his breath sped up. He held his arms in front of him like a shield, as if I was going to come at him.

"I'm so sorry," he whispered before stepping sideways toward the State Salon again. "I'll just go."

"Wait," I said. The man froze. "I don't even know who you are."

His eyes widened as he stared back at me, all the color leaching from his face. "Felix. Felix…" It was as if he was going to tell me his last name but thought better of it at the last moment.

"Come here, Felix Felix," I said, unable to stop from teasing the man. "It's okay. Nothing's broken. Relax."

He was wound up as tight as a top.

"I shouldn't have intruded on your privacy. I was admiring the glass in the floor and accidentally pushed the jewel."

Ah, now I understood. I felt my face relax into a grin.

"And were you surprised or freaked-out when the wall opened?"

"Um, both? And terrified?" he admitted with a small chuckle. "I thought for sure I'd broken a five-hundred-year-old masterpiece. I wasn't quite sure how I was going to explain it to Mari."

His face retained the blush, but it was nice to see his lips relax into a slight grin. As much as it shamed me to admit, my first thought at the sight of those lips hadn't been pure. *Those are dick-sucking lips. Red, full, luscious… biteable.*

I swallowed. "She'd skin you alive," I assured him. "Good thing you didn't actually break it."

His horror returned, and I noticed his Adam's apple raise and lower with a gulp.

"I'm kidding, Felix," I said softly. "Why don't you have a seat and warm up? If you were on your hands and knees in the State Salon, you could probably use a moment by the fire. It's pretty drafty in there."

My words replayed on a loop in my head, getting dirtier with every echo. Just the thought of him on his hands and knees mere feet away from where I sat sent all kind of blood rushing south.

Dammit, this was exactly what I'd run off to Gadleigh to get over: my attraction to men. The whole purpose of coming here was to man the fuck up and figure my shit out. And avoid being recognized. So why the hell had I asked this random stranger to join me in my hiding spot?

A faint reminder of my wish to have thinking time *and* sexy time whispered through my thoughts. Hmm, it was enough to get my mind racing.

Felix's dark eyes glanced at the chair next to mine. "Are you sure? It does feel good in here. Nice and warm. And the glass... it's exquisite."

I held out my hand to gesture for him to take the seat while I stood up to slide the panel to the salon closed again to help trap the heat in the small room. Once he settled in the chair, I noticed him let out a breath. "Thanks," he murmured, holding out his hands to the flames. His fingers were long and slim, and I couldn't help but imagine what they'd feel like skating over my skin.

We sat in companionable silence for a few minutes before he spoke again.

"Do you live here?"

Was he kidding? Didn't he know I lived in Monte Carlo? Where else would the prince of Monaco live?

"I... ah, no. Not really. I spent my summers here as a child though. It's my favorite place on earth."

Felix glanced around the room again with the same awestruck expression on his face. "I can understand why. It's amazing. This entire place is like magic. You're lucky to have spent so much time here. Do you know someone who works on the estate or something?"

He looked at me with such innocence, I realized there wasn't a hint of recognition on his face. Was it at all possible he didn't know who I was?

"Yes," I said, clearing my throat. "My family has ties to the estate. Now Mari and Bert put up with me from time to time whenever I need to escape for a little while. They're a bit like an aunt and uncle to me."

It was the truth, although clearly not all of it.

"Wow. That's incredible. You're so lucky."

I swallowed a laugh before it could come out. Lucky? In some ways, hell yes. I had money, security, parents, friends, an education. But there were many things I didn't have that others did. Privacy, freedom to choose my own way in the world, and the luxury of spontaneity.

"Yes," I murmured, bringing a mug of tea to my mouth. After taking a sip, I realized I was being rude.

"I have a kettle in here. Would you like some tea? I'm afraid I don't have any milk or sugar though."

His grin was smirky, and I raised an eyebrow in question. "Why are you looking at me that way?"

"Tea? That's very British of you even though you sound American."

"I'm neither, but I'll admit to having an American parent," I said with a wink. "And I studied at Georgetown University in Washington, DC, after going to American boarding schools."

"Ah, that explains the accent, then. Where are you from, if not England or the States?"

I studied him for a moment, trying to discern if he was putting me on. "I live near the border of France and Italy on the Mediterranean," I hedged.

"Isn't that where Monte Carlo is? How very James Bond," he said with a twinkle in his eye. "Have you ever spotted fancy yachts or met any movie stars?"

If he was putting on an act of adorable naiveté, he was damned good at it. But something in him tensed at the mention of movie stars, as if he hadn't meant to say it.

"Yes, that's where it is, and yes, I've seen both celebrities and fancy yachts. Enough to sink the proverbial ship. How about that tea?" My hope was to distract him from the subject of home.

"Sure. I'll try it. Mari offered me some yesterday, but I declined. Maybe I need to bite the bullet. When in Rome and all that."

I stared at him. "You've never had tea?" Now *for sure* he was putting me on.

His laugh was quick and easy. "Yes, I've had tea. Just not *hot* tea. Not much use for it in Texas."

I moved to the small corner of the room where I had a kettle plugged in and a box of my favorite teas. I selected a holiday mix I thought he might like.

"Where in Texas are you from?"

"Tiny town a couple of hours outside of Dallas called Hobie. Its only claim to fame is being located on a large boating lake. We get heaps of tourists in the summer."

"Ah, so you're familiar with yachts too, then," I teased.

He laughed, and I was struck by how relaxed he seemed around me. It was unusual for me to meet someone new who didn't treat me with kid gloves.

"Yes, but we call them jon boats," he said. I could tell he was messing with me, but his face began to pink immediately as if he couldn't believe he'd had the guts to tease me. Was he flirting with me?

I adored flirting.

"Hm, that's strange. I had a friend at Georgetown who was from Alabama. I could have sworn he said jon boats were crappy little things used for fishing."

Felix chuckled and turned his face away to hide his deepening blush. Oh god, the man was cute enough to eat.

I handed him the ceramic mug of tea I'd steeped for him and made sure he had to brush my hand with his when he took it. His face was still flushed, and his eyes widened up at me when our skin touched.

There was no mistaking the slight hitch of breath that came out of him. And if my ears hadn't heard it, my dick still would have.

*Well... Fuck. Me.*

# CHAPTER 6

## FELIX

I hid behind the thick mug as if it would be able to block my flaming face from view. The gorgeous man in the magical hidden room was turning me into jelly. I was a sucker for a handsome face, and his... *his* was almost regal in a way. Strong features, a prominent square jawline. Thick, dark hair with more than a day's worth of sexy beard growth. Confident body language in spades.

The man was like a grown-up version of me. Or who I'd be if I gained forty pounds of sleek muscle, matured about eight years, dressed in elegant but comfortable clothes like a Polo model, had mesmerizing blue eyes instead of shit brown ones, and finally got some poise.

It shouldn't have turned me on, but fuck if it didn't. He was dreamy as all hell. The kind of vision that made me seriously consider maybe I'd entered into a fantasy when I'd stepped from the salon into the hidden room.

"You never told me your name," I said in a voice too squeaky to ever be considered mature.

His intense cobalt eyes bore into me for a moment before he spoke.

"Leo."

"Ah, like the horoscope sign," I said. "You weren't born in August by any chance, were you?"

*Shut up Felix. Jeez. He'll think you're a moron.*

His face softened. "No. And I spell mine differently. L-I-O." He seemed to continue studying me as if waiting for a reaction.

"I like it. It suits you." I felt my face warm again and moved my chair back from the fire a little. As if it had been the flames heating my face rather than the intensity of Lio's gaze. "I guess the polite thing to do would be to ask what you do for a living." *Could I be any more awkward?*

Lio seemed to have mercy on me and leaned forward with a sparkle of mischief in his eye. "Why don't we try something different than the norm? What's your favorite vegetable?"

I thought for a second. "Zucchini. And you?"

"Hmm, I do like that one, but I'd have to go with artichoke."

"Dammit, can I change my answer? I love artichokes. My grandfather makes the best ones," I said, thinking of Doc's steamed chokes with homemade dipping sauce.

He shook his head, laughing. "Nope. You had your chance. Now you ask me something random."

"Okay. Let's see… Stuck on a deserted island or a snowy cabin in the woods?"

Lio made a show of looking out the windows and gesturing around us. "Deserted island, of course. And you?"

"Snowy cabin. Although, now that I'm here, I can see the allure of a deserted island for sure." I took another sip of my tea and tried to enjoy the nutmeg spices I could taste in it even though I'd decided I wasn't a fan of hot tea. "Your turn."

"Dresser or bureau?"

"What?"

He smirked at me. "My American friends seem to interchange the words, and I've never understood it. The chest of drawers you keep your clothes in. What do you call it?"

"Dresser, I guess. Although I've actually seen classified ads listing it as a 'chester drawer,'" I said with a laugh.

"No way. That's awful."

"That's Texas," I corrected. "What do you call it?"

"I don't. I have a wardrobe." His grin was cheeky and accompanied by a wink.

*Oh god. That wink. Kill me now. I might as well offer to suck his dick and get it over with.*

"Um, oh. Okay," I stammered, trying so very hard not to actually offer to suck his dick. "I-I didn't, uh, think of that."

He reached out to put his hand on my arm. "I'm teasing, Felix. We call it a chest of drawers."

I looked away, pretending to study the rest of the small room around us but really trying to pull myself together. I wasn't sure I'd ever been alone with someone so beautiful and elegant before. At least someone I wasn't related to. My grandfathers' words about indulging in a sexy adventure rattled in my head, making my face heat even more.

"You okay?" he asked. "I didn't mean to embarrass you, Felix."

The sound of my name on his tongue made me shiver. I still couldn't look at him.

"Are you cold? Maybe you should move back by the fire," he suggested. His voice was still quiet and low as if he was worried a louder sound might scare me off.

"I'm really hot."

*Oh god.*

He barked out a laugh. "Your lips to god's ears, man."

"No. Oh god. I didn't mean it like that," I groaned. I risked a peek back at him and saw a gentleness to his features despite his smile.

"I don't bite," he said. "Come back, please."

If I came any closer to him, I'd spontaneously combust. Instead, I shot out of the chair and lurched toward the carved windows.

"Tell me about your beautiful wood," I suggested.

There was a beat of silence as my words echoed around the small space.

I let out a breath and decided to admit defeat. I just wasn't cool enough to hang with this gorgeous man. Too much pressure to be someone I wasn't. I was completely out of my element. Plus, a man like him would never be attracted to a geek like me. It was a classic case of the quarterback taking interest in the band geek or math tutor. It just didn't happen in real life.

"I think I should go," I said with a wince. "Before I say something even stupider."

I heard him stand from his chair and approach me. My body was still angled toward the window so I didn't have to look at him, but as soon as I felt his large presence behind me, I slumped forward, bending my shoulders in and crossing my arms around my stomach.

This was so damned embarrassing. I honestly wasn't used to meeting new people. I spent most of my days alone with research books and my laptop or in a glass workshop. Why did I even accept his invitation to sit down for tea? Maybe a part of me had thought this was an exotic escape from reality where I wasn't the same introverted nerd I was at home. But it wasn't.

"Felix." The deep voice behind me made me want to whimper and beg. I'd never noticed how sexy something could *sound* before.

I shook my head and let out a chuckle. This entire situation was ridiculous. I was playing at living out a fantasy when, in reality, fantasy Felix turned out to be just as awkward and geeky as real Felix. "I'm a huge dork. Really. It's lucky I didn't break anything. I should really just go. It was nice to meet you, Lio."

I turned to make my escape and came face-to-throat with him.

"Fuck, you're tall," I blurted at his shirt collar.

"And you're adorable as hell. Have dinner with me tonight."

I leaned my head back to look at him in shock. "Are you crazy? Didn't you hear all the shit I just said? I'm a hot mess."

"You're fun."

"I'm awkward," I corrected.

"You're genuine," Lio said with a grin.

"You're insane. Are you looking for trouble or something?" I asked, noticing a seriousness behind his teasing.

"No, but I think I found it anyway. Meet me in the kitchen at seven o'clock, Felix. Dress warmly."

I shifted sideways to make my way toward where I remembered the panel opening having been. There was no obvious way to open it back up, though, so I stood there like an idiot trying to figure it out.

When Lio leaned around me to reach for one of the glass balls dangling above, I caught a whiff of his scent. He smelled like a hint of spicy aftershave mixed with the clean sea air and nutmeg from the tea he'd made. It was a unique combination I knew would always remind me of this bizarre moment in a hidden room at Gadleigh Castle.

As the panel slid open and I stepped forward into the colder air of the red salon, I heard Lio's voice behind me.

"Seven o'clock, Trouble. And don't forget to bundle up."

I nodded, but I didn't look back in case he'd be able to see the gigantic loopy grin on my face as I walked away. Maybe Grandpa and Doc were right.

It was time for an adventure. Of the sexual variety.

# CHAPTER 7

## LIO

I knew I was an idiot. And it wasn't like it was the first stupid thing I'd ever done. I was the king of stupid things. Or, as the press had called me on a few occasions, the Prince of Stupidity. It was a title originally coined by my sister and overheard by a reporter when I was sixteen. They'd relished being able to use it since then, and unfortunately, I'd given them many chances, especially every time I left the club with multiple hookups. If only they knew half of that shit was for show. Being seen with women was the best way of hiding the fact I was with a man more often than not.

But I justified my dinner invitation to Felix by acknowledging I was technically the host of the estate while I was there. It was my house after all. And while I was in residence, it was only polite to invite my guests to dine with me.

There was a tiny little problem though. If I had any hope of continuing the ruse of not being anyone special, I needed to get a few people on board with the plan.

I quickly made my way down to the kitchen to search out Mari.

"Lior, would you like something to eat?" she said as soon as I entered the cavernous space.

"No, thanks. At least not right now. Are you making something for dinner?"

She stared at me with daggers. "You ask me such things. Since when have I not fed you, Your High—"

"No! Shit. Jesus. Shhh," I squawked, looking around. "Zip it with the honorific, please."

Her eyes widened.

"Why are you even calling me that? You never say that shit to me," I accused.

"Because you were acting high-and-mighty, and I was reminding you that I've never let a royal—"

"Zzzt," I snapped again. "No mention of royal, please."

"William Triannon Frederik Harald Christien, what the hell has gotten into you?"

I clenched my teeth together and thought of how best to approach the topic. Before I had a chance to say anything, my bodyguard Jon came in.

"There you are, sir. I was looking all over for you."

I rolled my eyes. "Can we... Listen, is there any way we could all agree to put the whole..." I glanced around to make sure no one else was in hearing distance. "*Royal* thing away for a few days?"

They both looked at me like I was crazy.

I continued. "No 'sir,' no Lior, no prince or highness crap. Just Lio, plain and simple."

"But, sir," Jon began.

I held up a hand to stop him. "You work for me, right?"

"Yes, sir."

"Then you have to do what I say, right?"

"Unless what you say puts you in danger..."

"Then I insist you stop calling me anything other than Lio while we're at Gadleigh."

Mari looked at me with suspicion. "What's going on? What's gotten into you, boy?"

"I just want a break from it, okay? This is the closest I ever feel to normal. I want to leave all that shit behind for a little while." I pulled my upper lip between my teeth for a beat. "Okay?"

Jon studied me before responding. "Yes, s... Lio."

"Thank you." I turned to look at Mari. "And can you tell Bert also, please? And spread the word to the household staff?"

"If that's what you want," she huffed. "But if *I* was prince of—"

I cut her off. "You're not."

She glared at me again. "And you'd better thank your lucky stars for that one, kid."

I leaned in and kissed her on the cheek. "Thanks, Mari. I owe you one. Now, about dinner..."

AFTER ARRANGING EVERYTHING, I headed up to my rooms to shower and dress.

Arthur was there, reading the paper in front of the fire while griping about the cold wind coming off the sea.

"This is why I wanted to go to the Maldives, but no, you wanted to come to Gadleigh," he muttered. "Well, I hope you're happy."

"I am, as a matter of fact. Happy and hoping to get lucky tonight."

He folded the newspaper down and stared at me. "I beg your pardon?"

"I met someone."

He looked around behind himself as if there were sexy men hidden somewhere in the room. "Where?"

"Here. Downstairs," I said. "You should have come with me. Maybe he would have flirted with you instead of me. You snooze, you lose."

"I was hardly snoozing. I was *working*. You know, that thing some of us do for money."

"Pfft. Working is for losers. You should quit that boring crap," I teased. He was the most pampered man who worked in the palace, and he knew it.

"Don't think I haven't dreamed about it on occasion. So, who is this lucky local?"

"Not a local. He's an American. And his name is Felix. He's here studying the glass, and he's cute as hell."

Arthur rolled his eyes. "Glad you have your priorities straight, sir," he said, before leaving my room in the direction of his own.

That's when the stupidity of my actions hit me full force.

I'd escaped to Gadleigh to spend some serious alone time thinking through my future. The future that demanded my playing the role of dutiful king with a queen, an heir, and a spare. Not a string of secret hookups with men.

By the time seven o'clock rolled around, I was antsy as hell. My brain flipped back and forth between wanting one last fuck with an attractive man and trying to convince myself it was time to be done with foolish ways.

The fling argument was made in a voice that sounded suspiciously like Iggy's while the foolish warning was spoken in the voice of my father.

Both voices fell silent when I saw Felix approach the kitchen. He was wide-eyed and clearly nervous. He walked into the space as if ready to ask permission simply to exist in this world. Something about him made me want to kiss his vulnerability right off his cute fucking face. I wanted to hand him the keys to the kingdom—to tell him it was my house and he was as welcome in it as anyone.

But of course, I didn't.

"Hey," I said, low enough to avoid startling him. "Here comes Trouble."

He smiled shyly.

"Hey. I… um, is this okay?" He gestured to the thick dark sweater he wore, gray wool trousers, a heavy dress coat, a gray-and-black striped scarf hanging loose over his coat's lapels, and a hot-pink beanie perched on his head.

"Your hat is pink," I said, feeling my heartbeat speed up at the incongruous color topping an outfit of black and gray.

Felix's face began to match his hat. "My grandfather made it for me. His color choice was… let's just say, he was trying to make a point."

I strode closer to him and reached out to wrap his scarf properly around his throat.

"And what point was that?" I felt him shudder at the sound of my voice and wondered if I'd be able to walk to the door with a semihard cock.

"Real men wear pink," he said in a small voice.

"They do, indeed. Had you not known that before the hat?"

"No, I… I just prefer to keep a lower profile. You know, stay out of the way and try not to attract attention."

After reaching out to tuck the ends of the scarf into his coat collar, I kept my hands on the lapels. "Felix, no matter how hard you try, there's no way you'd ever fly under the radar. Nor should you. You're stunningly beautiful. Even in a bright pink hat. *Especially* in a bright pink hat."

His eyes darted to the ground behind the dark frames of his glasses. "Well, thanks. But I don't feel comfortable when people notice me."

"Why not?"

His eyes flicked back up to me accompanied by a hint of a smirk. "Because then they flirt, and then I try to flirt back and end up saying stupid shit."

I barked out a laugh. "You weren't wrong earlier. I do have some beautiful wood. In fact, I'd be happy to show it to you later."

Felix groaned and stepped back, forcing me to let go of his coat as we shared a laugh. I was happy to see him able to take my ribbing and even caught him shooting me a teasing glare in return.

"I hope you like stocafi," I said, picking up the picnic hamper Mari had prepared for me.

"I hope I do too," he said. "What is it?"

I gave him an exaggerated expression of shock. "You've never had it? How have you lived? It's the principal dish of Monaco."

His grin was devilish. "I guess I've been too busy living off the principal dish of Texas."

"Beer and peanuts?" I winked at him and gestured for him to follow me to the door.

Felix chuckled. "Close. It's chili. My grandfather has spent the past couple of months torturing us with different recipes. He tried to win a chili cook-off."

"You talk about him a lot. He must be a good man."

I led him outside to where Bert had left the utility vehicle for me. Jon sat in the back seat despite my refusal to have him join us.

"Get out," I grumbled to him.

"No, sir...reee Bob," he replied, catching himself but sounding like a fool in the process. "I'm coming with you to see the ah... sights."

Felix looked at me in confusion.

I cleared my throat. "Felix, this is Jon. My... friend. He's..." I felt my teeth clench instead of growling like I really wanted to do. "He's a little needy. Doesn't like to be alone."

Jon scoffed and looked away, mumbling.

Felix shifted uneasily on his feet. "That's fine. I don't mind. The more the merrier, I guess?"

He was obviously trying to be polite to put Jon and me at ease.

Before turning on the utility vehicle, I leaned in to whisper in his ear. "Thank you for understanding."

As we made our way along the gravel paths toward our destination, I noticed Felix looking out to sea. Darkness had come hours before, but the moon was bright on the choppy water.

Once we pulled up to the old stone structure perched on a small cliff overlooking the sea, Felix turned to me with excitement dancing in his eyes.

"What is this place?"

"A dovecote, originally, but now it's a bit of a picnic shelter for tourists in summer. There's a fireplace inside we can use to warm up so it won't be quite so bad."

The wind coming off the water was biting through even the thickest coat, and I knew once we were inside the shelter of the dovecote, we'd be somewhat protected from it.

I grabbed the picnic basket from the rear seat next to Jon and reached for Felix's hand.

"Come on, let's get you out of this wind."

Once we'd entered the round space through an old wooden door, I heard Felix take in a breath. He spun slowly around, trying to make out the features of the place in the dark. I handed him the small flashlight I'd stashed in my pocket.

"Here, turn this on, and I'll get the fire started."

There were cement benches around the edges of the circular enclosure, and two wooden picnic tables sat abandoned in the center. I made my way over to the large stone fireplace and lit the kindling that had already been laid. Once it caught, I added a few small logs from the wooden bin off to the side and watched as the fire began to grow.

"Where did your friend go?" Felix asked from over my shoulder. I turned to look at him and saw worried creases between his eyes. "Do you think he's okay?"

I glanced behind Felix through the giant open windows and saw Jon walking a perimeter around the dovecote. He'd have known to wear high-tech warm gear and would be sufficiently supplied with a thermos of hot drinks from Mari.

"He's fine. He just hitched a ride out here so he could brood along the cliffs like some romantic hero," I joked while lighting some candle lanterns around the space. "Jon just went through a bad breakup. He wants some time to himself but doesn't want to really be alone. Does that make sense?" I hated lying to him, but I couldn't bring myself to tell him Jon was my bodyguard. Not only did it make me feel weak, but it would also reveal my true identity. I wasn't quite ready for the wall that would go up between us when Felix learned who I really was.

He followed my gaze and noticed Jon making his way along the footpaths surrounding the dovecote.

"He's kind of odd, isn't he?" Felix murmured. "Poor guy."

"Yeah, well. Aren't we all?" I threw a couple more logs onto the fire before retrieving the picnic basket and bringing it over to one of the tables closest to the fire. "Have a seat and let me show you what I brought."

While I unpacked a tablecloth and plates from the basket, I noticed

Felix wrap his arms around himself in a kind of hug. I stopped what I was doing and sat next to him.

"You still cold?" I asked gently. "We can go back if—"

"No!" He seemed to realize how loudly he'd spoken and softened his voice. "No, this is good. It's… special. I am still a little cold, but I don't want to go back, Lio. Please."

I noticed his warm hat had ridden up over his ears, and I reached out to pull it back down again on both sides. His eyes widened in surprise at the gesture, but I felt him lean into my touch nonetheless.

His dark eyes drew me in, and I marveled at how sexy a man could be in eyeglasses. There was something about those tortoiseshell frames that set off his dark hair and dark brown eyes. His lashes seemed obsidian and endless. I realized I was staring.

"You're sexy as hell," I admitted in a low grumble. "The things I want to do to you…"

His eyes widened comically farther, and his lips parted in surprise. "Me?"

How could he not know? "Of course you. Who else?"

"But I—"

I cut him off because I just couldn't wait any longer. I slid my hand around to cup the back of his head and leaned forward to taste his lips.

# CHAPTER 8

## FELIX

Surely I was dreaming. I'd landed on an enchanted island and straight into a fairy tale. Either that, or things happened very, very differently in Europe than they did at home. Because this kind of thing didn't happen in Hobie, Texas.

My breath caught in my throat as the tip of Lio's warm tongue teased the edges of my lips.

"Oh god," I groaned. While my lips were open, he took the opportunity to slide that tongue inside my mouth, and I completely melted against him.

My cock was rock hard despite the cold, and I realized there was very little cold left in the stone room around us. The entire space had been heated up by Lio's passionate attention. My face felt like it was on fire, and my heart thundered in my chest. Desire pulsed through my veins while I wondered idly if it would be okay if I climbed directly into the man's lap. Or mouth, or body...

"You're so fucking sweet, Felix," Lio murmured as he moved his kisses across my cheek to the side of my neck. One of his hands cradled the back of my head while the other grasped the scarf around my neck and pulled me closer to him. "And sexy. Want to fuck you."

I whimpered a little and winced before letting out another whim-per. *Dammit, no one wants to fuck a whimpering douchebag.*

"You're driving me crazy with those noises," Lio mumbled as he nosed my scarf away and nibbled on my neck.

"Sorry," I said through labored breaths. *I knew it. Stupid whimpering.*

Lio pulled back and studied me. "Sorry for what? Do you want me to stop?"

"What? No. *No!*" I winced again at my loud cry as it tore through the air. Why the hell did I need to sound so goddamned desperate? *Um... maybe because I am so goddamned desperate?*

Jon came storming into the room. "What's wrong?"

At the sound of the man's deep voice, I jumped and clutched at Lio's coat. He pulled me against his chest and turned to Jon with a frown.

"We're okay. Everything is fine," he told Jon in a soothing voice. The big guy studied the pair of us as if looking for signs of trouble.

"You sure, Your Hi..." He seemed to grit his teeth before continu-ing. "Hi... hidey-hole is warm enough? It's awfully cold outside," Jon stammered.

Lio's eyes narrowed at him. "Is that right?"

Jon rolled his eyes before grunting and turning around to walk back outside.

I looked up at Lio. "What was that about?"

"He's protective."

"And weird," I muttered under my breath. Lio laughed and squeezed his arms around me before dropping a kiss on my head and letting me go.

"Let me get something warm inside you."

I gulped. *Surely he didn't mean...*

"This is like a fish stew," Lio said, pulling a container out of the basket.

*Oh right. Something warm like soup.*

"It smells good," I said with a cough. "What's in it besides fish?"

"Tomatoes, garlic, onion, black olives. All the good stuff," he said with a wink in my direction. The wink made my heart do little twirly things.

"Sounds delicious. You said it was a Monaco specialty?" I wondered if I sounded as awkward as I felt.

"Yes. And this is a recipe that has been in my father's family for a very long time. Mari has made it for me for years."

I helped him unpack the supplies from the basket and set out soup bowls, spoons, and water bottles.

"There are only two of everything," I said with a frown. "What about Jon?"

"He already ate."

Something about the Jon situation seemed off to me, but I didn't dwell on it. I inhaled the steamy aroma of the soup as Lio ladled it into the pair of bowls on the table, and I moaned after bringing the first spoonful up to my lips.

"This is amazing," I admitted. "Beats the hell out of chili any day."

Lio laughed and settled onto the bench beside me. We still wore our bulky coats, but as the fire took hold in the nearby fireplace and the warm soup hit my stomach, I realized I could take off my hat and scarf. Lio did the same.

"I brought some wine but didn't know if it would make you too cold," he said. "Would you like some?"

"No, I'm good with the water and coffee. I'm kind of a coffee junkie if you want to know the truth."

"Is that right? Why is that, do you think? Just like the taste of it?"

"No. Well, yes, I do. But I got addicted to it when I started graduate school. I was juggling two specialties—art history and glassmaking. All the time spent between the library and the studio meant little time left over for sleep."

"Mari told me you were here as a student. Are you studying Gadleigh glass as part of your master's?"

"My doctoral dissertation," I corrected. "I finished my master's a few years ago."

Lio set his spoon down and shifted until he was facing me. "You're pursuing a PhD in glassmaking?"

I felt my face heat up with embarrassment. "It's actually a PhD in chemistry. My hope is to teach at a university as a professor instead of a TA."

"Why would a chemistry professor come study at Gadleigh?"

"Well, the study of chemistry is part of glassmaking, which is my real love. The chemistry of the different minerals creating the various colors of glass. Gadleigh boasts the most unique sand mineral combinations on the planet. It's one of the reasons Gadleigh is known for its glass. It's always been a dream of mine to come visit the island in person and study the glass up close. I'm kind of a stained glass nut."

Lio's face relaxed into a smile. "Well, then, you've certainly come to the right place."

"Right. And that's why I made the mistake of pressing the jewel in the floor earlier today. I couldn't keep my stupid hands off it," I confessed. "It's just so… exquisite."

I found myself gazing past Lio's face into the warm light of the fire. The colors of the flames were their own study in chemistry, and I began to babble.

"The gold that's prevalent on the beaches here makes the most amazing shade of rose. But when you combine it with the neodymium, you get a completely different result. The fact that the island is controlled by a singular owner who won't allow the gold to be mined for its cash value means it can go into the glass. Obviously, it's rare to get glass with gold used in its coloration. That's one of the reasons Gadleigh glass is so unique. And there's also erbium here, which was originally discovered in Sweden. That gives the glass a lighter pink coloration than the gold."

"Go on," Lio said, encouraging me. "Tell me more."

Rather than second-guess myself, I took the opportunity to talk about something I loved. "These beaches have magical sand," I explained with a grin. The subject made me a little giddy. "It's like a glassmaker's wet dream. So, one of the main ways of coloring glass is by adding metal oxides, which absorb certain wavelengths of light. Manganese, one of the metals found in the sand here, can be used to achieve a lovely purple color. There's also a coloration process using heat treatment to create colloidal properties. The colloidal properties basically scatter light in the glass to cause the color effects. Then a third way of coloring glass is simply to add already colored particles to the glass. Milk glass is made this way by adding tin oxide."

"What got you interested in stained glass originally?"

I thought about the first time I'd ever noticed stained glass and felt a chill come over me. Despite the warmth of the fire, the fullness in my belly, and in the mug of hot coffee in my hands, I shivered.

"I saw some as a child and just… fell in love I guess," I said quietly.

Lio's large hand came up to pull one of my hands off my mug and enclose it in his warm grip.

"There's a story there, Felix. What is it?" he asked.

I shook my head and cleared my throat before looking back at him and trying to hide my sad memory with a smile.

"Doesn't matter. Anyway, my grandfathers always encouraged my love of it. So when I went to college, that's what I studied. My under-graduate degree was in art history with a minor in chemistry. Then I got a Master of Fine Arts in Glass. Now I'm finishing a doctorate in chemistry. Kind of geeky, I know." I chuckled and shrugged. "But there it is."

Lio's thumb caressed the back of my hand as he peered at me with his intense blue eyes. I could tell he wanted to push me on the story I was obviously hiding, but in the end, he didn't.

"Why do you want to teach instead of make glass?"

"I'm not good enough to make a living as an artist. If I want to be around stained glass, there aren't many options. Glass preservation would require lots of travel. I'm a bit of a homebody normally. So teaching is the natural place for me to end up. Chemistry, art history, glassmaking… any of those things, really. As long as I'm able to keep studying and appreciating the glass, I'm not picky about how. My grandfather gives me hell about not making more glass, but… I don't know. Honestly, I'm happy just being around it."

"You've mentioned your grandfather before. I take it he's been important to you?"

This time, my smile was genuine as I thought of Grandpa and Doc. "Both of them, yes. They raised me from the time I was nine."

His lips turned down. "What happened to your parents?"

"Um, I never knew my dad. And my mom sort of... decided it would be better for her to pursue her career unencumbered by a kid." I didn't dare mention who my mother was. The last thing in the world I wanted was that weirdness that happened whenever someone realized who I was.

Lio's other hand came up to cradle mine in both of his. "I'm sorry."

"Don't be. It was definitely for the best. Doc and Grandpa were... *are* amazing. They're funny and smart, sweet and caring. I loved growing up with them. They're still my greatest champions."

Lio smiled at me. "Tell me about them."

I felt my entire body relax and my mouth turn up. "Doc was married when he was pretty young. To a woman, I mean. They had several kids before my grandmother passed away. When Doc hooked up with Grandpa, they raised the kids together. Grandpa was a rancher, and Doc was the family physician in town. So when I moved in with them, it was onto a ranch."

"You grew up on a Texas ranch? How the hell did you wind up going into academics?"

Lio's teasing grin washed over me, and I felt myself relax even further.

"I know, right? People in Hobie think I'm a little nuts," I admitted. "Hopefully I can get a teaching position at UT Dallas or University of North Texas. Otherwise, I'll have to leave all my family and move for the job. In addition to my grandfathers, I have a bunch of cousins in Hobie and Dallas whom I adore." I gazed at Lio's deep blue eyes. "Do you have siblings or cousins?"

"I have a sister," he said with a smile. "Typical sister. She drives me crazy."

"What's her name? Do you live near her?"

He seemed to hesitate before answering. "Henriette—Hen—lives close to me in Monte Carlo." I sensed his body tense up and wondered if his sister was a sore subject.

"You don't have to tell me about her if you don't want to. I didn't mean to..."

"It's fine. I like talking about Hen. She's actually very funny and sweet. She's my best friend."

We continued talking while we finished the dinner he'd brought for us. Once we were warm, Lio had opened the bottle of white wine and poured us each a couple of glasses as we kept finding things to talk about. Getting to know Lio was easy and relaxing—way less stressful than I'd anticipated. Something about him tamped down my shyness and put me at ease. We talked about everything from family members, to embarrassing moments in college, to our favorite binge-worthy movies and shows.

At one point, he told me about serving in the French army.

"Why the French army if you're from Monaco?" I asked.

"The French military defends Liorland. We don't really have our own armed forces," he explained.

"What did you do while you were in?"

"I was part of a division that provided support to global health initiatives in war-torn countries. Basically, we protected the doctors and nurses trying to help the civilians caught up in the fighting."

"Wow. That must have been both horrible and amazing," I said, imagining the evils he must have seen during that time.

"Witnessing innocent bystanders hurt because of political shit going on without their input was heartbreaking," Lio said. "Especially the kids. Seeing children growing up in a town that's been decimated by bombs and starvation, lack of clean water or medical help... it's devastating."

"I can't imagine. How long did you stay in for?"

"Only three years. I was able to leave early to work directly with a global children's charity."

"And what do you do now? For a living, I mean?"

His eyes shifted to his hands, where he twirled the stem of his wineglass. "I work for the government. And I still try to spend as much time as possible supporting that charity."

"That's admirable, Lio. One of my grandfathers is a doctor and would love to hear more about your experiences. He works on some of our local rural health initiatives for children living in poverty. Even though he's retired, he still volunteers for projects when they need him. Things like vaccinations during flu season and helping with wellness exams before each new school year."

Finally, I remembered his poor friend outside, wandering the cliffs in the cold December night.

"Shit, your friend Jon!"

"He's fine."

"He's got to be frozen solid, Lio. Maybe we should head back so you can put him to bed," I suggested.

Lio's blue eyes smoldered at me. "I'd rather put you to bed, Felix."

I felt my heart lurch into my throat and my cock hop in my pants. Then my mouth just fell open and out came stupidity. "Oh… um… yes, please? That would be nice. Good. I mean… yes. Please."

*Way to stay cool, Felix*, I thought.

Lio's eyes lit up in a predatory glint. "Then it's settled. Let's pack up so I can get you into bed."

My stomach nearly fell to the floor, and I wondered if I'd be able to even walk as far as the vehicle parked outside. A stupid gathering of brain cheerleaders shook their asses and cheered loudly in my psyche. *Gonna get fucked! Can I get an F? Can I get a U? Can I—*

"Felix, you coming?"

I shook myself out of my mental pep rally to glance at him. He stood by the wooden door with the picnic basket over his arm. At some point he'd managed to pack everything up and douse the fire while I was mentally calculating the distance between the dovecote and naked time.

"Hell yes."

*I am definitely coming.*

# CHAPTER 9

## LIO

I'd tried to tell myself hooking up with Felix was some kind of last chance intimate connection with a man, but the more time I spent with him, the more I realized sex might not be enough. He was interesting in a way I hadn't come across before. His entire face lit up when he talked about glass, and passion simmered under his skin anytime I got near him.

I wanted to fuck his brains out, but I also wanted to hear more about what made him tick. He had intellect and a kind of sweetness I was unused to seeing in anyone I partied with. Maybe it was simply that I'd never really given anyone the chance. I didn't date, really. I hooked up. I was beginning to realize there was a noticeable difference between the two.

Despite Jon shooting me evil eyes the entire drive back to the castle, I was giddy with excitement. The voice of reason had long since deserted me, leaving me free to anticipate sex with Felix. I kept trying to remind myself it could only be physical. Two men using each other to meet some needs. It wasn't like it was even possible for there to be more between the future king of Liorland and a small-town Texas college professor. But I couldn't help the twinge I felt in my chest every time I thought of using Felix for sex.

I really liked the guy. He was cute and smart and sweet. I had to admit, the fact he didn't know who I was checked a major box in the pro column of whether or not I could get away with sleeping with him. Not that I thought he was the type to sell me out to the tabloids, but I'd learned early on, looks could be deceiving when it came to who one could trust not to blab to the press.

After we ditched Jon and the picnic supplies in the kitchen, I grabbed Felix's hand and led him toward my royal bedroom. It wasn't until we were halfway up the stairs that I realized he'd know a visitor, no matter how close to the family, would never sleep in the royal apartments. Plus, how the hell would I explain having a valet?

Without realizing it, my feet stopped midclimb.

"What is it?" Felix's voice sounded unsure. "Lio, if you don't want to..."

I turned to look at him, our hands still clasped together. His gaze had darted down to the floor, and I could see the pink tips of his ears. He thought I'd changed my mind and didn't want him anymore.

I reached out with my free hand to tilt his chin up.

"Oh, I want to, Felix," I murmured in a low voice. "Never doubt how much I want to. I'm just wondering if you'd be more comfortable in your own room."

I leaned in and distracted him with a line of soft kisses to his jaw to keep him from overthinking why I'd changed our direction so quickly.

"Oh. Ohh. Yes, that's... oh." He began to tremble under my touch as I slid both hands to his hips and moved him back against the heavy wooden handrail of the massive staircase. "So good," he groaned. "Please don't stop."

"I love the noises you make, Felix," I grumbled. "You're making me hard as a damned pipe." I grabbed one of his hands and held it against the front of my pants so he could feel me. His sharp intake of breath made my cock even harder as his slender fingers tested the hard length under my fly.

"Fuck," he gasped, hot air wafting over my ear. "Oh fuck, Lio."

"Invite me to your room, Felix," I coaxed as my hands slid down to cup his firm ass through his soft wool trousers. "Want to see you naked. Want you underneath me. Want to make you come screaming my name."

His entire body shuddered as he groaned again. I moved my mouth back up to his and nibbled hotly on his lips. They were full and warm, perfect for spending hours licking and teasing.

"Mm-hm," he hummed against my skin. "My room." His mouth opened for more kisses before continuing. "My room and the naked. And the screaming," he murmured. I wasn't sure he was quite with me any longer. He seemed fucked out already, and we hadn't even taken the first stitch of clothing off.

I released him and stepped back, keeping my hands on his hips to steady him. "Lead the way, Trouble."

WHEN WE PASSED back through the kitchen on the way out the side door, Jon's head snapped up in surprise from where he sat by the fire trying to warm up.

"Where are you going, sir… *Certainly*, you're not heading back out now?"

The rule for the royal guard on my watch duty was that as long as we were in the same building and it was deemed safe, he didn't have to stay in the same room with me. He could hang out nearby and wait until I needed to leave the house before joining me.

But Felix's guest quarters were across one of the gardens and above the carriage house.

Fuck. This was going to be a problem.

"I'm fine. I'll see you in the morning," I tried.

His eyes narrowed as he began to sit up straight in his chair. I felt Felix tense next to me, and I scrambled for a way out of the confrontation that was brewing with my bodyguard. I could ask Jon many things, but I could not ask him to break protocol. He could lose his job.

"Jon, why don't you walk with us to the carriage house? There's a… a really interesting chair you might want to see there."

After the words were out of my mouth, I felt my back teeth clack together in frustration. *A chair? Really, Lio? Christ.*

"Sure thing, *Lio*," Jon said with a smirk. He reluctantly unfolded himself from the cozy chair by the fire, causing me to feel a twinge of guilt for making him get up. I reminded myself that there was a very comfortable sitting room in the carriage house that he could hang out in and do… whatever it was he did when he was waiting around for me. It wasn't like waiting on me was anything new for him, but I still felt guilty about it.

After entering the small stone building and leaving Jon on the main level, we made our way upstairs to the guest apartment.

Once the door to the small suite closed behind us, Felix turned to me with wide eyes.

He was nervous.

I reached out to cup the sides of his neck gently and rubbed my thumbs along the angle of his jaw. "Hey, if you've changed your mind, that's okay," I told him softly. "I don't want you to do anything you don't want to do."

His nostrils flared and his eyes heated up. The sudden pique made my heart speed up. The man was adorable anyway, but when he was annoyed? Fuck, he was irresistible.

"What makes you think I've changed my mind? I'm not a kid, Lio. Just because I'm smaller than you are and… and… I don't know. But don't treat me like a stupid farm boy from some… some…"

I couldn't help myself. "Ranch in Texas?"

His eyes rolled behind his sexy glasses, and he threw up his arms. "Why do people think I can't handle shit? It's annoying as hell. Just because I'm from a small town—"

"Woah," I said, holding up my hands in surrender. "I never said you couldn't handle shit, Felix. I only wanted to check in with you to see if this was still okay."

"Of course it's okay," he snapped. "Why wouldn't it be okay?"

I bit my tongue to keep from laughing. He was so fucking cute, but I didn't dare tell him that.

"If I'm being honest, you look a little freaked."

"I *am* freaked."

His words froze me on the spot. "Why?"

Felix narrowed his eyes at me. "Because you're you and I'm me. Because this doesn't happen in real life, so I'm wondering what the deal is. When is the other shoe going to drop?"

"What doesn't happen in real life? Sex? Hookups? Jesus, Felix, tell me you've had sex before." The words were out of my mouth before I realized how condescending they were. "Wait."

Instead of the scream of annoyance or demand to exit the premises I was expecting, I was attacked by a hot Felix, intent on sucking my tongue out through my teeth.

"Mmpfh!" My arms went around him to keep us from falling over backward as his body landed against my chest. His legs wrapped around me, and his arms pulled tightly around my neck. Once I realized what he'd done, I moved a hand under his ass to steady him and couldn't help but sneak a few grabs at the delicious roundness there.

Felix ripped his lips off mine long enough to mutter, "Yes, I've had sex, you jackass," before diving back in for more. "Stop talking. That's the problem here. The damned talking."

His mouth tasted like heaven. Like wine and spices and himself. His body was warm through his clothes, but it wasn't enough. I couldn't feel his skin. I desperately needed to feel his skin.

"Clothes," I managed to get out between kisses. "Off."

His entire body was trembling in my arms, and it made me even hotter for him. He was the most responsive man I'd ever been with, and we hadn't even gotten to the good stuff yet. How would he sound when I slid inside his body? How would his breathing hitch and his pupils dilate? I felt my own muscles begin to shake.

His slender legs tightened around my hips, thrusting his hard-on against my belly.

"Oh god, Felix. I have to get you naked. Please," I begged.

"Bedroom," he said between sharp pulls of breath. "Let me down. I'll show you."

Of course, I knew where the bedroom was already. It was my damned house. I'd had friends stay in the carriage house apartment before and knew every inch of it. Instead of letting him down, I walked with him still clasped to me.

His lips traveled down the side of my neck in openmouthed kisses.

"You smell good enough to eat," he murmured against my skin. "It's been driving me crazy all night. When you were sitting next to me at the table, I wanted to jump you right there."

I closed my eyes for a moment to suck in a breath and get my bearings. "Why didn't you? Jesus, Felix. You should have. It took all of my self-control not to grab you and kiss the hell out of you."

He pulled back and grinned at me like a cat with the cream. "Really?"

I rolled my eyes as I stepped through to the bedroom. "Yes, really. Are you truly so blind that you don't know how sexy you are?"

"I might be cute in a nerd way, but it's never been the kind of attractiveness that gets the attention of a guy like you. You know, the hot guys. The popular guys." His face began to blush as if he realized he'd admitted an inner thought he'd meant to keep secret.

"Liar," I said, tossing him down on the bed. "Take off your clothes."

Without looking away from my eyes, he began to unbutton and unfasten.

I stood stock-still, watching. His long, slender fingers carefully removed his glasses before lifting the soft sweater over his head and dropping it on the floor next to his bed, leaving only a soft undershirt covering his trim muscles. Felix was a smaller guy, smaller than I was anyway. But his clothes had clearly been hiding a nice toned body.

I watched his rounded shoulders move and his small biceps flex as he crossed his arms to pull his undershirt off.

As the cotton moved across his stomach, it revealed the shallow ridges of ab muscles with a dark, delicious happy trail bisecting the lower bumps.

"Good god," I said under my breath.

Felix's eyes were still locked on my face as he lifted one eyebrow. "Is this a solo strip show, or were you going to participate?"

I wondered if drool had escaped the corner of my mouth. "Um, if it's all the same to you, I'd like to watch."

He barked out a laugh, startling me out of my reverie and spurring me into action. I quickly shucked off my own clothes, realizing the sooner I was naked, the sooner I could slide my naked self along Felix's naked self.

As his fingers toyed with his belt, I felt my cock grow even harder than before.

The leather slid through his fingers slowly, like the worst kind of tease.

"You're growling," he said with a smirk. "I like it."

"You're teasing me. Take it off, Felix, or I'll take it off for you," I growled.

His chest raised and lowered faster while his fingers fumbled to remove the leather strap from around his waist. Once his belt was gone, he flicked open his fly, revealing a bright pink pair of boxer briefs.

"Oh god." I quickly grabbed for my cock to squeeze it into submission. "Real men wear pink underwear too, huh?"

# CHAPTER 10

## FELIX

I was sure my face matched the color of my underwear by now. I shrugged and admitted the truth. "I wasn't expecting anyone to see them."

Lio's eyes rolled back in his head with a groan. "You're killing me, Felix."

I felt the corner of my lip tip up. "Well, I *hoped*, but I wasn't *expecting* it," I clarified.

He smirked and slid off his trousers until he was standing beside the bed in nothing but a pair of sexy-as-fuck black briefs doing very little to conceal a giant, intimidating package.

His olive-toned skin seemed to go on for miles, and the dark hair on his legs continued up a slim trail from the waistband of his briefs to his navel. He was a goddamned Greek god.

"Jesus fuck," I muttered. "I'm leaving the rest of my clothes on. Matter of fact, I'm putting some extra back on. Where's my suitcase?"

Lio's eyes sparkled at me. "No you're not."

I looked up at his face. "Yes I am. I can't compete with all that..." I gestured wildly at his entire body. "All that... that... You know, all *that.*"

His laugh was a sexy deep rumble that went straight to my gut and down to my groin.

Lio crawled over me on the bed on his hands and knees. "All *that* wants desperately to get inside all *this*," he said in a silky voice. His eyes roamed slowly over me before his mouth dropped to run the flat of his warm tongue up my happy trail.

I could see the muscles shift and bunch under the skin of his shoulders. The firm, round globes of his ass in those black briefs could be seen above the strong plane of his back.

"Fuck," I breathed. "Do I have to get naked to enjoy all *that*?" My hands skimmed across his shoulders and down to his shoulder blades.

"Mm-hm, you sure do," he rumbled. His scratchy chin dug into the skin above the waistband of my underwear and began to shove it lower, exposing the top of my pubic hair. "I'm going to suck you off, Felix. I can't do that with all this fabric still in the way."

Lio was deliberately teasing me with his flirty, sultry tone of voice. Out of the corner of my eye, I could see my own chest and abdomen heaving up and down as I struggled to suck in enough air to stay alive.

I'd never been so turned on in my entire life, and I still had on my fucking pants.

*Oh god. What if I come before you get my pants off?*

I didn't realize I said it out loud until I felt his chuckle vibrate against my thighs where he lay sprawled on top of me. His chin still held my boxer briefs down, and I felt his tongue snake its way into the nest of curls there.

"Felix, I want you to come. Feel free to do so at any point," he purred. "There's no hurry and certainly no limit to how many times I can make you come tonight."

I reached my fingers into his thick hair and squeezed my eyes closed in disbelief. My cheeks tightened as I felt myself grin like an idiot.

The hottest man on the fucking planet was going to go down on me. Lio was going to suck my dick. I thought about all of my insecurities and decided I was going to miss out on enjoying this aberration if I continued to be apologetic and weird.

Instead of a stammering, nervous geek, I decided to fake it—to act like a confident, sexual beast who took what he wanted. Why not? It's not as if this guy was anyone I was going to see again after this trip. Why not try for once in my life to embrace the moment and fly by the seat of my pants?

My eyes opened again to catch him peering up at me, his tongue dragging lazily across my hip. "Did you leave me?"

"No. Hell no. But I need you to take my clothes off and suck my dick," I told him with a grin. His own grin widened, and he rolled over and stripped off his briefs, exposing a glorious cock, uncut and hard as hell.

I groaned and salivated. I'd never been with an uncircumcised man, but I'd porned the hell out of them.

I tried not to swallow my tongue. "Gnpfh."

Lio's eyes lit up as he began to pull my pants and underwear off. "Like that, huh?"

"Mpfh," I agreed.

As my clothes came off, my hard-on got caught up in my underwear and slapped back to my belly. I reached for it to stroke myself, but Lio grabbed my wrist and pinned it to the bed next to my head instead.

"Let me. Someone had certain ideas about what I should be doing with your cock, and if I recall correctly, it didn't include your hand."

"Your mouth," I breathed.

He stuck out his tongue and gently swiped it over the tip of my cock, where a bead of precum lay waiting.

"Shit," I gasped, throwing my head back onto the mattress and squeezing my eyes closed. "Shit, I'm going to come already. Fuck."

Lio's laugh vibrated its way around my shaft as he swallowed me down in a quick down-up motion.

"No, Felix. I changed my mind. No coming until I say so. I want to play for a while first."

A whining sound escaped my throat, and I brought my feet up flat on the mattress next to Lio's sides. I wanted to thrust up into his wet warmth, but I wasn't sure if that would be rude. My fingers threaded through his hair, and I scraped my fingernails lightly along his scalp. The man practically purred with pleasure, my cock in his mouth and my balls in his hand.

I looked down at the sight in front of me and felt dizzy.

"Fuck my mouth," Lio said in a gravelly voice. "Want you to feel good."

"Jesus," I muttered as I thrust immediately up into his throat, feeling the lure of his tight heat. "Fuck. Fuck, Lio. God."

If only I had more coherent words to say, but I didn't. It was all pleasure and gasping and mumbling out expletives.

The slurping and sucking sounds coming from his hot mouth turned me on even more, and I thought I might lose it right there.

"Lio," I cried in warning.

He quickly pulled off my cock and shifted forward in the bed. I cried out a complaint before his mouth crashed into mine in a searing kiss. Just like that, my attention went from a close climax in my cock to an absolute ravaging of my mouth. His tongue licked into me as his cock thrust against my thigh in rhythm.

I gasped between kisses. "Lio, gonna—"

"Not yet," he commanded in a stern voice that made my stomach flip. "No, Felix."

"Agh, god. Fuck," I panted against the side of his face, trying every sort of mental gymnastics to keep myself from coming too soon. "Ffft."

"Tell me you have lube and condoms, baby," Lio purred. His tone was like a roller coaster ride in the dark—unpredictable but exciting as hell. "I want to get inside of you right now. Pound you into this bed, Felix. Where's your stuff?"

My heart dropped. "I... I don't have any stuff," I admitted in a broken voice. Who the hell brought condoms and lube to an island in the North Sea when they hadn't had sex in years? "I mean, I have lube, but... no condoms."

"Fuck," he muttered before lurching off me and reaching for his pants. "Fuck. My wallet's back in my room." He looked up, revealing the most adorable frown lines between his eyes. "Guess we'll have to get creative, then. Where's the lube?"

I reached out a shaky hand to point toward the bathroom. "In my shaving kit."

He strode over to retrieve it and had a mischievous smile on his face when he returned.

"Hands and knees," he commanded. The man was obviously used to being in charge.

I wasn't complaining.

I blinked up at him and swallowed a gulp before moving into position. Lio moved over top of me, his cock grazing the skin of my ass and his knees landing on the mattress inside of each of mine to nudge my legs farther apart. I felt the scratch of his body hair against my inner thighs and sucked in a breath.

Warm lips landed on the base of my neck and began trailing kisses slowly toward one shoulder. Lio's arm wrapped around my waist while the other grasped my cock with a cool, slick grip.

"Mmm, someone's still hard for me," he murmured into my ear. "You have no idea how hot that is, feeling your cock and knowing it's hard for me. Does that feel good, Felix?"

"Uh-huh."

I felt his lips curve into a smile against my neck before he licked a light stripe down my spine to the top of my ass.

"Do you like my mouth on you here?"

"Uh-huh."

*Suave, Felix. Super cool.*

"Yes, I mean. *Yes*," I said.

His lips and teeth took turns nibbling at my ass cheeks before his hands opened me and cool air hit my hole.

"Ungh," I gasped. "Lio, please. You're teasing me."

I was owning this role as a sex-confident player. I hadn't whimpered once. Well, not more than a few times anyway.

"You want me to kiss you here, Felix?"

"Fuck yes… Please." *Okay, that might have been a whimper.*

I felt his fingers tighten on my skin and his hot breath land on the sensitive bundle of nerves between them.

"Oh," I moaned, before his mouth even landed on me. "Oh god."

Lio's hand stroked my cock while his tongue began to dance around my hole, and white shards of light began to creep around the edges of my vision.

I'd never been rimmed before, and it was goddamned nirvana.

# CHAPTER 11

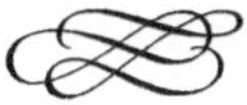

## LIO

It occurred to me at some point while I was tongue-deep in Felix's body that I had never before given so much attention to someone else's pleasure. Every movement, every sound he made was like fuel on the flame of my own desire until it became a game of getting myself off by getting Felix off.

It was like the higher he flew, the higher I would as well.

"That's it, baby," I murmured against his inner thigh before grabbing some more lube and playing at his entrance with my fingers.

I'd gone from being desperate to fuck the man to desperate to make him feel good. And, boy, was he feeling good.

"Please, please, let me come," he whimpered. "I need to come. I need to come." His words were barely audible through his labored breaths. He was teetering on the edge.

I pressed my slick index finger inside of him and felt his entire body react. His spine arched, his head went back, and his ass drew closer, searching for more. I took the risk of pushing in deeper in hopes of finding the magic spot.

"Holy Christ, fuck, fuck!" Suddenly, Felix's channel contracted around me as he cried out, warm jets streaking across my hand as I stroked him through his release with one hand and fucked it out of him with the other.

The orgasm wrecked him in the very best way, and I wondered if he was always like this, if he was this responsive with the other men he slept with.

At the very thought of him with other men, I felt like I'd been doused with frigid water. I released him and pulled away, falling onto my back and closing my eyes to steady myself. I covered my face with an arm and tried to even out my breathing. My cock continued to pound in rhythm with my heart, and why shouldn't it? I was still in bed next to the most beautiful soul and the hottest body around.

"Lio?" He sounded small and unsure, and I hated hearing his voice like that. I turned to look at him. Worry creased his face. I wanted to run my fingers through his hair, but they were manky with lube.

"You okay?" I asked quietly, trying to give him a reassuring smile. It must have worked because his face softened into a relieved grin.

"Hell yes, I'm okay. Very okay. Better than okay." He glanced down at my cock, standing up like a jackass from my groin. "Lio, will you hop in the shower with me?"

It wasn't what I expected him to say, and it must have shown.

His grin turned a bit evil then. "I have plans for you. In the shower. Come on."

He wiggled away from me and hopped off the bed, showing me a tight little ass still pink from where I'd worked the hell out of it with my hands while rimming him.

Felix's body was gorgeous. I could stare at it all day.

*Or you can go put your hands on it and rub up against it in the shower, you imbecile*, I reminded myself.

I followed him into the bathroom, idly stroking my cock along the way.

While we waited for the water to heat, my hands began exploring his ass again and I dropped kisses behind his ears. "This ass. Fuck. I can't keep my hands off it."

"No one's asking you to."

Felix's hand came back to cup the back of my head as I continued to kiss his neck and fondle his front. His nipples were stiff peaks in the cool bathroom air, and his stomach contracted into little bumps beneath my touch.

"Never thought I'd get lucky at Gadleigh," I teased. "Who would have expected to find a sexy scientist here in the middle of winter?"

I turned Felix around to face me before backing him into the tiled space and making sure he was under the hot spray. His eyes were warm brown pools of lust, and his pupils remained wide open as he gazed at me.

"It's like a crazy fantasy," he murmured before catching himself and giving a self-deprecating laugh. "I mean, sorry. That sounds silly."

"No, it sounds accurate," I assured him. "A fantasy I'm sure to revisit in my head for weeks to come." I winked at him then and leaned in to kiss his reddened lips. They were soft and firm at the same time, and his tongue began to taste familiar, as if the night's kissing had been enough to imprint his taste on me forever.

He pulled away and shifted us so I was the one under the water. I leaned my head back to get my hair wet for a moment, and when I opened my eyes again, Felix had lowered himself to his knees.

The man was looking up at me as if waiting for permission. Silver water droplets caught in his dark lashes and on his full lips as the tip of his tongue came out to swipe it away. I squeezed my eyes closed for a moment and thanked my lucky stars for not walking away from Felix like my conscience had tried to tell me to do.

"Correction," I said in a low voice. "*This* is the fantasy I'll replay. The sight of you on your knees for me, Felix. Christ."

His eyes stayed on me while his face nuzzled my cock, the prickle of his stubble rough on my tender skin. I brought my hand up to brush wet strands of hair off his forehead. Felix's tongue came out and began to lick up and down the length of me, always, always keeping his eyes glued to mine.

It was hot as fuck.

He took the head of my cock into his mouth and began to toy with my foreskin, clamping it gently between his lips and tugging slightly. I groaned and tightened my fingers in his hair.

After a few pulls with his hand around my shaft, he pulled back the skin and teased the tip with his tongue, letting the skin loose again but continuing to roll his tongue inside of it. I thought I was going to lose my fucking mind.

"Fffuck, Felix. Feels so good. Just like that."

His eyes stayed on me as his hand jacked me firmly and his tongue played along the sensitive head of my cock.

Felix pulled off just long enough to lick his lips and ask, "If I'm doing anything wrong, please tell me."

His eyebrows were up in concern, and I reached out to smooth the worry lines between them.

"Not possible. Your mouth feels amazing. Keep going." I tried to steady my breathing, but I couldn't. It came in gasps and moans as his mouth and hands went to town on my cock. Sure fingers clasped my balls and made my knees shake.

"Not going to last," I warned through my teeth. My hands had come out to brace against the walls of the shower in case I lost my footing. My legs were shaking so hard, I thought it was a real possibility.

A finger I hadn't noticed before snaked behind my sac and pressed against my perineum, sending sparks of pleasure all through my groin and warning me of the coming orgasm.

"Baby, shit," I cried, trying to pull him off. He stayed on his knees, mouth firmly wrapped around my cock as I released into his throat. "Fuck. Oh god." My hand came down hard on Felix's shoulder to support myself, and he reached up to hold my wrist.

He never once took his gorgeous eyes off me.

I'd had intense sexual experiences with other people before—men and women—but I'd never before felt something quite like this. It was as if Felix had seen straight into my soul somehow, which was ridiculous because the man didn't even know who I was. And, hell, I didn't even know who he was. Not really. A glass professor from Texas. That was it. It wasn't like we'd exchanged phone numbers or anything.

The thoughts and feelings I had were well and truly inconsistent with a hookup. I'd thought that was all this was.

But then we'd talked. And kissed. And touched.

And now… now I knew it was about more than just sex.

And that was not okay.

# CHAPTER 12

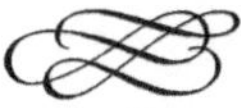

## FELIX

Waking up to an empty bed was decidedly shitty compared to falling asleep in Lio's strong arms the night before. I knew before I even opened my eyes he was no longer there. The bedding was cold, and I was curled into a tiny ball in a subconscious effort to conserve heat under the covers.

"Crap," I mumbled into my pillow. It wasn't like it was a surprise. Clearly Lio was the type to fuck and duck, but that didn't make it any less disappointing.

And I was most definitely disappointed. The sex had been out of this world, but the companionship had also been a rare treat. I'd enjoyed talking to him and flirting with him. Would have enjoyed sleeping all night in his arms even more.

That was one of the shitty aspects of being single. No one to touch, no warm body to cling to on a cold night in bed, no one to complain to when things didn't go your way.

I blew out a breath and thought about the day ahead of me. Calum had offered to teach me a few things in the glassworks later in the morning. I wondered if I could scrounge up my own breakfast in the little apartment. I knew I had coffee, but I wondered if I still had some of the instant oatmeal packs I'd thrown into my bag at the last minute.

After visiting the bathroom and dressing warmly, I set about making breakfast without sparing Lio another thought. I wasn't at Gadleigh to get laid. I was there to finish my dissertation and study glass.

There were still hundreds of examples of hidden glass in the castle, but I knew right away I wouldn't have the guts to go anywhere near the main house today. Not when there was the very real possibility of running into Lio and having the awkward morning-after weirdness. No. I'd concentrate on the glassworks and picking Calum's brain as much as he'd allow me. Then maybe I'd return to my apartment and work on my dissertation.

Once I'd downed a cup of coffee and a granola bar I found in my backpack, I bundled up in my coat and hat to make my way to the glassworks building.

When I entered through the wide door, I saw the glow from the fire right away. Calum was sitting back drinking from a mug while reading a paperback book that seemed as old as he was. Two of his assistants puttered around the studio behind him.

"Morning," I said with a smile. "You ready for me?"

"Do I have a choice?" he asked in his rough voice. I would have thought his question was rude if I hadn't noticed the twinkle in his eye. "Come on over here. We're making glass today."

My heart sped up. Had he really meant *we*?

"Why do you look so surprised, young Felix? I thought you'd done this before."

I was in the process of taking off my coat when I laughed. "Yes, sir. I have. I have a degree in glassmaking. Not the same as being master glassmaker at Gadleigh but enough to keep from embarrassing myself with a blowpipe and marvering table," I joked. "And I'd do just about anything to make something in the Gadleigh glassworks."

"Well, then. I guess you'd better get an apron on. Let me tell you what I have in mind."

We spent the next hour going over his process. Calum was like a completely different man than he'd been before. He apologized for being "quiet" when we'd first met, explaining only that he'd been knackered from the exhausting schedule of the holiday ornaments.

"Every year Gadleigh makes a special design and sells it around the world as a collectible. They're done in the summer, believe it or not, but the royal family itself gets a unique design that's made in November and early December and given out as personal gifts to friends and family."

I quirked my head at him. "What royal family?"

"Monaco, son. The royal family who owns Gadleigh. Surely you did your homework if you've been studying this place."

"Oh, right. Yes. I forgot. So much of my study is about the glass-makers and the history, I forget it's still connected to the monarchy today. I can't imagine being on the list to get one of the royal orna-ments. Do you have one from this year? I'd love to see it." That explained how Lio had ties to Gadleigh. He was from Monaco.

Calum wheeled his metal stool over to a worktable and reached for a wooden box. When he returned to where I was sitting, he opened the lid, revealing four or five glass pyramids. They were exquisite, with colored spirals twisting from one inside corner, through the clear pyramid, to another corner. It was like a colorful glass version of Untangle the Knot.

"My god," I breathed. "How in the world did you manage to do this? It's breathtaking."

Calum puffed up with pride. "I could tell you, or..." His eyes flicked to the melting furnace. "I could show you. What do you reckon is best?" His wink sparked off my excitement, causing me to sit up straight on my stool. I caught one of Calum's assistants smiling at me with understanding. Surely, he knew how damned lucky he was to work with the Gadleigh glass master.

"I believe you know the answer to that question." I felt like a kid in a candy store.

Once we got our hands dirty, time passed in a flash. Before I knew it, I was covered in sweat and dust, my face was surely beet red from the heat of the fire, and I'd finally gotten a few hours' respite from my

Lio-based anxiety. Calum's assistants were funny and crass, and their banter made the time even more fun.

Obviously, my glass pyramids didn't look nearly as breathtaking as Calum's did, but I did manage to complete two of them before our lunch break. I planned on giving one to Doc and Grandpa and giving the other to the newest Wilde, my cousin's baby, Pippa. One of my aunts had made a point of giving each niece and nephew a new ornament every year, and I'd always thought it was a special tradition.

"Ready for a hearty meal?" Calum finally asked after two in the afternoon, wiping a rag across his face. His grin was large in his ruddy cheeks, and I realized just what a different man he was than the one I'd met only a couple of days before.

"Lead on, master," I teased.

None of us put a coat back on for the walk to the main house for lunch. The cool wind off the sea felt amazing on my heated skin. I wondered if I'd run into Lio in the kitchen and hoped the later hour meant he'd come and gone from Mari's lair already.

Sure enough, the only people to be found were Bert, the estate manager, Mari, and a man I hadn't met before named Arthur. He appeared to be older than my oldest cousin, Hudson, but younger than fifty. The man had short dark hair with threads of silver in it that only served to make him more attractive. If he hadn't been so stiff and formal, he'd be downright droolworthy.

Bert sat reading a newspaper while Mari fussed around making plates for the four of us. Arthur studied me like I was something of interest. It was a little creepy, so I tried ignoring him.

"Sorry, I'm a sweaty mess," I told Mari.

She beamed up at me. "Nothing wrong with the results of hard work, Felix, and if'n you keep that large grin on your face, I'd imagine it'll do to serve the likes of you regardless."

I followed Calum's helpers to the large sink and washed my hands before taking my place at the thick wooden table in the center of the room. The heat from the kitchen fire was hardly noticeable compared to the heat in the glassworks, and I relished some time away from the hot air.

When I realized Calum and Arthur were speaking familiarly, I asked Arthur what he did at the castle.

He opened his mouth to respond but seemed to freeze before a single word came out.

"Uh, sorry," I stammered. "I didn't mean to pry. It's really none of my business."

"No, no. It's fine. I am one of the assistants to the royal family. When they are in residence, I help with… clothing. Packing, unpacking, pressing, and whatnot. It's… yes. That is what I do. The service I perform. For the royal, ahem, family."

Mari hid a chuckle in a dish towel, and I noticed her face flush pink. Were they making fun of me? I didn't know much about the royal family of Monaco, but that didn't mean I didn't know they had valets.

"You're a royal valet?"

Arthur's eyes widened before his smile did the same. "Yes, Felix. I am a valet. Have served the royal family for almost twenty years. They are good people."

I wasn't quite sure what to say to that. "Well, they're lucky to have you, then."

Once we were all finished eating, Mari pulled me aside and handed me a slip of paper. "Your grandfather called while you were out this morning. You can use the phone in my office to call him back if you'd like."

My heart began to hammer in my chest. Doc and Grandpa had the phone number to the castle in case of emergencies since my cell phone wouldn't work on the remote island. "Did he say if anything was wrong?"

Mari's eyes softened and she reached out to pat my shoulder. "Didn't sound like it, my boy. Go and call him, then. You'll see. I'm sure everything is fine."

I excused myself to Calum and his men before making my way to the kitchen office and closing the door. After dialing the long string of numbers to reach home, I calculated the time difference.

It was almost three here which meant almost nine in the morning at home.

I heard the click of the phone connecting and didn't wait for the man to speak. "Grandpa? Is everything okay?"

The deep, familiar sound of his voice washed over me, making my eyes sting. "Of course it is. Everything's fine, son. We were just calling to wish you a Merry Christmas in case we couldn't get a hold of you tomorrow."

I let out a breath and ran my hand through my hair in relief. I'd forgotten today was Christmas Eve. "Shit. You scared me to death."

I heard Doc's familiar chuckle join Grandpa's scoff. "Don't say that, or I'll owe Doc ten bucks."

I felt a laugh bubble up. "It's good to hear your voice. Hey, Doc."

"Hey, Felix. Met any hot glassmakers over there?" Doc's teasing voice was light, reminding me of the advice he'd given me to relax and have some fun.

I thought about Calum's two assistants. One was almost as old as dirt, and despite being cute as a button, didn't spin my wheel. The other was a nice enough guy about my age, but married to a woman who worked in the stables.

"No, no glassmakers."

They must have heard something in my voice because the two of them both began chattering excitedly.

"Tell us everything," Grandpa insisted.

"Spill," Doc agreed.

"Well, there *is* a hot guy here. Seems like a friend of the family of the couple that runs the place. I guess he's here for vacation or to get away from the city maybe. He lives in Monte Carlo."

They tittered back and forth. "Wonder if he's famous," Doc mused.

"Or rich," Grandpa speculated.

I sighed. "Does it matter? We're only here together temporarily. It's not like a dating situation." I tapped a nearby pen on the pad of paper by the phone. "More of like…"

"Like?" Doc asked.

"More of like a hookup thing," I admitted, feeling my face heat before they even had a chance to tease me.

"Hoooo-boy!" Grandpa whooped in the background as Doc laughed his fool head off.

"You staying safe, Felix? I should have stocked your bag with condoms and lube," Doc muttered. "Knew I forgot something, dammit."

"No, I mean, yes. I'm staying safe. But I have to admit, I'd have given anything for you to have stowed that shit in my bag. As it was, staying safe meant not getting too lucky."

My friends at school had never understood how I was so open about sex with my grandparents. But then again, they didn't fully grasp that my grandparents were not only cool, but also gay men themselves. Which meant, they knew shit. Lots of shit. *Good* shit. My cousin West told me early on that Grandpa and Doc were cool like that and just wanted what was best for all of us.

It had been hard for me to open up to them about personal stuff like sex since they were like fathers to me, but once I had, it was like opening floodgates. We'd only gotten closer, and I knew I was lucky as hell to have them.

"Well, shit, Fee," Doc said. "Sorry about that. I guess there's no drugstore on every corner there at Gadleigh, is there?"

I snorted. "I wish. And I doubt the sixty-year-old caretakers have condoms to spare either."

"Does FedEx deliver there?" I heard Grandpa ask Doc in the background.

"Never mind. It's fine. I'm actually more interested in the glass," I lied. "It's amazing." Okay, that part wasn't a lie. It truly was amazing. "The master glassmaker taught me some new techniques this morning. We just finished our lunch break, and now he's going to teach me a new cane-braiding method this afternoon."

"Sounds like a dream come true, son," Grandpa said, the love clear in his voice. "We're so proud of you."

"I can't thank you guys enough for sending me here," I told them with a lump in my throat. "It means the world to me to see something I've only ever dreamed about."

"You deserve to have all of your dreams come true, Felix," Doc said in a gentle voice. "We love you. Oh, before I forget, Ruth was trying to get in touch with you. You might want to shoot her an email if you can't call."

Ruth Lawson was one of my favorite art history professors. During my graduate program, I'd been her teaching assistant and discovered how much I loved teaching college kids. We'd stayed in touch over the years and remained friends.

When I finished the call with my family, I called Ruth.

"Oh, thank god I caught you," she said in her typical frenzied rush. "You're in England, right? I mean, not England. Gadleigh."

"Yes. I'm at Gadleigh. Why?"

"Is there any way you can fly to Paris to give a talk for me before you fly home? I'm scheduled to present at a symposium right after New Year's, and I broke my damned foot slipping on the ice at my daughter's house in Denver. I could still do it, but I really don't want to go through all the hassle of trying to travel to Europe on crutches."

"What's the presentation about? Surely I wouldn't be able to—"

She cut me off. "I was going to be talking about William Morris, but everyone's heard it all before. I want you to give a talk on Etienne DesMarais."

I took a deep breath and tried not to cuss her out. "God fucking dammit, Ruth." So much for not cussing her out.

"Just listen," she said. "This is the perfect opportunity to present your dissertation, Felix. Consider it practice. You know Etienne's work like the back of your hand, and by the time you're done at Gadleigh, you'll even have all the firsthand knowledge of it you need to sell the thesis that he's the mysterious Gadleigh glass artist."

"I don't feel like I have the proof I need. I'm not ready, and the dissertation sure as hell isn't ready," I whined.

"Bullshit. The dissertation has been done for months, and you're never going to be ready. No time like the present. Suck it up, butter-cup. This is happening. I was all set to sweet-talk you into it and play the broken-bone card, but I can see you need a little tough love instead. So here's the deal. You're doing it. If you don't show up, I'll be considered a no-show among my peers. You wouldn't do that to a broken-down old lady, would you?"

"You're going to burn in hell," I muttered.

"As long as they have an espresso machine, I'm cool with it. Thank you, Fee. I owe you one," she said before promising to email the details.

"You owe me a million," I corrected before she hung up.

As I made my way back out to the glassworks studio, I had a heart full of love for my family back home, even if it was besmirched by some resentment toward my old mentor. Doc and Grandpa had reminded me today was Christmas Eve, which meant my mother's big blockbuster movie debuted in theaters all over the world tomorrow. And thanks to them, I was a million miles away from the attention it would bring to both my family and my tiny hometown. Now, thanks to Ruth, I could justify extending my exodus a little bit longer.

God bless the ability to hide from the tabloid media.

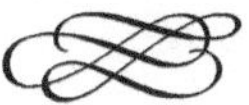

# CHAPTER 13

LIO

I'd snuck out of his room in the early hours of the morning like a fucking coward. Fear had gripped me as multiple crazy thoughts compounded in my head. What if Felix really knew who I was and was playing me for some kind of media exposé? What if he didn't know who I was but would sell me out the minute he found out? And, possibly most importantly, why couldn't I stop thinking about him for more than two fucking consecutive minutes?

After gathering Jon and heading back to the main house, I'd paced the floor of my bedroom for at least an hour, lecturing myself about how stupid it had been to take such a risk with a stranger. I thought about how I was not much better than my father—unable keep his dick in his pants long enough to avoid a royal scandal.

*But Father is married, and I'm not. Why can't I have a fling while I'm young?* My thoughts had betrayed me.

*Because the fling was with a man.*

And that was the truth of it. What the entire thing boiled down to. I could sleep around as much as I wanted to and only get a reputation for being a playboy. But the minute the press discovered I preferred men to women? Then it would be another story entirely.

It was a moot point, though. I'd always known when it came time to settle down, it would be with a woman. Someone to play the role as my wife and mother to my children. Someone to represent the monarchy with the same elegance and grace my mother had.

Maybe it was crass, but in my mind, men were for fucking while women were for marrying.

By the time dawn had arrived, I'd talked myself into my decision to walk away from the temptation of Felix. I'd avoid him and get my mind back where it needed to be—on the assumption of the throne and the mantle of responsibility it would require of me.

I was determined. I'd had my one night with Felix; I'd gotten to taste him and touch him and watch him let go. It was enough. It *had* to be enough.

Arthur, however, didn't seem content for me to move on. Especially without sharing the details with him first. From the moment he arrived in my room to help me dress – or rather, sit by the fire while he watched me dress – he'd been waiting for me to spill.

"None of your business," I grumbled over the crumbly basket of breakfast breads Mari had reluctantly sent up to my room.

Arthur raised an eyebrow at me. "You know you're going to tell me eventually, so you might as well do it now and get it over with."

"You're going to judge me," I whined.

"And? What else is new?"

I rolled my eyes, but I knew he was right. I was going to tell him anyway. I told him everything. Even though I was close to Iggy and my sister, it was really Arthur who knew every little thing about me.

"I wanted to sleep with him, so I did," I said before picking up my coffee mug like it was no big deal.

Silence for a beat and then a loud guffaw. I stared at my ex-valet.

"Stop laughing, asshole," I warned. "You work for me."

"Oh please. Like you'd ever fire me. Have you forgotten about the night you proposed to me?" His eyes were sparkling as he tried not to laugh.

"I had appendicitis, and you distracted me from the pain with your stupid-assed stories. I remember thinking how good you are in a crisis. I still feel that way. You're a good man to have around when the shit goes down," I admitted.

Arthur snorted. "You were so high on morphine, I couldn't stop giggling. I regret not taking video. Could have made millions. You suggested at least twenty original names for my new puppy."

I stopped and looked at him. "Hell. What did you end up naming her?"

"I've never had a puppy, Lio, and you know it."

We both laughed at that. It was a bit that never got old and reminded me he was right, of course. I'd have Arthur with me as long as he was willing or as long as I lived. He was one of the best men I knew.

So I told him the truth. "Felix is special."

Arthur's eyes turned serious. "Oh."

"Yeah. *Oh.*" I sighed. "It's a problem."

"It doesn't have to be, Lio. There's nothing wrong with being attracted to another man."

He and I had spent hours discussing my sexuality in regards to the monarchy. Thankfully, he understood my predicament rather than just trying to convince me to come out publicly and throw up the middle finger to my family's history.

"He lives in Texas. I live in Monaco. How is that supposed to work? It's not like I can date him like a normal person, even if I could be gay."

"Lio, you *are* gay. There is no 'if' about it," he corrected.

"He's really cute. Have you seen him?"

Arthur gazed at me with twinkling eyes. "You're grinning like a fool. Yes, I've seen him. Cute as a button."

I snapped my eyes over to him and narrowed them, causing him to bark out a laugh.

"Down, boy. I have no interest in fiddling with your boy toy. He's definitely not my type."

"Why not? What's wrong with him?" I asked, affronted on Felix's behalf. "He's sexy as hell."

"Oh my god, you're besotted. Yes, he's fine. But I prefer the big beefy type, if you want to know the truth. Someone like that new guard who's been looking after your sister recently."

Arthur's eyes glazed over, and it was my turn to laugh. "That guy? The one with the man bun? He's like an empty pocket. There's nothing upstairs. Surely you want your partner to be able to read a restaurant menu?"

"Sir, I never said I was looking for scintillating conversation. Have you seen him in his workout clothes?"

I shuddered. "Go for it."

"I believe that's what I was advising you to do," he corrected.

"Mm," I scoffed as I got up and left the room. "Maybe."

I spent the entire morning hiding in the treasury room with my laptop. Father's advisors had sent me heaps of email in order to get me up to speed on several diplomacy issues as well as a budgeting memo, a notice of a new judicial assignment, and an article on sustainable development.

By the time I stopped for a lunch break, my head was spinning. I'd always worked closely with my father, but I'd never been the decision-maker involved in any of the issues he managed. I was grateful his minister of state was a good man—intelligent, capable, and trustworthy. I'd be able to rely on him while I got my feet under me.

A couple of hours after lunch, I decided to take a walk to clear my head. I hadn't had the chance to say hello to Calum yet, which was unusual. Normally, I'd run into him at mealtimes in the kitchen, but I wanted to make a point to thank him for all of his hard work this season.

I somehow convinced Jon to watch me from the utility vehicle parked next to the building rather than following me into the studio itself.

"I'm just going in to have a quick word with Calum. Nothing too dangerous," I said before stepping out of the vehicle and walking along the crushed-shell path toward the building.

As I approached the large open door of the glassworks, I heard Calum's deep laugh. I'd known the man since I was a teenager and had always enjoyed his gruff personality. He was a cross between a moody artist and a hardworking laborer. It may have taken time to get to know him properly, but once I had, he'd been one of my favorite people to share a cup of tea with at Gadleigh.

As I rounded the corner and saw into the studio, the first thing I noticed was the thin, sweat-soaked T-shirt plastered to Felix's back. Damp hair stuck out in wayward spikes all around his head where he'd obviously been running his hands through it. His arm muscles bunched and moved under slick skin as he moved and rotated a long pipe with a gob of molten glass on the end. He was joking around with Calum and his men, responding to some innuendo about his skill with the blowpipe.

"Show us what you got, greenhorn," one man teased. "Put that pretty mouth to work."

"Watch and learn, my friend. I'll show you how we blow things in Texas," Felix joked before bringing the long pipe to his lips.

My entire body seized up, and I froze where I stood.

Felix's wide red lips wrapped gently around the pipe, but it might as well have been around my cock. I felt the memory of his lips on me and shuddered.

"Holy fuck," I breathed, watching him.

As he blew and worked the pipe with his mouth, his arm muscles continued moving. The pipe spun in his nimble fingers, and the glowing gob began to expand. He placed a colored cane onto the glass and continued spinning the pipe. The color swirled around the glass gob, making a unique design. He quickly added another colored cane and began intertwining two more while adding them to the object. While he was twisting the colored canes onto the gob, he kept glancing up at Calum and his men and joking with them.

Watching his face bright and full of happiness was breathtaking. He looked so easy, so free. I could see how much fun he was having and remembered with sudden clarity the reason for his visit to Gadleigh.

It wasn't to sleep with a prince. It wasn't to fuck around with someone he'd just met. And I could tell now for certain that it wasn't to lie his way into a celebrity exposé for the tabloid press.

He'd come for the glass. He'd come to appreciate something that had been a part of my family's history for hundreds of years. Something I knew very little about but that clearly he embraced with every part of his being.

I suddenly felt like I was missing something important—something I never knew I'd been lacking.

Felix put his design back into the fire and spun it for a while before bringing it out. It was clear there was more molten glass on the design now. He brought the pipe back to his lips again and blew.

The clear glass around the original design began to open and expand, encasing the design in a clear glass ball.

It was mesmerizing. The man wasn't just the chemist geek he'd portrayed. He was an artist.

He moved to a steel table and pressed the item to the table, flattening its sides until it resembled a pyramid with a colorful twisted design inside.

As Felix walked the pipe back to the fire, Calum followed him with another pipe.

"Punty here, Felix. Whenever you're ready," Calum offered.

I saw them transfer the item Felix was making from one pipe to another before Felix put the item back into the fire. As he leaned over, his damp shirt rode up his back, revealing a strip of skin above the electric blue waistband of his underwear. Andrew Christian underwear.

Fuck.

I wanted to see him in nothing but that underwear. With the sweat of the glassworks still running down his back and the heat of his skin under my palms.

My heart thundered in my chest as I continued watching him work from my semihidden spot by the doorway.

I couldn't take my eyes off the muscles of his back and arms, the way he shifted his weight as he moved around the space. The easiness to his interactions with Calum and his men. He was a completely different man than the nervous guy who'd stumbled into my hidden study the day before.

This Felix was confident and strong, creative and engaging. Relaxed and happy. I wanted to throw the man over the large steel table and fuck him six ways to Sunday. My dick pounded in my jeans, and blood roared in my ears. The man was a damned masterpiece, and I wanted him all to myself.

"Sir!" The bark was so sudden, I jumped, nearly tripping over my own feet. Calum stood just inside the door gazing at me. "Didn't you hear me? I called your name twice."

"Sorry," I mumbled, brushing nonexistent dust off my knees in an effort to hide my erection in my lap. "Woolgathering."

Once the fear had deflated my cock, I straightened up and followed him into the studio. He held out his hand toward Felix with obvious pride.

"Look who's surprised the hell out of us with some moves," he declared. "Young Felix here is a glassmaker himself."

I watched as Felix turned from his position near the melting furnace and recognized me. The pipe he held swung in an arc toward the ground, and I shouted at him to take care. He jerked his arms back up, narrowly missing smashing the delicate design against the hard wall of the furnace.

"Shit," he blurted. "Fuck."

One of Calum's assistants tutted over him, offering to take the apparatus and hold it until he was ready to continue working on it. Felix handed it to him and shook out his arms, as if cramping muscles had caused the inattention rather than surprise at my arrival.

He flicked his eyes over to me again.

*Sorry*, I mouthed, trying with my eyes to communicate how sorry I was to have bothered him while he was clearly having a nice time. He shot me a small smile and shrugged before turning back to the assistant. I could tell from his body language he'd gotten my blow-off message from the night before loud and clear.

The realization tightened my chest and made my fingers clench into a tight fist, but before I had a chance to say anything to him, Calum clapped me on the shoulder.

"Want to see what we're working on these days?"

I followed him through the studio, trying my best to pay attention as he showed me the latest designs his team had created. They were beautiful and unique, as always. I'd been a big fan of his from the early days of his arrival at Gadleigh but had shunned his efforts to teach me anything about the process of glassmaking. My father had demanded too much of my time for me to spend it on "art."

But now I realized I'd missed out on something by not allowing him to teach me. I could see how much joy it brought all of the men in the studio and how they took great pride in their work. I wasn't sure I could say the same about the hours I'd spent toiling over memos and diplomatic documents earlier that morning.

The entire time I tried listening to Calum's voice, I couldn't help but sneak glances at Felix across the big open space. After a few awkward minutes, he was finally able to forget I was there and go back to his work. He returned to the easy camaraderie with the other glassmakers, and I even overheard him talking to them about their favorite bands. When the subject moved on to favorite movies, Felix seemed to go quiet. The two men with him chattered on endlessly about new releases coming out that week and didn't seem to notice Felix's body stiffening and his complete departure from the conversation.

I continued to watch him, concerned about what had caused him to shut down, when Calum's hand landed on my arm. I glanced at him and found him looking at me with knowing concern.

"We're begging off early today, so I'll leave you to it," he said quietly. I arched an eyebrow at him in question. "Christmas Eve, yeah? Gonna let these boys go home to their families."

I'd completely forgotten about the holiday.

"Oh shit. Yes, of course. Please," I stammered. "Merry Christmas. Go on."

Calum studied me again for a beat. "Would you mind terribly staying to help Felix finish up?"

"I... I don't know how to help him do anything here," I admitted. Not that he didn't already know this. Plus, since when did he ask the prince of Liorland to do a cleanup job in his workshop? It wasn't that I minded at all. In fact, it was nice to be spoken to normally for once—as if I was just a regular man lending a hand. "Of course," I added.

The truth was, I wanted them to leave. I wanted to be alone with Felix. To nudge him out of his sudden funk and find a way to bring him back to the easy joking from before.

"Cheers, sir," he said with a twinkle in his eye and a pat on my arm. "And a Merry Christmas to you too, Your High—"

I rushed to cut off the honorific. "Go! Get on out of here and have fun. You too, guys," I called to the men helping Felix put his design into some type of special cabinet.

The men turned to gawp at me but quickly tidied up and gathered their belongings to leave with Calum. Felix watched them in shock as the three men rushed out of the large front doors, and quiet descended on the studio again.

"What—" he began. "What the hell just happened?"

"They're headed home. It's Christmas Eve."

"Well, yes. I know. I guess… I guess I just thought they'd help close down the shop or something?" He glanced around the space at the items left out.

"I told Calum I'd do it," I said, walking toward him. "But, to be honest, I don't really know what I'm doing. Maybe you can help?"

He nodded.

I picked up one of the tools scattered on a workbench. "What's this?"

Felix hesitated before stepping forward to stand next to me. "It's an optic mold. You can put the warm glass down inside it to help shape it."

I switched out the mold for another tool. "And these?"

"These are jacks. They're kind of like scissors to cut your item off the base." He ran his hands along some of the other items one at a time. "These are tweezers for grabbing and manipulating the soft glass to shape it. This is a block. If you place the glass in here and spin it, it helps shape it evenly. Let's see… these are tongs and forceps, pliers and clamps… And this," he said, gesturing to another long pipe. "This is a pontil. It's a rod that holds your design while you add decorative flourishes."

"I thought it was called a punty," I murmured, distracted by his nearness.

Felix's eyes widened. "Yes, it is. They're the same thing."

I leaned closer to him and reached across his body to another tool. The scent of his sweat nearly brought me to my knees. It was a complete contradiction to the bookworm I'd met in my study. This guy was all man, and he smelled like he'd been hard at work using every muscle in his body. My dick was hammering in my pants.

"And this one?" I breathed into his ear.

His body shuddered, and he began to stammer.

"It's, ah… it's… ah… this one is—" He took a deep breath and closed his eyes for a moment before continuing. "Jacks. Like the other one."

His chest was heaving breaths in and out, and his pulse flitted frantically in his throat. While I stared at it, he swallowed. Hard.

"You're still sweating," I murmured against the thundering pulse point.

"It's… it's hot in here. I'm… hot."

"True enough."

My tongue came out to draw a line down the cord of his throat, to taste the salty residue of his hard work. The sharp intake of his breath echoed in the cavernous studio, and the only other sound was the faint hiss of the gas furnace nearby.

"God," he groaned. "Good god, Lio."

"Mmm. I want to lick every damned inch of your body right now. Do you have any idea how sexy you are?"

He continued to gasp as my hands roamed across the curve of his denim-clad jeans and up onto his moist lower back under his shirt.

"I'm filthy with glass dust," he muttered. "Need to shower."

"Later," I said, pulling him into my arms and aligning our hips together. I noticed he had a leather apron on, and I quickly untied it and set it on the worktable next to us. When I pulled him close again, I felt his cock press into my inner thigh. "Fuck."

My hands wandered down into the back of his jeans, causing his cock to get even harder against my legs. Despite my mouth all over his face and neck, he seemed to be in a kind of passive trance. His hands rested on my chest, but he wasn't grabbing me and kissing me back with the same fervor he'd done the night before.

I pulled back and cupped his face to look at him. "Felix, are you okay?"

He stared at me for a minute before shaking his head. "No. I'm not."

My heart dropped. "What's wrong?"

"You left. Without a word. I assumed that meant… you know," he trailed off, and his eyes flicked away.

I blew out a breath. "I'm sorry. I know I did, and you didn't deserve that. That was shit."

Felix stepped back from me and began putting away the tools in a nearby crate with sections labeled for each one.

"It's fine. You didn't owe me anything, Lio. It's just that I don't… I mean, I didn't want… I'm not really good at the casual-sex thing. I'm sorry. I know that makes me lame, or whatever, and I'm sure you're used to guys who are more put together and know the score, or something, and—"

I cut him off with a hand on his shoulder. I stood behind him and noticed a damp curl against the slim tendons on the nape of his neck. I ghosted my thumb over it, trying to touch it without actually touching him.

"Don't apologize. You don't have anything to apologize for, Felix." My voice sounded rough in my ears. "I'm the one who's sorry. For making you feel that way."

"What way?" he asked, turning to me.

"Like that's all it was," I muttered softly.

"Wasn't it?" he challenged.

I felt my nostrils flare as the truth of it left a bitter taste in my throat. What else could it be but a one-time thing? Even if I could admit to wanting more, I couldn't allow myself anything more than physical with Felix. So that was it—one last fling with a gorgeous man before accepting my life with a nice woman. But I couldn't tell him any of that. And, besides, something inside of me knew I was fooling myself.

"Maybe at first," I began. He turned back around and moved quickly to switch off the gas to the furnace. "Felix, wait. It was at first, maybe. But then I got to know you more, and it… it freaked me out a little. I wasn't expecting to… like you like that. And the fact of the matter is… I'm not in a position for something more than physical right now." *Or ever*, I thought.

I could see his face from the side and noticed his jaw ticking in frustration like he was holding back from saying something.

"Talk to me, Felix."

He threw up his hands and laughed. "This is ridiculous. I'm acting like some stupid kid when the truth of the matter is, what else could it be but just physical? We live in different countries, and I don't even know your fucking last name!"

I felt a familiar panic well up in my gut. Was this the moment I confessed who I truly was? He deserved to know.

But the minute he knew my identity, things would change between us. It was inevitable.

"Grimaldi," I said quietly, wondering if it was enough for him to put two and two together. "My last name is Grimaldi."

# CHAPTER 14

FELIX

Something about the name was familiar, but I was too distracted by the man in front of me to figure it out. Worry lines etched between his eyes, and the eyes themselves were deep blue pools of… something.

*Longing.*

But he'd been right. It could only be physical. Once I left Gadleigh, I'd be heading thousands of miles away, back to my regular old life. And he'd be winging back to fancy Monte Carlo—to whatever life he had there.

"My last name is Wilde," I offered in return. "Felix Wilde." I stood still, wondering if by any chance he'd mention the famous actress with the same last name.

He didn't.

Instead, Lio's face melted into a relieved grin, and he held out a hand as if to shake.

"Nice to meet you, Felix Wilde."

I rolled my eyes but took his hand, only to have it yanked forward so Lio could pull me into a tight hug. The clean scent of the skin on his neck drew my nose to it like a flower.

"Mm, you smell good," I murmured against him. "I'm getting you all dirty."

"I like you all dirty," he admitted in a low voice.

The sound of a throat clearing came from the direction of the doorway, and I jumped back from Lio as if we'd been caught necking in the high school corridor.

It was Lio's friend Jon.

"Call for you," he said to Lio, holding out a mobile phone. I noticed Lio's nostrils flare in irritation and wondered why Jon was carrying Lio's phone.

"Tell them I'm busy," Lio said.

"No sir...ree bob, it's your sister," he stammered. The man was clearly a little slow in the head.

Lio looked at me with an apology in his expression. "I need to take this. Sorry."

"That's okay, there isn't much left to take care of anyway. Thanks for sticking around to help me put everything away."

Lio approached Jon for the phone as I gathered my coat and hat and made my way out the front door. Jon shot me an apologetic glance, and I wondered for the millionth time who the man was to Lio. Were they friends from home? From college? From work? Had they ever slept together?

After finishing cleaning up the shop, I returned to my guest apartment and took a long, hot shower. Scrubbing off the sweat and dust felt amazing, and I enjoyed the feeling of sore muscles after several hours' making glass. When I stepped out of the shower, I heard banging on the door.

"Coming. Hold on," I called, wrapping a thick towel around my waist and grabbing a second one to rub the water out of my hair. "Who is it?" I asked as I approached the door.

"It's me," Lio said. I felt the grin pull at my cheeks.

As I opened the door, I saw Lio's face change from pleased to full-on hungry. His eyes raked over my exposed chest, and his fingers twitched where they hung by his sides.

"Well, now. That's the way you should always greet someone at your door," he drawled.

"I'll remember that the next time Mari comes to offer me a meal," I replied with a cheeky grin.

"Dammit, I missed the sweat," Lio growled as he stalked me, closing the door behind me with a kick. "The dripping water will have to suffice. Tell me I can touch you, Felix."

His eyes were so feral, the words stuck in my throat. I nodded instead.

I expected him to attack—to maul me to within an inch of my life. But he didn't. He ran one index finger along my collarbone. His eyes remained riveted on mine.

"You drive me crazy, you know?" His voice was low and rumbly, sending shivers through me straight to my toes. I felt my cock push against the terry cloth of the towel around my hips.

"Nngh," I managed around the lump in my throat.

Lio's eyes brightened and his lips curved into a grin. "Cat got your tongue, Felix?" His finger lowered and circled around one of my nipples.

"Eungh." It came out high-pitched and needy, but when it seemed to only egg Lio on, I decided to not let my desperation embarrass me.

"Fuck, those noises make me crazy," he murmured before leaning in to drop kisses along my jaw. His mouth nibbled its way over to my ear and clamped down gently on the lobe. The feelings he was bringing out in me were so hot, I was surprised there was still water on my skin that hadn't evaporated yet.

I finally managed to find my tongue. "I want... *oh god*... I want you to... *jesusfuckingchrist right there*," I stammered. "Want you to fuck me so badly, Lio."

As he continued to run his fingers lightly over my wet skin and kiss along my throat, I wondered if I'd even make it to any actual fucking or if I'd blow it right there by the front door in my towel.

"And what if I said you were in luck?" he asked, pulling back to gaze at me. "I brought a condom."

My stomach dropped to the floor, and before I knew it, I'd dropped the towel as well and hot-footed it to my bedroom. I heard the sounds of Lio's laughter echoing behind me. I lunged onto the bed and turned around to lie on my back, knees folded toward my shoulders in the sluttiest offering I could think of.

I had no idea what had gotten into me, but I wanted Lio to fuck me so badly, I wasn't at all willing to pretend otherwise.

When he stepped into the room and saw me like that, his eyes widened and pupils darkened. "Christ, Felix. Look at you."

"Please," I whispered. "Don't make me beg."

I was completely bared to him—as vulnerable as I could possibly be—while he remained fully clothed and standing.

Lio pulled off his shirt and approached the foot of the bed slowly —slow enough to make me reconsider my position. I let go of my knees, but before I could put my feet on the mattress, Lio stopped me with a command.

"No. Put them back. I want to see you."

I closed my eyes and arched my head back in anticipation, his deep, commanding voice like a tight, slick hand to my cock.

Suddenly, I felt his grip on my hips as he hauled my ass close to the end of the bed. His hot, wet mouth descended on me, and I felt his tongue hit my hole with even more aggression than the day before.

I cried out in relief and pleasure as his teeth gently nipped and his tongue sucked. My nerves were lit up like a Christmas tree, and the sparks traveled through my entire groin. My cock leaked all over my stomach, and my balls felt heavy. I wondered if it was all going to be over before Lio was even naked.

"Don't come," he warned, pulling back just enough to make eye contact with me.

"But I—"

"Felix, baby, please don't come yet," he said in a more gentle, pleading tone. I felt my stomach flip at the endearment and couldn't take my eyes off his. Something seemed to pass between us then, and I wondered at it until I felt the slick coolness of a finger enter me.

"Oh god," I whimpered. "Please. Please, Lio."

His finger began moving in and out of me until he added a second. "Love it when you beg me."

"Now. I'm ready," I pleaded.

"No, you're not."

"I am. I promise."

"Baby, I don't want to hurt you."

My eyes rolled back in my head, and I stopped breathing for a moment while his fingers danced along my prostate like a mother-fucking pro.

I wasn't going to last. I would embarrass myself in front of him, and he'd think of me as even more of an inexperienced idiot than he probably already did. I tried to think of complex chemical formulas to stave off my orgasm.

"Formers, fluxes, and stabilizers," I murmured. "Silica, soda, lime…"

"Felix, look at me."

I opened my eyes to see Lio propped above me, grinning from ear to ear. I could feel the fat head of his cock pushing against my hole. Thank god. It was time for the really good part.

"Welcome back," he teased. "You ready?"

"Uh-huh," I said with an overly enthusiastic nod.

Lio's warm palm came up to smooth over my jaw in a gentle touch. "You're so beautiful, Felix," he murmured. I felt my eyes widen at the compliment and wondered if he had any idea what his words did to my heart.

I turned and pressed a kiss into his palm before tilting my pelvis toward him in invitation. As his cock began to stretch me out, I winced and focused on relaxing. I hadn't been telling the truth earlier, obviously. Of course I wasn't ready. I hadn't had anal sex in ages. I'd probably revirginated in the time since I'd last had it.

The burn and stretch reminded me of just how long it had been, but I tried to keep it from showing on my face. I must have done a terrible job because I saw Lio's face crinkle into worry.

"Baby, talk to me. Are you hurting?"

"It's okay, just been a while. Keep going."

He slowed down his movements and pulled back before pressing slowly forward again. This time he went at a snail's pace, which was both good and bad. Good in that it gave my body time to accommodate him, but bad because, despite what my ass wanted, my libido wanted a pounding. I wanted Lio to fuck me into the floor.

My hands gripped his arms where they held him up on either side of me. I saw the tendons and muscles vibrating with his efforts at holding back. Clearly I wasn't the only one with pounding in mind.

Finally, I felt my body give way, and the burn changed from unpleasant to acceptable, bordering on good.

"Go. Yes," I stammered. "Move."

Lio's lips crushed mine as his body surged forward. He caught my yelp in the kiss and began to explore my mouth as thoroughly as he fucked me. I felt the delicious sensation of his cock sliding past my prostate, and the sounds that came out of me were incoherent—babbling, begging, whimpering.

Lio had his own incoherent sounds between kisses. I caught expletives and words like *tight, perfect, hot, need you.* His mouth moved to my ear as he began to urge me toward my own climax. His hand moved between us to grab my cock, and my eyes, yet again, rolled back in my head. It was a sensual overload of the very best kind.

"Not gonna la—" I began.

"Come for me, Felix," he groaned into my ear. "Want to see you let go, baby."

That low grumble was all I needed to push me over the edge. My entire body contracted and arched into him—my head went back on the pillow, and my mouth dropped open in a guttural cry. I felt my ass clench around Lio, and his hands tightened under my shoulder blades in response. My brain stuttered and shut down for a moment while the best vibrations of pleasure I'd ever felt washed through my entire body.

"Holy fuck, Felix. *Ahh.*" Lio exploded into me, clutching me even tighter as he came. I noticed a slick sheen of sweat on the skin of his back when my hands moved up and down his spine. It was several moments before he managed to move off me to dispose of the condom. When he rolled back against my side, I peered over at him.

His eyes studied me like I was an unexpected data point in a predictable experiment. My hand reached out to sift through his hair, causing his eyes to soften.

"That was… that was…" I tried, unable to put words to what I was feeling.

"Yeah. It was."

Lio ran a thumb along my cheekbone and across my lower lip. I felt the heavy weight of his leg across mine and enjoyed the masculine roughness of his leg hair on my skin.

He was propped up on an elbow, gazing at me, and I couldn't take my eyes away. We just stared at each other for a while as our breathing leveled out and our skin returned from nuclear levels of heat.

All the while, Lio's thumb lightly traced my features, my hairline, the angle of my jaw, the cords of my throat, the curve of my collarbone. Goose bumps prickled over every inch of my skin.

Finally, Lio lowered his mouth onto mine, and I slid my arms around his neck, pulling him down to lie on top of me. We kissed lazily for a while, exploring each other's mouths with gentle lips and tongues. Hands wandered down each other's sides and across curved shoulders and muscled thighs.

It was the single most intimate and erotic experience I'd ever had.

And I couldn't help but wonder if it would remain so for the rest of my life.

# CHAPTER 15

LIO

Even though we eventually got up to find something to eat for dinner, the atmosphere of quiet intimacy surrounded the two of us. I held Felix's hand while we walked to the kitchen and only leaned over to distract him with kisses when I thought he'd catch sight of Jon trailing behind us from the carriage house to the main building.

I'd insisted on Mari taking the night off to spend it with Bert, and she'd promised to leave the fixings for a homemade pizza behind in one of the refrigerators. She knew how much I loved making a pizza in the brick oven built into the main fireplace.

Sure enough, she'd left the fires going, and Felix was more than happy to help move some of the embers and hot logs up into the pizza oven. I arranged all of the ingredients on the huge wooden table in the center of the room and teased Felix about his taste in pizza toppings.

"I should make you an American pizza," I joked. "Bet you've never had one quite like mine."

He rolled his eyes at me. "Dude, I live on American pizza. And might I point out that, technically, all pizza is American?"

"Actually, that's a myth. It started thousands of years ago in the Middle East."

Felix lifted a brow at me. "Ah, know your pizza history, do you?"

"I'm extremely well educated in the area of history," I admitted. "It's one of my special skills."

"Yet, you don't know much about the stained glass here in the castle," he teased. "How is that? I'd never even set foot on the island before and I have all kinds of theories about Gadleigh glass."

I poured the tomato sauce over the two dough rounds laid out on the table while Felix sliced the mozzarella. "I know some think the maker is a mystery even though it was credited early on to da Lodi."

Felix looked up at me in surprise. "Shit. You really are a history buff."

I shrugged. "That's about all I know. Well, I know where most of the hidden glass is, only because I've spent so much time here."

I thought about telling Felix the truth of who I was. There was something about the new closeness we'd begun in his apartment earlier that made me feel like I was lying to him now. Every moment I withheld the truth from him felt like a kind of nasty betrayal.

After we finished adding toppings to the two pizzas, I showed Felix how to use the pizza peel to slide them into the oven.

While we waited for them to cook, I found us some bottled beer and sat down at the large table next to Felix. Mari had left a stack of mail and magazines on the table, and Felix pulled a copy of *GOTCHA!* Magazine from the stack. On the cover was a photo of my parents coming out of the hospital with the headline "Is the King of Liorland hiding a terminal illness?" emblazoned across the photo. Even though it was an old shot taken after they'd visited sick kids as part of some charity work, I felt my gut clench. Those kinds of covers and articles were nothing new, but I realized now might be as good a time as any to tell him who I was.

"Felix, I—"

"This is absolute shit," Felix spat. "This poor family is dealing with a health scare, and the fucking tabloid press turns it into a circus."

I watched him to see if any part of what he was saying was insincere. He seemed really upset. He began leafing through the magazine for more information.

"It says here that the king claims it was only a panic attack, and yet the reporter is convinced it's all some big cover-up. He even goes on to say this panic attack was brought on by some secret shit going on in the king's personal life. As if anything going on in the man's personal life is any of our business."

"You're right. It's not," I agreed. "I'm glad to hear you say that because—"

Felix looked up at me, and I noticed his eyes were full of tears. The sight caught me completely off guard.

"Felix? What's wrong? Why is this upsetting you so much? It's a tabloid. This is what they do." I reached out to pull the magazine away and bury it under the stack of mail before pulling him into my arms.

"What if they have kids, Lio?" he asked with a sniff. "That's not fair to those kids. Being dragged through the press like that. What if there's a story there and the press gets a hold of it? What would it do to their kids? It's not like anyone asks to be born into royalty."

I wondered if he knew who I was and that's why he was taking this so hard. Was it possible?

"They do have kids," I said quietly. "But maybe their kids are used to it by now."

Felix pulled back and looked at me with a lifetime's worth of anguish on his face. "They can't possibly be, Lio. You don't ever get used to it. It's impossible."

My heart slowed to a crawl as I realized he was speaking from personal experience. I brushed the hair from his face and placed a kiss on his forehead.

"Tell me," I said.

He turned away and began to fiddle with the corner of an envelope on the top of the mail stack, flicking it with his thumbnail back and forth with a *ticktick* sound.

"My mom is an actress."

I thought about what he'd already told me about his personal life. He was raised by his grandfathers and didn't know his dad. Suddenly, I recalled that his mom hadn't wanted a child to hold back her career.

As an actress.

There was only one actress I could think of with the last name

Wilde. Jacqueline Wilde. The age would fit with being Felix's mother, especially if she was young when she'd gotten pregnant. Jacqueline Wilde was the Sharon Stone of our generation. She was known for being beautiful but ruthless—a power player in Hollywood. Despite a now highly publicized early career in porn, she'd wound up earning hundreds of accolades including Golden Globes and an Oscar nomination.

"Stop staring at me," Felix said in a small voice.

"You look just like her," I couldn't help but say. "I can't believe I didn't put two and two together."

He rolled his eyes in disgust and began to stand up. I pulled him back down and tucked him against my chest.

"I'm sorry. Forgive me. I'm just surprised." I ran my fingers through the hair at the nape of his neck. "I guess this is a sore subject?"

He scoffed. "You could say that."

I pulled him back and kissed his forehead again before cupping his cheeks and looking into his eyes. "Do you want to talk about it?"

He shrugged. "It's one of the reasons I'm here, actually. She has a new movie coming out, which means I suddenly become the catch of the day with the entertainment media."

"Even living in a small town like you do?"

"Especially living in a small town. They come in droves, news vans and camera crews. The entire town thinks it's the greatest thing since sliced bread. They make money hand over fist with the influx of new consumers, and they beg me every time to play up to the press to drag it out as long as I can. The more exposure Hobie gets, the better our summer lake season is for all the business owners. They act like I owe it to the town to help out by letting it happen."

"Felix, that's terrible."

He blew out a breath. "Yeah. It is. That's why I couldn't stand it this time. This movie is going to be huge, and I know it will be the craziest media frenzy yet. I just couldn't deal. I hate the paparazzi. *Hate* them. And I hate my mother for bringing me to their attention." The last part was mumbled, but I still caught it.

I realized with sudden clarity that the same thing would happen if word ever got out that we'd slept together. He would be the center of attention once again, but this time it would be because of me. *I'd* be the one responsible for putting him in the spotlight he so desperately hated.

"Oh fuck," I breathed.

"Yeah. Sorry. I didn't mean to bring down the mood." It was an attempt at a joke, but I couldn't even fake a chuckle. "Do you think the pizza is ready yet?"

I stood up to check the pizza. My entire body seemed to have gone numb at the realization that I was no better than Felix's mom if I was willing to risk his exposure for my own benefit.

As we sat at the table eating our dinner, my mind spun. Surely Felix knew something was up with me, but he didn't ask. Instead of our usual easy conversation, there was silence.

Finally, after we'd finished and cleaned up the mess we'd made, Felix turned to me.

"Listen, I get it. Now that you know who my mom is, you're not interested. It's fine. You don't need to worry about hurting my feelings or anything. Honestly, it's actually better than the opposite. Usually guys want *into* my pants when they find out, not out of them."

"Felix—"

He held up his hand. "No, really. It's cool. I'm just going to head back to my room and turn in. I have lots of work to do on my dissertation anyway."

"Felix," I said again. I could not let him leave like that, thinking I didn't want him. What would the harm be in spending one more night with him in the comfort and security of the private estate? It's not like anyone could catch us here.

"I don't want you to go," I admitted. "I... I really like you." And that was the absolute truth. Even if there was no future that included the two of us together. "Please may I stay with you tonight?"

His face softened into a shy smile that squeezed my heart. "Really?"

I nodded. "Yes, really. But first, I was hoping we could take a glass tour of the castle. You can explain your theories to me."

The sparkle returned to his eyes, and I let out a breath of relief.

"Let's go," he said. "I'll show you my favorite first. It's in the portrait gallery."

I thought about the recent addition of my own portrait in the gallery. Surely, he'd seen it. "Actually, have you seen the hidden glass in the king's bedchamber?" I said quickly.

Felix's eyes widened. "Of course not. It's off-limits."

*Not to me it's not*, I thought.

I grinned at him and grabbed his hand. "I'm sure Mari will overlook a little innocent snooping."

Thank god, I had enough time to message Arthur to prepare the room for visiting before disappearing to his own room.

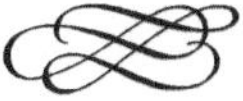

# CHAPTER 16

FELIX

After hours and hours of the most exciting and intriguing treasure hunt of my life, Lio and I returned to my room and fell into bed.

"That was amazing. Best Christmas present ever," I gushed. "I can't believe how many hidden passages you know about. And the glass handles in the royal water closet… they were amazing."

Lio turned to look at me with a satisfied grin. "I'm glad you liked it. It was fun hearing about all the different techniques, especially considering those pieces were made hundreds of years ago."

"I'm sure a good chunk of Calum's job is maintaining the existing glass in the castle. He has to keep it from glass disease and—" Lio cut me off with a kiss.

"Merry Christmas, Felix," he murmured against my mouth. "I'm so glad you're here with me."

"Me too," I breathed. "Wouldn't want to be anywhere else."

We made out like teenagers, kissing and touching and humping against each other until we couldn't stand another minute with fabric between us. As we stripped each other bare, our eyes met and locked on to each other—the intensity in Lio's deep blue gaze struck me like a jolt to the heart. I'd never before felt at once so exposed and so protected.

"Lio," I whispered.

"Shh," he said, reaching for my face and pulling it in for a kiss. "Let me make you feel good, Felix."

And he did. Over and over again for hours until I fell into an exhausted sleep curled up against his strong body.

I AWOKE to banging sounds and shouting, deep voices I'd never heard before and the broken static of walkie-talkies. Before I could figure out what was happening, I felt Lio's body cover mine, his arms wrapping protectively around my head.

"Lio?" I asked, trying to shake myself out of a deep sleep. "Is that the TV?"

"Shh, everything's fine, Felix. I'll explain in a minute," he whispered quickly in my ear. "Please just trust me, okay? I'm sure it's a false alarm." I could hear slight fear in his voice, but what I didn't hear was surprise. Did he know what was happening?

I tried to shift so I could see, but Lio kept me covered.

"Sir, you need to come with us now. It's a full call." The voice was low and commanding. "We'll keep Mr. Wilde safe."

I blinked up at Lio, whose head was tilted to the side.

"He's coming with me. He needs to stay with me," Lio said.

"You know we can't do that, sir," the voice responded. "And I don't have time to argue. We go now."

I felt Lio's body being pulled off me, and I cried out. "What's happening? Lio?"

A man in dark clothing was forcing Lio off the bed and leading him out of my room by the arm. Lio's bare ass was exposed for everyone to see.

"Lio!" I called. The fear was stark in my voice. "You can't take him!"

I scrambled off the bed, pulling a sheet around myself and charging after him, but another man stopped me with a hand around my biceps. It was Jon.

"It's okay, Felix. He's all right, I promise. You need to come with me."

"The hell I do," I snarled, yanking my arm out of his grip and trying to follow Lio. When I got to the door of the guest apartment, I saw someone had thrown a blanket around Lio's nakedness. He looked back at me, his face full of apology.

"I'm sorry, Fee. I'll explain everything when I see you again. I'm so sorry."

And just like that, he was gone.

I turned back to look at Jon, who'd grabbed me around the shoulders to keep me from following Lio.

"You need to come with me, quickly," he said.

"Why? Let me get my clothes." My head was spinning, and I didn't even know what to think. Had Lio just been kidnapped? "What the fuck is happening, Jon?"

Without even allowing me more than the sheet around my waist, he quickly led me out of the apartment and toward the main house. Instead of entering via one of the regular doors, we entered through a space that looked like a cellar door. It took us straight down into a level below ground, and I immediately recognized the stone arches of the basement corridor.

"Where the hell are we going?" I asked, hearing the panic in my own voice.

"To a secure room. There's a security protocol in place we follow until we get the all clear."

"I don't understand."

Jon sighed and glanced at me. "This is a royal house, yeah? So when there's a threat to the monarchy, the royal house goes into a lockdown protocol. In this case, that protocol includes you."

"But what..." I thought about where to begin with the questions. "What about you? Why are you the one bringing me here, and why can't Lio be with us?"

Jon led me into a room where I saw a woman about my age sitting curled up on a worn plaid sofa. She was slender with pale skin and delicate features. Thick waves of messy dark hair tumbled down over her shoulders, and she held an e-reader in her lap.

A space heater was trying and failing to warm up the space, and I noticed a table with a coffee maker in one corner. Everything was slightly blurred without my glasses.

I shivered in the thin sheet wrapped around me.

The woman looked up at the commotion of our entry, and her eyes flew wide at the sight of me. The same dark blue eyes as the man I'd been curled up with only moments before.

"Who are you?" she asked.

I looked from Jon to the woman and back. "Um… Felix? Who are you?"

"Henrietta. Hen."

That name rang a bell. "Henrietta, Lio's sister?"

"Yes. And you?"

I wondered if he was out to his family. "Oh. I, ah… I'm a friend."

Out of the corner of my eye I noticed Jon roll his eyes, but it was the valet named Arthur who spoke up from where he'd been sitting reading a book. "They're sleeping together," he said with a sniff, not even looking up from whatever he was reading.

My head spun around to glare at him. "That's none of your damned business."

But the woman, Hen, just laughed. "Ah-ha. I see. Even when he hides away at Gadleigh, he manages to get laid. Little shit."

The comment soured my stomach, making it seem like all there was between Lio and me was a cheap fuck.

Hell, for all I knew, maybe it was. I swallowed and looked around for a place to sit.

"I don't suppose anyone happens to have an extra pair of sweats lying around," I muttered.

Henrietta looked me up and down with a smirk. "No, but there are extra blankets in that cupboard over there," she said, nodding toward a wooden wardrobe against one wall. I shuffled over to it and found stacks of wool blankets. Despite smelling musty, they were nice and thick and warm.

"Thanks. Much better." I exhaled and found a spot in an over-stuffed chair. "How long until we get an all clear?"

"It depends on what the threat is," Henrietta explained. "Some last only a couple of minutes. Some last days."

"Days?" I sputtered. "I can't stay down here with no clothes for days."

"Well, maybe you should have thought about it before sleeping with the prince of Liorland," she teased.

I stared at her while I waited for my brain to catch up. When it did, I felt the blood drain from my entire body.

"What?"

"Oh hell," Arthur said before standing up and approaching Jon to whisper something into his ear.

"You heard me," Hen continued. "Everyone wants a piece of Lio thinking it's all fun and games, but then this sort of shit happens and they realize it's not all nightclubs and fancy clothes."

"Wait, what?"

I couldn't feel my lips. Or my tongue. Or my feet.

Henrietta's eyes narrowed at me. "What's wrong with you?"

"I didn't sleep with a prince," I insisted, knowing full well it was a lie. "I slept with Lio."

Henrietta stared at me for a beat. "You're serious, aren't you? You really don't know who he is. How can you not know who he is?"

I thought about the magazine cover from the night before, the one with the king and queen of Liorland on the front. Liorland with an *L-i-o*. As in, the royal family of Monaco. The house of Grimaldi. I thought about Lio, who seemed so at home in a royal fucking castle. *Grimaldi.*

"Oh fuck," I breathed. "Oh god." I thought about how stupid I sounded complaining about the paparazzi to *him*, of all people. How stupid I felt for not knowing who he was. For letting him keep me in the dark about it.

Henrietta glanced up at Jon. "Is he breathing?"

I felt like an absolute fool.

"Shit," Jon said. "Felix, put your head between your knees for me." His hand guided my head toward my lap.

I noticed Arthur leave the room out of the corner of my eye.

"Oh god," I moaned. "I can't breathe."

Hen came to perch on the arm of my chair and rubbed my back. "Honey, it's okay. Just calm down." She mentioned something to Jon about finding Lio.

"But, Hen," he argued.

"Find him!" Her shout made even me jump, and I noticed Jon's feet disappear from view. A few moments later I heard multiple sets of footsteps clamber into the room. Jon, Arthur, and the face I most wanted to see.

"Shit." It was Lio, and he didn't sound happy. "Felix, baby, just breathe. What happened?"

Henrietta began lecturing Lio about being an insensitive jerk. She seemed to go full sister on him and lambasted him while he tried to calm me down.

I opened my eyes to find him squatting in front of me, lines of worry carving divots in his forehead. His hands held mine on my lap, and I soaked in the warmth of them as my brain spun.

"You're a prince," I said.

His face fell. "Yes."

"Of, like, a country."

"Yes."

"Oh god," I groaned again. "It's true. I'm an idiot."

Lio's hands came up to cup my chin, forcing me to look at him. "You're not. You're smart as hell."

"Why didn't you tell me?" I asked. "You could have told me. I wouldn't have treated you any differently."

Arthur mumbled something that sounded like *I told you so*.

One of his hands moved to push hair back from my face. "I'm sorry. I'm so sorry, Felix. I wanted to, but then…" He looked up at his sister and the other men in the room, who I'd figured out by now were some type of security personnel. "But then you saw that magazine and…"

And I'd gotten upset. Very upset. And I'd raged against the tabloid press when his entire life was most likely lived in front of the exact same paparazzi.

No wonder he hadn't told me.

# CHAPTER 17

## LIO

The minute the security team had barged into Felix's room, I'd known it was all going to go to shit. Regardless of the reason for the alert, Felix surely wasn't going to get through the experience without finding out who I was. And, sure enough, he hadn't.

He looked so small and pale sitting on the chair with old blankets wrapped around him. I wondered if I'd fucked it all up. If I'd ruined whatever respect he might have had for me.

"I'm so sorry," I said again. I honestly didn't know what else to say to him.

His brown eyes peered up at me from under his dark lashes. "I understand why you didn't want to tell me," he said in a soft voice. "You just wanted to be normal with someone. Be with a person who didn't know the public bullshit side, right?"

I felt a breath of relief exit my tight chest. "Yes, exactly. How did you know?"

Felix's eyes darted away from mine. "Because I know that feeling. I-I mean… not like you do, of course. I could never know what that's like. But with my mom… well, I know what it's like to be the focus of the media's attention. And if it's bad for me, I can't even begin to imagine what it's like for someone in a royal family."

I still held his hands in mine and rubbed them idly while he spoke. "Still," I began. "I'm really sorry. I didn't want to lie to you. I really wanted to tell you."

My sister spoke up from her perch on the edge of the sofa to my left. "Then you should have. No one wants to be with a liar, you freak."

I glared at her. "Thanks a lot, Hen. What are you even doing here?"

"I told you I was coming to keep you company for Christmas."

"Yeah, and I thought you were joking. You haven't been to Gadleigh in years. You hate it here."

She rolled her eyes, but I could still see affection soften her face. "Maybe, you idiot. But I don't hate *you*. And I was worried about you. Didn't want you to be alone on Christmas. Turns out, I needn't have worried so much." Henriette's grin was mischievous, and I worried at the teasing she had in store for Felix.

"Hen," I warned.

"What? Introduce me properly to your boyfriend, Lior," she said with a false innocence.

I blew out a breath and looked back at Felix. "I'm sorry," I murmured. "Sisters are assholes."

His grin curved the corner of his mouth slightly, causing me to imagine teasing it with the tip of my tongue.

"Why does she call you Lior?"

Before I had a chance to downplay Hen's slip of the tongue, she cut in.

"Because that's his name—the name of the king of Liorland and all of the kings before him."

If it was possible, Felix's complexion went even paler. I shot daggers at my sister.

"Cut it out, Hen. Can't you give him a minute to wrap his head around this? And, besides, I'm not the king."

Her delicate eyebrow arched. "That's not what I heard."

"Fuck," I snapped through clenched teeth before looking over at Jon. "Can we go yet?"

"No, sir. We don't have the all clear. Someone was spotted on the grounds, so we need to finish securing the estate before we can let you go."

"Then can you at least send someone for Felix's clothes?" I gave Jon a look that brooked no argument and saw him say something to the other guard by the door. Before the guard could respond, Arthur offered to go up to my room and grab something of mine. When I turned back to Felix, I noticed he was shaking. "Scoot over and let me sit with you."

I nudged him over to the side of the chair and then pulled him back on my lap and wrapped my arms around him, forcing him to curl against my chest. "You're freezing," I murmured into his hair. "I'm so sorry. This whole thing must have freaked you out."

"I thought they were kidnapping you," Felix admitted. "So, yeah. You could say it freaked me out."

I kissed his hair and forehead before tucking his face back into my neck. "I'm sorry."

"You don't need to keep apologizing, Lio. I told you I understand."

"You shouldn't have to," I muttered. "It's fucked-up. I hate it."

"I can't imagine."

Silence descended for a moment before I remembered my sister was on the sofa next to us. I glanced at her and noticed her shocked expression and wide eyes.

"What?" I asked.

"You… you like him." Her voice was reverent, and the tone of it caused Felix to lift his head up to look at her before turning to look at me.

I felt my face heat up.

"Well, yes. Of course I like him. What's not to like? Look at him," I babbled. "He's beautiful. Plus, he's smart and sweet and—"

As I spoke, Felix's eyes widened comically until Hen laughed.

"I'm not sure he knew that, brother," she teased. "Maybe you should tell him instead of me."

Despite my burning face, I forced myself to meet Felix's eyes. "I do. I like you," I said stupidly before clearing my throat. "In case that was somehow unclear."

"I like you too," he whispered. "But..."

And there it was. *But.*

Of course there was a but. There could be nothing *but* a but.

But the press. But the fact that the king couldn't be gay. But Felix lived in Texas and I lived in Monte Carlo. But we only just met. But... but...

"Yeah," I murmured, running my hand through his hair before tucking his head back down on my shoulder. "But."

Hen's forehead creased in worry as she caught my eye over Felix's head. She mouthed the word sorry, and I shook my head to dismiss her. It wasn't her fault things were the way they were.

They just were.

Two hours later, the security team gave us the all clear and we were able to move up to the kitchen. It was still very early morning, but there was no way anyone was falling back to sleep so soon after the flurry of activity that had awoken us.

Mari and Bert had most likely been secured in a different antechamber and made their way to the kitchen shortly after we did.

"Merry Christmas, Lior!" Mari's face was bright with holiday cheer, and I was happy to see the security protocol hadn't diminished her good mood. "Henriette, dear, how did you sleep? Wait, where is young Felix?" She craned her neck to look around the large space.

"He's changing his clothes in the other room," I said. "He'll be here shortly. And, ah, he knows about me now. Obviously." I tilted my head toward the handful of uniformed guards helping themselves to the coffee machine.

Mari's face fell. "Oh dear. Is he upset?"

Before I had a chance to answer, Felix wandered in and beat me to the punch.

"Yes," he said with a wink toward me. "Upset he let me feel guilty about sneaking around the royal wing of the castle last night."

I could tell despite his attempts to be congenial about everything, the news was bothering him.

Mari turned to me with a glare. "You didn't."

"Oh, come on. Isn't it more fun to sneak around a place than to feel like you own the damned thing?" I was kidding, of course, just trying to make the conversation light to keep from ruining the morning. But I could see the moment the words sunk in with Felix.

"You own the damned thing," he repeated faintly before glancing up at me. "You own Gadleigh Castle… This is—" He swallowed. "This is your house. One of them. One of your houses. A royal castle is… is one of your houses."

I approached him slowly, the fear of scaring him off a very real thing tightening in my chest.

"Felix," I began.

"No. Oh, no. It's fine. I mean, yeah. It's a little crazy, right?" His eyes were bright with burgeoning panic. "But it's cool. Totally fine. No big deal."

His breathing quickened and his eyes darted around the large kitchen space, landing on the royal guards, the giant medieval fireplace, and the rich tapestry hanging above with the Grimaldi coat of arms on it—a majestic lion surrounded by the royal crest.

"Oh god," he croaked.

"Felix," I repeated.

"I need to go back to my room," he said before swallowing and turning to go. "I'm sorry."

"Fuck," Hen said quietly from behind me. "Don't let him go, Lio. He's freaking out again."

But my feet were frozen in place. There wasn't a damned thing I could say to halt his panic. And considering we weren't really more than an extended, albeit fantastic, one-night stand to each other, I wasn't sure it was my place to try and reassure him. What exactly did Hen expect me to say? That I was there for him? That I cared about him and didn't want him upset?

Well, that last part was for damned sure true, so maybe it was worth trying to at least be there for him right now. Even if there was no such thing as long-term potential between us. I couldn't bear to see him confused and hurting.

I moved quickly toward where he'd disappeared out the side door. Jon noticed and followed me as I bolted across the gravel pathways toward the carriage house.

Once I was inside, I slowed my pace on the stairs to his apartment, racking my brain to try and come up with something to say. I knocked softly on the door before trying the handle. It turned easily and allowed me to crack the door open.

"Felix?"

I heard his muffled voice come from the direction of the bedroom where we'd been curled up together only a few hours before. Part of me wished we could go back in time, even if just for a minute so I could enjoy the final moment of peace between us. But then again, knowing it was the end of our peace together wouldn't have felt that great either.

"It's okay, Lio," he said. "I'm fine."

He sounded anything but fine.

"I'm coming in," I warned him before making my way through the doorway and locking the door behind me. Through the opening to the bedroom, I could see him sitting on the edge of the bed with his face in his hands. He raised his eyes up to look at me.

"I'm fine. You didn't have to check up on me," Felix repeated.

"I wanted to. You may be fine, but *I'm* not fine." I sat down next to him and reached for one of his hands. I noticed it was shaking, so I clasped it between my own in an effort to stop it. "I'm sorry about all of this. I didn't want you to find out this way."

His eyes lifted to mine, and I saw a myriad of emotion in them. Confusion, sadness, determination, and longing. The mix of feelings in those deep brown eyes made my chest tighten.

"How did you want me to find out?" Felix asked with a small smile. "I keep picturing what it would have been like to go home after this trip and run across your photo on the cover of a magazine at the grocery store. I'm not sure that would have been any better, Lio."

I couldn't help but smile at the mental image of his jaw dropping at the checkout line.

"I guess not."

Silence descended as I peered down at our joined hands. One of my hands clasped his while the fingers of the other brushed lightly across the smooth skin of his knuckles. After a moment, I pulled his hand up to press a kiss onto it.

My thoughts tumbled around in my head like knotted rope, and I searched frantically for one end of it so I could begin to untangle the situation.

I cleared my throat before speaking. "I didn't... I didn't really intend to do more than sleep with you, Felix."

His entire face crumpled as I realized how my words had sounded.

"Oh god, no. Wait," I said quickly.

Felix tried to pull his hand from mine as he began stammering apologies again. I held on tightly with one hand and grabbed his chin gently but firmly with the other.

"Stop. Stop, Felix, and let me finish what I did such a piss-poor job of starting." I watched as his eyes lowered to his lap. I hated seeing him so unsure of himself. It made me fucking crazy. "Baby, please look at me for a minute. I didn't realize I'd start to have feelings for you, Felix. At first I thought it was just sex. But now... now I... *fuck*. Now I care. Do you understand? I care about you, and I want... I want..."

I took a deep breath and felt my back teeth clench together.

"I want you." There, I finally got the truth out. I'd said it out loud. But it wasn't the whole truth. The whole truth made my stomach churn with acid and made me fantasize about being born into any other family besides my own.

"I want you, Felix. But I can't have you."

# CHAPTER 18

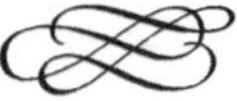

## FELIX

It was the emotional equivalent of seesawing with a psychopath. One minute I was flying high and the next I was smacking the ground with a teeth-rattling crash.

"Oh." The word was out of my mouth before I could stop it. And then the words just kept spewing forth as if from a broken fire hydrant. "Right. Of course. I understand. It makes sense. Of course you can't do... that. I mean, I assume it's the... well. A prince can hardly be gay, really, so you can't... I mean, you and I can't... nothing could come of—"

Before I could make even more of a fool of myself, Lio's fingers tightened on my chin, and his mouth sealed firmly over my own. Thank god for nonsense-stopping kisses.

I whimpered into his mouth as the familiar taste of him assaulted my senses. God, how was it possible his mouth felt like home to me? How was it possible I felt most alive when I was touching him?

Lio's lips were soft and full, nibbling and sipping mine as tenderly as if I was daydreaming it. His large sure hands slid into my hair and moved my head gently to one side as his lips trailed from my mouth down my jaw to my throat.

"Lio," I breathed. "We..." I'd meant to say we shouldn't, but I couldn't bring myself to do or say anything to stop his delicious attentions. I moaned and arched into him as his hands began roving down my back to the waistband of my sweater and under it to the bare skin just above the waistband of my jeans. "Yes, please," I whispered. "Please, Lio."

I couldn't think when his hands were on my skin. In the back of my head, alarm bells were trying their hardest to clang, to remind me that Lio wasn't really available to me, that we needed to talk about stuff, but I honestly didn't give a shit. All I cared about in that moment was feeling Lio's warm hands on me and smelling the familiar scent of his body next to mine.

My cock throbbed, begging to rut against Lio for release. The sexy fucker pressed me back onto the bed and shifted me until I was lying in the middle of the mattress, completely at his mercy.

When he climbed over my body to lock eyes with me, I saw a range of feelings in his glittering eyes. "What?" I asked.

"I don't just want you for sex, Felix."

His voice was low and certain, almost as intense as his gaze on me.

"I believe you," I breathed.

Lio's face softened into a relieved smile, and he lowered his face to kiss me on the lips. "Good. Because I don't ever want you to think that you're not the complete package, Felix Wilde." His words were spoken between soft kisses dropped across my face. Every move of his mouth and word he spoke raised the hair on my neck and the pace of my heart. "You are smart, and talented. Sweet and adorable. Hot, passionate, responsive…"

I brought my legs around his back and pulled him in closer with them until he let his weight drop on me. "Stop talking and start taking my clothes off," I suggested with a grin. "You can respect me later."

Lio laughed and began undressing me, still sneaking soft kisses onto every body part of mine he uncovered. Eventually, I was completely naked beneath him and he was still fully dressed. Something about that made me even hornier.

My hips bucked up into his in search of more. I felt the rough fabric of his fly against the sensitive skin of my dick and thought about how much better it would feel to be skin against skin instead.

"P-pants off," I stammered as his tongue did crazy things to the side of my neck. I felt his answering smile against my skin before his hand moved down to work on his button and zipper while his mouth stayed on me.

"Oh god," I pleaded. "Hurry."

Lio's hand moved to stroke my cock, and I heard the sharp intake of breath when he felt the precum I'd been leaking all over my stomach.

"Jesus, Felix," he murmured, stroking me up and down as he pulled back to look at his hand jacking me. "I want to make you feel incredible." His eyes flicked back up to mine, and the dark intensity of them made my stomach flip. "What can I do to you to make you feel incredible?"

My heart thundered in my throat. Had I ever been the focus of such intimate attention? Did I have the guts to tell him what I really wanted?

*I want your mouth on my ass. I want you to rim the hell out of me again.*

"Anything," I said instead. "Everything. I don't know."

He must have seen something flick across my face because he smirked at me. "Nuh-uh, baby. Fortunately for me, you're a terrible liar. You want something specific. What is it? What dirty thoughts are in your head right now, beautiful?"

As he spoke, his hand stroked my cock and moved down to tug at my balls. There was no blood flow left in my brain at all.

"Mouth on me," I gasped just as one of his fingertips brushed my hole. "Mouth on me *there.*"

Lio's entire face lit up like he'd tortured state secrets from his prisoner.

"Hands and knees, Felix."

I was so far gone, I didn't remember much after that.

# CHAPTER 19

## LIO

After rimming Felix and then fucking him into a stupor, I fell asleep wrapped around his sated body. We'd been woken up so early that morning, both of us clearly needed a few more hours' sleep.

When I came awake a little while later, I heard the tapping of a cell phone keypad and realized Felix was sending an email or text. My body was still spooned around his, so I was able to open my eyes and peer over his shoulder.

With his fingers flying angrily over the keypad, the only word I could make out on the screen was the name of the contact he was texting. *Jackie.*

His mom. At least I assumed so. But why would he have her listed as "Jackie" instead of "Mom"?

I tilted my head down behind him until I couldn't see it anymore. There was a tiny, delicate mole on the sharp edge of his left shoulder blade. I traced it softly with a finger, eliciting a wave of goose bumps breaking out on the skin of his back. He was so damned responsive, it drove me crazy in the very best way. I felt my lips curve into a grin before I dropped a kiss on his shoulder.

"Proud of yourself?" he asked in a sleep-roughened voice. "Maybe I'm just cold."

"Mm-hm. That's probably it." I continued pressing gentle kisses along his shoulder to his neck and into the back of his hair. "Everything okay back home?"

He harrumphed and shifted to set the phone back on the bedside table. In the process, his ass pressed back into my groin, and I couldn't help but grab his hip and return the gesture.

"Fuck," I groaned. My cock was already wide-awake from waking up nestled against Felix's bare ass, but feeling him press against it made me even harder. Felix turned to face me with a grin of mischief.

"Before we do any of that again, you need to feed me."

His face was creased on one side where he'd slept on a fold of his pillow. Warm brown eyes peered at me expectantly from under bed-rumpled hair, and I had a moment's clarity that I was really quite gay. I'd spent much of my time since puberty self-identifying as bisexual, but in that moment, I couldn't imagine a single woman on earth who could ever come close to being as attractive and enticing to me as the man in front of me.

But then again, there couldn't be another man that beautiful either. Perhaps I was Felix-sexual.

A furrow formed between his eyebrows. "Why are you staring at me? Aren't you hungry too?"

I nodded. "Yes, yes, of course. Late breakfast is just the thing. Surely Mari left something out for us." Without lingering further, I turned to exit the bed and find my clothes.

IT WASN'T until much later in the day, after a big Christmas meal Mari and my sister insisted on serving to the rest of us in the castle, that I found myself alone with Felix again. I'd invited him into the hidden treasury room, and we were kicking back in front of the fireplace with full bellies and Irish coffee.

Felix's shoes were off, and he stretched out his legs toward the fire. He wore red-and-green-striped socks which, for some reason, made me think he was even more adorable than I already knew him to be.

What the hell was wrong with me? I'd never been so attracted to another person in my life.

Was this some kind of last-minute panic? Like a manifestation of my unwillingness to give up my life for the crown? Maybe I was clinging on to a man in hopes of not having to face my real life. As long as I was seeing a guy, I couldn't take the throne.

I was so much in my head that I didn't hear what Felix asked me until he nudged my leg with his toes.

"You okay, Lio? You've been super quiet all afternoon. I think Hen is worried about you."

There had been at least twelve of us for the meal, including three to four royal guards. I'd noticed Henriette talking Felix's ears off from her spot between him and Jon. She'd told him about growing up in the palace with nannies and tutors until we were old enough to go off to boarding school and have a somewhat more "normal" childhood. Not that it was ever normal by any stretch of the imagination. Arthur had piped in several times and left Felix in stitches telling "teenage Lio" stories.

My eyes moved from the golden glow of the fire to Felix's worried gaze. I'd intended to give him a smile of reassurance, but he continued speaking before I had a chance.

"Is it me? It's okay. I should probably give you some space anyway. I feel like I've been monopolizing—"

"No," I blurted. "Stay. Please, Felix. That's not the problem. You're not the problem at all."

I ran a hand through my hair and looked back at the fire. Felix shifted, standing up quietly from his chair and stepping over to mine. I looked up at him and saw his sweet face in the light of the fire. Without even thinking about it, I reached out my hand to him and pulled him onto my lap until he was straddling me with his knees on either side of my hips.

"I'm sorry," I said softly. "Just have a lot on my mind. It's not you at all."

Felix's hands smoothed up my chest to my neck. "Do you want to talk about it? I mean, you don't have to, of course, but if it would help..."

The divot between his eyebrows had returned, and I reached up to rub it with my thumb.

"Soon it's going to be my turn on the throne," I said quietly, as if anyone could hear us from our hidden space inside a semideserted castle on a sparsely populated island in the middle of the North Sea.

In winter.

I moved my hand to cup his jaw before continuing. "And I don't want it, Felix."

There, I'd said it. I'd confessed my deepest secret thought to a practical stranger.

*Well done, Lior.*

Felix didn't say anything immediately, just studied me. As if I hadn't just said something explosive and monumental.

"Say something," I breathed. "Tell me I'm being a spoiled brat. Tell me to suck it up."

Instead of saying either of those things, he just leaned in and hugged me.

Felix's hands came around my neck and pulled me to him until I felt like his entire body was holding me in unspoken support. I turned my face into the side of his neck and inhaled the comforting scent of him. There was something so soothing about the man. He radiated calm unlike anyone I'd ever met before.

When he pulled back to meet my eyes, I saw the twinkle of mischief in his eyes.

"You're just having cold feet, Lio. You're going to make a wonderful king someday."

I realized he didn't understand how imminent my reign would be. Of course he didn't. That information was a massive secret. One that, if it got out, would throw the media into a frenzy.

"What if it's sooner rather than later, Felix? I'm gay. I can't be gay when I take the throne."

Felix snorted. Actually snorted with laughter.

"It's not funny," I cried. "It's my fucking life, Felix."

His eyes shot wide, laughter dying immediately as his face

dropped. "But, Lio. You *are* gay. Which means you will be gay when you take the throne. There is absolutely no way to stop being gay. We both know that. Plus, it's the twenty-first century, Lio. The world can handle it."

"No. The world can't handle it."

"But Luxem—"

"Stop. Please. I know all about the prime minister. That's not the same thing as a hereditary monarchy reaching back hundreds of years. Can you even imagine if Prince William were gay?"

I noticed his jaw clench and his nostrils flare. "Yes, as a matter of fact, I can. I think it would be fucking fantastic if Prince William came out. Someone needs to be the first."

"Well, it's not going to be me."

So what if I sounded like a child?

Felix paused for a beat before trying a different tactic. "Then what's your plan, exactly? Be celibate for the rest of your life or try and stay hidden in the royal closet?"

And there it was. The story of my fucking life reduced to one simple question.

# CHAPTER 20

## FELIX

It wasn't my place to interfere with how he made his life decisions. And, quite frankly, it wasn't even like me to get involved in discussions about someone's personal business. I tended to keep myself to myself, but for some reason, it rankled me to see Lio so upset. It was almost like an itch under my skin. I sensed his discomfort and frustration and wished like hell I could fix it for him.

"I'm sorry," I said. "I didn't mean to push. It's really none of my business."

Lio's hands snuck up the back of my shirt, and I felt my skin prickle at the touch of my bare skin.

"No, Felix. I'm the one who's sorry. It's just a shitty situation, but it's nothing new. I've known this was coming for a long time. I'm having a hard time accepting it; that's all."

"So, what's your plan, then?"

He shrugged and looked past my shoulder to the fireplace. "Go home, grow up. Marry a nice woman who'll make a fine mother to my children."

I felt my stomach pitch into my throat. The very idea of him marrying a woman just to appease tradition made me want to throw up.

"Seriously? You'd do that?"

Lio's forehead leaned against my chest, directly over my heart. I brought my hands up to brush through his thick hair.

"I don't have a choice, Felix," he murmured. It was so soft, I almost didn't hear the words over the snapping of the fire. "It's what I was born to do. I've always known that was my path."

"That's not exactly fair to the woman involved," I grumbled, grasping at straws.

"Maybe not. But whoever signs up for this will obviously be getting a lot out of the bargain." His voice held sarcasm, and I knew he'd spent hours upon hours in his head trying to justify his future actions.

"I guess so." It was all I could think of to appease him and let the subject drop. I wondered if there was a way I could get him out of his head and out of the funk he'd fallen into. "Will you take me to bed, Lio?"

When he lifted his head, there was a sexy smirk on his lips and a hint of relief in his eyes.

"Hell fucking yes."

Before I even had a chance to crawl off his lap, the panel to the red salon slid open and his sister stepped into the room.

"There you are. I should have known," she said. "Been looking all over for you."

I shifted to get off Lio, but his arms tightened around me to keep me in place. My cheeks flamed in response to Henriette seeing us that way.

"What's up?" Lio asked.

Before Hen could answer, Jon stepped through the doorway as well. The four of us filled the small space to the brim. Hen's eyes flicked between Lio and me.

"I just wanted to make sure you were okay. You were awfully quiet this afternoon."

Lio's hands tightened almost imperceptibly where they rested on my hips.

"Just frustrated. That's all."

Hen moved forward to take a seat in the chair I'd been sitting in. "Is it the thing with Dad? You and I haven't had a chance to talk about it yet, but I knew you'd be upset."

I squirmed and shot a glance at Lio before speaking. "Please let me leave you two in peace. Clearly you need some time to catch up."

Lio's dark blue eyes met mine. "Will you wait for me in my room? It's the one with the stained glass in the bedpost."

He'd shown me the room the night before when we'd "snuck" into the royal apartments upstairs. I'd gone apeshit over the glass bedpost. Of course that was his room. Jesus.

I felt my nerves kick up at an external confirmation he was, in fact, the royal personage in this castle. "Yes. But please take your time. I'm going to call home first and wish Grandpa and Doc a Merry Christmas."

When I stood up, Lio grabbed my hand and pulled it to his lips for a kiss before winking at me. My heart did stupid shit, so I turned to leave the room as quickly as possible. Before I got to the doorway, however, Hen stood up and pulled me into her arms for a hug.

The gesture shocked me.

Her smooth voice whispered into my ear. "Thank you for being here for my brother. Merry Christmas, Felix."

I gave a sort of freaked-out nod before hotfooting it out of the room like my ass was on fire. What had she meant by that? It was weird enough to even meet the sister of a hookup, but to have her thank me for... what? Having sex with her brother? Fuck. What was that about?

I made my way back to my guest quarters and pulled out my laptop to do a video call back home. While I didn't have cell coverage at Gadleigh, I did have access to their Wi-Fi.

After the call was answered on their end, I saw a clear image of Doc and my cousin Saint in the background. Before Doc even had a chance to greet me, I spluttered. "Saint! Holy shit, what are you doing home? I thought you were still overseas."

The big guy turned and grinned at me. Despite the muscle-bulked frame, his face was all baby, and I felt a wave of relief pass over me to see him safely home.

"Otto and I decided to pack it in once and for all," he said into the camera. I could see they were in the kitchen and assumed Doc had kept the laptop set up in hopes I'd call.

"What do you mean? Like, retirement? For real?"

He nodded, and I could see Doc's grin grow wider. Doc slipped his arm around Saint's waist. "Can you believe it? They got in late last night as a surprise. Didn't tell a soul they were doing it."

I felt a small tick of homesickness niggle at me. Saint and Otto had come home from the Navy, and I hadn't been there to celebrate with everyone.

"I'm so happy for you. What are you going to do with yourselves now?"

In the background, I could see the familiar hunched shoulders of my cousin Otto as he grabbed a beer from the fridge before approaching the computer and edging Doc out of the way.

"Hey, Felix. Sorry we missed you, but Grandpa and Doc said you'll be home soon," Otto said with a kind smile. God, how I'd missed those two guys during their deployment. They'd both been in for several years, and I'd always imagined at least Saint would be a lifer. I wondered what had caused him to change his mind.

The reminder of my dwindling time at Gadleigh left a hollow in the pit of my stomach, but I tried to hide it with a smile.

"Yep. I'll be home soon. Hope you'll still be there in Hobie when I get back?"

Otto glanced at Saint before nodding at the camera. "Yeah, buddy. We've got some job leads in Dallas, but in the meantime we're staying here in the bunkhouse with the pups. I think Grump has officially fallen in love with Saint here."

I laughed. My grandparents' coonhound was a sweet old thing with long ears and a grizzled face. "Don't let Sweet and Salty see you guys playing favorites, or Salty will bite your ankles off. She's a bitch."

Doc came back in the frame with a mock glare. "Hey now, that's my sweet baby you're talking about."

"Sweet baby, my ass," Saint muttered under his breath. "Damned thing near took my feet out from under me this morning on my way over here for breakfast."

Seeing them all acting like their normal selves made me happy. I realized I really had missed being there for Christmas even though I wouldn't have wanted to leave Gadleigh for anything.

"Was everyone there for Christmas today except me?"

Grandpa leaned into the frame, his chin resting on Doc's shoulder. "Mostly. But we missed you. Especially when Hudson's girlfriend gave him a Christmas ornament made out of stained glass. You should have seen how red his ears got."

"Darci was there? I thought they broke up."

Doc's eyes glanced up as if looking at something off-screen, and I realized maybe Darci was still there and had heard me.

"Oh shit," I said quietly. "Is she… are they still there?"

"No," Doc said quickly. "They left a little while ago. I just thought I heard Pippa crying and realized the monitor isn't turned on in here. I'm gonna go check on her. Love you, son."

"Love you too," I said before watching him disappear down the hallway toward the bedrooms. Grandpa watched him go before turning back to me.

"Darci and Hudson are still going out. That poor girl looks at him like he's the last pint of ice cream at the grocery store," Grandpa scoffed. "If it weren't for him being in Dallas and her being here, I think she'd have wrangled a commitment out of him already by sheer force of will."

I thought about how it could be worse for them. "Dallas to Hobie isn't that far apart. Compared to, say… if she was in Europe or something."

Right on cue, my face heated up like a solar flare. I hadn't meant to be so specific, and Lord knew Grandpa never missed a beat.

"Something going on there, Felix?"

Saint and Otto had wandered off to join Hallie in an argument about something in the background. It was just Grandpa left on the call with me.

"I met someone."

Somehow, he knew when to keep his jokes to himself.

"Sounds serious. Where does this someone live? There on the island?"

"Monte Carlo."

There was no way in hell I could tell him who it was. Obviously I trusted Grandpa, but his house was probably full of friends and family members, and who knew how much everyone had been drinking at Christmas dinner.

"Damn, Fee. How's that supposed to work?" Grandpa's face was creased with concern, and I felt his love for me across the ocean.

"It's not. He's not in a position to start something," I admitted. "I'm just feeling sorry for myself."

"Is he already in a relationship?"

I blew out a breath. "No. That's not it. More like… more like the deepest closet possible. A closet he'll never come out of and one that wouldn't have room for me in it even if I wanted to squeeze in there with him."

Grandpa was silent for a moment. No doubt, he was trying to figure out how to solve the unsolvable problem, and I loved him for that.

"It is what it is, Grandpa. Doesn't mean I have to like it."

He peered into the camera at me. "I love you, Felix. We all love you. When you come home, we'll make sure to distract you, all right? I don't know what else to say."

I felt my eyes prickle and my chin tilt in a nod.

"Love you too, Gramps. Tell Doc the same. Gotta go."

Once I disconnected the call, I sat back on the sofa and closed my eyes to think about the situation I was in with Lio. Talking about it to my grandfather had clarified it for me. There was absolutely no future for me with Lio. I knew that now.

Lio clearly had no plan to be the first openly gay king, and who could blame him? Talk about a life in the media crosshairs. I couldn't even imagine the scrutiny he'd be under if he tried to make history that way.

So I had two choices. I could cut it off now and spend my remaining days trying to focus on the glass, or I could accept the thing with Lio was a temporary fling and enjoy it while it lasted.

I stood up and turned toward the door of my guest apartment. There was a stained glass bedpost calling my name. For tonight, at least, I could have both.

# CHAPTER 21

## LIO

I knew something was up with my sister. She had that look about her that sisters get when they're getting ready to lay down some truth. I wasn't sure I was in the mood for any of her truth, but I was definitely sure she was going to lay it down regardless.

"He's cute," she began.

I couldn't help but smile. "He's fucking gorgeous and adorable as hell. And it goes without saying, I call dibs."

I noticed Jon's eyebrows quirk up as he glanced at Hen, but Hen only chuckled. "No worries, Lio. I'm not shopping around at the moment."

The fire crackled as quiet descended. I thought about my father and his pregnant mistress. No wonder Hen was put off looking for someone. Falling in love was dangerous business in our family. Not that I was in love, of course. Because going down that road was a nonstarter for me. I couldn't even consider the possibility of falling for someone I really wanted. Even if Felix had been the right gender for my life's plan, I still saw how many relationships ended in disaster. I wondered if Hen did too. If so, I hated that my father's lack of responsibility to this family would cause my sister to lose her hope of finding love.

Between the two of us, at least she had the chance to go for it. Maybe once the scandal came out and subsequently died down, she'd try again.

"How did you get here?" I asked, trying to change the subject.

"I swam, Lio. What are you going to do about Felix?"

I blinked at her in the firelight. Her dark hair was caught up in a messy knot, and her dark eyebrows bunched together in concern.

"What do you mean?" I asked, genuinely confused. "What is there to do about Felix?"

"You like him."

"Yes."

She twisted the fingers of her hands together. "He likes you."

"You think so?" The very idea he liked me back made me happy even though it didn't really matter in the long run.

"You're smiling just thinking about him." Hen's own face was curved into a smirk. "It's sweet. I've never seen you smile like that about someone you liked."

"Yeah, well. I told you I liked him, and I do."

"So, I'll repeat. What are you going to do about it?"

I felt my back teeth grind together. "Hen, what are you getting at? Because you and I both know there's no future there. I can enjoy him this week as long as he's willing and then say goodbye. That's it."

"Sounds pretty shit if you ask me."

My teeth began to ache in my jaw. "I didn't ask you."

Hen tapped her fingers against the arm of the overstuffed chair. "You could always—"

I cut her off. "No. Sorry, Hen, but there's no good solution to this. Just drop it."

I noticed her glance back at Jon, who sat with his ass propped on a windowsill. I wondered why he was even in here with us. He usually left me in peace inside the castle.

Jon noticed me look at him and spoke up. "I could help you hide—"

"No!" I barked. "Felix deserves better than that, and we all know trying to hide shit doesn't work. It would come out. It always does."

I noticed Hen wince, and I felt guilty for my outburst. After a few minutes, she spoke again.

"You could refuse to take the throne," she offered quietly.

I glanced at her. "And then what? Let Laurence have it? I'd rather die celibate." My father's cousin was a nightmare. A womanizer, a bigot, and all-around narcissist. There was no way in hell my family would allow him to take a leadership position in our beloved country.

"Hell no. I mean, you could ask Father to stay on despite his scandal. That would at least be better than Laurence."

"I'd bet all of Gadleigh our father wouldn't stay on even if I begged him. I got the feeling he wants to escape somewhere and play pretty family with his new conquest." Even I could hear the bitterness soaking my words. I still couldn't wrap my head around the decisions my father had made, but it was done. There was no avoiding the upcoming coronation.

I peered at Hen out of the corner of my eye. "What about you? Why don't you take the throne?"

She snorted in a very un-queen-like manner, and I could have sworn I heard Jon's sharp intake of breath at the same time. "Right. As if."

"Why not? We can bring this ancient monarchy into a new era."

"If we're going to do that, we might as well have a gay king, Lior," she insisted with a smirk. She deliberately used the regal version of my name to make her point. "Explain to me why you think it's a nonstarter."

"The reasons are too obvious to state," I said, more petulantly than I'd intended. "And besides, why come out until there is someone worth coming out for? Until then, it's really just a hypothetical."

"Bullshit. And you don't think someone like Felix is worth coming out for? I saw the way you looked at him, Lio. Don't you want a chance to see if there's the possibility for more with someone like him?"

If I didn't help her understand this soon, I was in danger of losing my hold on my frustration about this situation. "Even if it was perfectly acceptable for me to date a man, it still couldn't be Felix. He hates the paparazzi. And when I say hate, I mean despises them. He wouldn't even consider a real relationship with someone like me. The media scrutiny would destroy him."

"You don't know that," she began.

"I do. I really do, Hen. His mother is Jackie Wilde."

My sister's mouth opened in surprise. "You're kidding?"

"No. I'm not. And I get the feeling he's had his share of shit from the tabloid press, just like we have. He's a quiet man. Felix deserves to pursue his dreams without people all up in his business. Now, can we stop talking about it, please? I'd like to spend some more time with him before we all have to return to our real lives. I have a feeling this is the last week I have of peace before all hell breaks loose at home."

I stood up and banked the fire to allow it to finish burning down safely. After dropping a kiss on my sister's cheek and tilting my head at Jon, I left the room in search of the man in question. I could feel myself mentally shoving away the serious shit in favor of losing myself in the physical connection with Felix.

If only for a few more days, I could pretend that the shy, beautiful man from small-town Texas was mine, and we were just a couple of regular guys enjoying each other's company far away from the madding crowd.

THE NEXT THREE days passed in a kind of deliberate nonchalance. It was as if Felix and I had some unspoken agreement not to bring up any serious topics such as a certain royal situation or the impending date of his departure. We spent daytime hours exploring Gadleigh Castle, goofing off in the glassmaking studio, or just talking by the fire in the treasury room. Sometimes my sister joined us, but often it was just the two of us. At night, we spent hours exploring each other's bodies, talking and laughing, or just curled around each other in sated sleep. It was like having a boyfriend but in the present tense only. There was no past, there could be no future, and the present was simply easy and fun.

As long as we stayed in the present.

By the time the end of his visit approached, it was impossible not to think about our impending separation and my upcoming ascension to the throne. There was no telling how Felix was feeling about it all, but I, for one, had begun to feel slightly panicky.

We were asleep in my bed in the castle early on the morning of Felix's last day at Gadleigh when I heard my sister scream from her room down the hall. At first I thought it was part of a dream, but Felix shot up in bed, displacing my arm from around him and almost elbowing me in the face.

"What is it?" I mumbled. "Bad dream?"

"Shit. It's Hen. Something's wrong." He scrambled from the bed and grabbed clothes from the floor. I took a microsecond to appreciate the rounded bounce of his pale ass as he stepped quickly into the plaid flannel pajama pants. His words finally sunk in when I heard a muffled thump from the direction of my sister's room.

"Hen? Fuck." I moved quickly then, grabbing for my own sleep pants before reaching for a fleece pullover. Felix had thrown on a hoodie over his bare chest and shoved his feet into thick socks before flying out of the bedroom.

I was only a few beats behind him when he reached her bedroom door and flung it open. Felix screeched to a halt, causing me to run into him at full speed. After grabbing him with my arms to keep us from tumbling to the floor, I noticed what had caused him to stop in his tracks.

# CHAPTER 22

FELIX

As soon as I stepped through the doorway to the bedroom, I saw Jon's naked ass kneeling on the bed next to Hen. His arms were up in a calm-down gesture, and he was clearly pleading with Hen to stop screeching.

Which wasn't working.

Hen was in full-on hysterics. Her face was blotchy red, and tears wet her cheeks. She clutched her phone with a death grip and waved it around like it was the weapon in a jittery bank robber's shaky grasp.

"How did this happen?" Her screech pierced the cold air of the castle room as Lio barreled into me from behind.

I sucked in a breath as Lio crashed into me, and I tried to keep from landing face-first on the decadent rose-and-cream carpet beneath my feet. As soon as Lio steadied us with a grunt, I felt his arms tighten around me as he took in the scene: his bodyguard naked in bed with his sister.

"What the fuck?" His shout would have decimated the hearing in my right ear if he hadn't put his hand over it a second before bellowing the words. I felt the warm hand cup my ear gently as his other arm continued to hold me against the front of his body.

Jon bolted under the covers before turning to face us. "Oh god,

Lio. This isn't what it looks like." Considering the words were spoken while actually naked in bed with his sister, I couldn't help but snort.

Even the corner of Hen's mouth twitched in amusement before she muttered, "Yes it is."

I heard another snort from over my shoulder and turned to see Arthur standing in the hallway wearing formal pajamas and a bathrobe. Besides the nightclothes, he was immaculate as usual.

Jon turned to stare at Hen with a desperate expression on his face. "Are you kidding? Do you have any idea what he's going to do to me?"

It was as if the question gave Lio ideas. Suddenly, his body moved from behind me as he approached Jon. I grabbed the back of his fleece to stop him.

"Wait. Wait, Lio. Let them explain." I thought for a moment before continuing. "Actually, they're both adults. They don't need to explain."

"The hell they don't," Lio roared. "What the fuck are you doing in bed with my sister?"

Despite his anger, Lio reached his hand back for mine, lacing our fingers together and squeezing. It was almost funny that in the midst of giving Hen a hard time about an illicit liaison, he was claiming his own illicit liaison with me.

I wasn't sure he'd appreciate the irony in that moment, so I kept my mouth closed.

Hen sniffled loudly and shook her phone at him. "They know. They were here! Someone was here!"

Her voice carried a hysterical tone I didn't like. Fear, maybe. Or at least worry.

Jon looked almost as panicked as Hen, and Lio was on the verge of shouting again. I realized I was the only sane one in the room and took action.

"Stop. Everyone just calm down. Lio and I are going to step out for two minutes and let you both get dressed. When we come back in, we'll figure this out. Hen, try to take a few deep breaths, okay?"

Without waiting for a response, I pulled Lio out of the room and closed the door behind us. He stared at me.

"What?" I asked.

"You just took charge like you owned the place," Lio said, astonished.

"Like a true leader," Arthur deadpanned. "Someone should take notes."

I didn't have to worry if Lio was angry with me because I could see the corner of his mouth curve up a little.

"Well, someone had to," I muttered. "You are all a little high-strung."

Lio chuckled and ran his free hand through his messy hair. I tried not to wish I was his fingers right now.

"What do you think happened?" I asked.

Arthur held up a hand. "Whatever it is, I don't want to know. I left a thick slice of beefcake cooling in my bed. Thank your sister for staying in last night, will you?"

Lio and I stared at the valet as he sauntered down the hall toward his room.

"What the—" I began.

"You don't want to know. Or at least, I don't want to think about it," Lio grumbled with a shudder.

Just then, the door opened and a now dressed Jon peered out to invite us back in.

I moved into the room, pulling Lio behind me, until we could perch on the small love seat in front of the large stone fireplace. Hen and Jon sat in side-by-side chairs across a coffee table from us. Hen was dressed in a navy velour tracksuit and had pulled her dark hair up in a messy pile on the top of her head. Her eyes were red-rimmed, but she appeared to have gotten her breathing regulated.

"Tell us what happened. Whatever it is, we can handle it." This time, it was Lio who spoke with calm authority. I caught a glimpse of the royal leader in him and was struck dumb for a moment. There had been times that week when I'd remembered with breathtaking clarity that he was a royal prince, but they'd been few and far between. He seemed to work very hard to keep us on an even keel, just two regular guys spending a week together in a faraway castle.

As if that was a thing.

Hen sniffed and reached over to grab Jon's hand. I noticed his eyes flick to Lio, and his forehead creased in worry. But through it all, he never let go of Hen's hand.

"Jon and I are together," Hen began.

I noticed Lio's nostrils flare, but he managed to keep his anger in check. Jon, on the other hand, looked ready to explode.

"Listen, Lio," Jon said. "Before you say anything, you have to know I never planned on dating your sister."

"Dating? You're… this isn't just a onetime…" Lio gave up and looked at me with raised eyebrows as if asking me if I'd somehow known.

I hadn't.

"We've been together for five months," Hen hissed. "So back off."

I rested a hand on Lio's thigh before leaning forward to ask a question. "Who found out? Earlier you said 'they know.' What did you mean? Who knows? Your parents?"

Both Lio and Hen groaned at the idea of their parents finding out. Jon met my eyes.

"The press. Apparently there was a photographer on the grounds of the castle, and they got photos of us through a window… together."

The way Jon emphasized the final word implied it had been more than just a shot of the two of them chatting on a park bench around the property.

I felt Lio prepare for battle next to me.

"Are you fucking crazy? That's exactly why you don't risk it! What the hell did you think was going to happen when the press found out the royal daughter of Liorland is banging a fucking *commoner*! How the hell did this happen, Jon? What if they'd gotten photos of me with Felix for god's sake?"

Silence descended with a whoosh as if all the air had been sucked from the room. I felt my own body begin to tremble as his words hit me like airgun pellets, but before I could even remove my hand from his leg and bolt to the safety of my guest apartment like I wanted to, Lio stood up.

"I'm going to call Milane. The PR department is probably having kittens," he spat before storming out of the room.

The three of us sat there staring after him for a beat before Hen's eyes came back to mine with sympathy.

"I'm sorry, Felix," she said softly.

"For what?"

"For my brother being an asshole."

I shrugged, trying to pretend that Lio's outburst hadn't completely gutted me. "It doesn't matter really. I'm leaving tomorrow. You're the one who has to live with him." I tried to laugh it off, but the words tasted like the lies they were. Of course it mattered. I cared about the asshole even though he'd just pointed out how impossible a relationship was between us. Even without the whole "gay prince" thing, the two of us together would be ridiculous. A royal couldn't build a life with the bastard son of a former porn star.

Hen let out a big sigh and looked over at Jon. "Are you ready for this?"

Jon's face softened, and I noticed something I'd obviously missed all week.

He loved her.

"Of course I'm ready, sweetheart. The question is, are you? It's going to suck. You know how the paparazzi are when they get a story like this."

Hen looked up at Jon with the same strong affection in her eyes. "You're worth it."

Before they had a chance to sprout goddamned lovey-dovey angels out of their eyeballs, I skedaddled and made my way as quietly as I could to my quarters.

It was time to pack my bags and say goodbye.

# CHAPTER 23

## LIO

Half the day was spent on the phone with my parents and the family's public relations liaison. Milane was professional as always and handled the situation with as much grace as possible despite the rest of us losing our fucking minds with stress about the fallout. Or, as in the case of my father, hypocritical judgment.

I'd finally called him on his hypocrisy once he'd complained for the millionth time of Henriette not thinking about the family before she jumped into a relationship with "the help."

"Are you fucking kidding me right now?" I'd railed at him through the phone. "First of all, she's not in line for the crown, so who gives a fuck. Secondly, you have the audacity to sit there on your high horse and rant about people jumping into a relationship? Have you lost your goddamned mind? Prepare yourself, old man, because this is nothing compared to what's coming for you and Eleanor as soon as your own news breaks."

I heard the sharp intake of breath from my mother as someone most likely scrambled to turn off the speakerphone function on their end. My mother's voice was cool when it came on.

"Lior, control yourself," she warned. "This is no way for a man in your position to act. You're supposed to be the sane one, so I expect you to act like it. Now come home so we can deal with this as a family. Milane says the optics will be better once we're all together."

I let out a breath and ran my fingers through my hair for the millionth time. "We're scheduled to fly out tomorrow morning, Mother. Jon's family will meet us at the palace."

Another sharp intake of breath. "And why is that?"

"They're going to announce their engagement." It was a total lie, but I couldn't help myself. My parents were acting like the biggest snobs on the planet, and I was sick to death of it. I'd had a chance to see my sister and bodyguard through different eyes today and realized they seemed to have found the real thing with each other. I couldn't help but feel envy.

At that point, my mother completely lost her cool. "Over my dead body," she growled. "I'll see you tomorrow, Lior. Fix this."

The call ended before I had a chance to reassure her. I put the phone down and dropped my face into my hands.

I thought about how Hen and Jon's scandal in the media was nothing compared to what would happen if news of, or god forbid, photographs of Felix and me got out.

Just the thought of it made my stomach churn.

The photos published that morning were of Hen and Jon kissing by a window in the front of the castle. Because the photo had to have been taken on the estate property, even with a long lens, it meant a serious breach in security for the royal guards. That meant Jon was in double trouble for his part in not fully securing our privacy while at Gadleigh, and Arthur's beefcake was history.

I wanted to rip Jon and the beefcake in half for putting my sister's private life in jeopardy that way, but I knew what was done, was done. The only way out was through.

After sending another email to my assistant, Lucas, letting him know I'd be back in the office later tomorrow, I realized I hadn't seen Felix in hours. I looked up from the desk I'd been sitting at and saw I wasn't alone.

Arthur sat calmly in a leather chair opposite me.

"How long have you been sitting there?" I asked.

"Since right after I overheard Hen tell Jon she was worried about Felix. Apparently you said something stupid in front of him, and he's been quiet ever since."

My stomach dropped. "Why? What did I say?"

"Something about a royal personage sleeping with a commoner as if the very idea was disgusting?" His eyebrow raised in accusation. The man wasn't subtle when he thought I'd done something wrong.

"Ugh, Arthur. I didn't mean him. Surely he knew I was just upset."

Again with the eyebrow.

"Lio, may I make a suggestion?"

"You're going to anyway," I mumbled. "Go ahead."

"Your sister is a grown woman with her own staff. Let her handle her situation the way she sees fit. Until you are the actual head of the family and on the throne, it's really not your place to go off half-cocked like you did today."

"But I—"

"Save it," he said calmly, holding up a hand. "Do you know what Hen did today while you yelled at everyone back home?"

"No."

"She stayed in her pajamas and cried through a bunch of chick flicks on television while eating an army's worth of carbohydrates."

It didn't surprise me. "Yeah? And?"

"And Felix was right there next to her the entire time, consoling her, bringing her snacks, and making sure she had a fresh stack of tissues handy."

I pressed my fist into my chest and felt my throat tighten. "Dammit," I whispered.

"Go find him, sir," he said gently.

I always knew when Arthur was done lecturing me because he would throw in an honorific to put us back on official footing.

"Thank you, Arthur. I owe you one. You're a true friend." The words were sincere even when I tacked on another few. "Sorry I had to fire your boy toy."

He shrugged. "Meh. He was hardly a ten. Better luck next time. I think you should let me help with the interviews," he said as he turned and wandered out of my office.

I made my way out of the room behind him and found Mari baking some bread in the kitchen.

"Have you seen Felix?"

Mari narrowed her eyes at me before exchanging significant eye contact with her husband.

"Not since I served him lunch a couple of hours ago. He might be back in his room packing," she said.

"Packing?" I asked before I realized what she meant. "Oh shit."

"Yeah, oh shit," Bert muttered. "Seems to me you've got some explaining to do, son."

My heart dropped into my stomach. Bert stood up from the heavy table and rinsed his tea mug in the sink before kissing Mari on the cheek and heading for the door. Before reaching it, he turned back to me with a rare scowl.

"That there is a nice man, Lio. He doesn't deserve to be on the used end of this mess. He came here to discover Gadleigh's unique treasure —to fall in love with it in person. Shame what he fell for didn't turn out to be the glass."

When he left, he seemed to take something of mine with him. I felt gutted and breathless, desperate and off balance. Felix was leaving in the morning, and there was fuck all I could do about it.

I made my way through the door Bert had just used and walked the short distance to the carriage house. Without looking behind me, I knew one of the royal guards had followed me out of the kitchen. Two of them had been sitting at the table with Bert and Mari when I'd walked in.

When I reached the carriage house and ascended the staircase, I found the door to the guest apartment propped open with a chair. I knocked on the doorframe rather than striding directly in without permission. Had it been like that the day before, I would have walked straight in. But this was different. Everything had changed since that morning, and things felt awkward as hell.

"Felix?" I called.

"In here." The voice came from the bedroom, so I followed it. He was folding clothes and stacking them inside his suitcase with precision. Just the sight of the suitcase made my stomach ache.

"Hey," I said, trying to act cool even though I knew I was failing miserably. "The door was open." As if he hadn't known that. What the hell was my problem? I'd never had a hard time talking to him before.

"Yeah, I accidentally turned the heat up instead of down before I left the room yesterday, and it was stifling when I got back."

I realized he hadn't spent much time in his room for the past couple of days since he'd been spending every spare moment with me and sleeping in my bed inside the main house.

Felix continued folding clothes.

"Ah, sorry I raced out this morning," I began. "Things were—"

He cut me off. "It's fine."

More packing. I felt my back teeth grind together in frustration and my eyes prickle.

"It's not fine. Felix, will you stop for a minute and talk to me, please?" Something in my voice sounded wobbly, and I swallowed in an attempt to squelch it.

He slowly placed the last T-shirt on the stack and turned to face me.

"I'm sorry about your sister," he said. The man was so fucking sweet, and that was not helping the wobbly bits inside of me.

"It'll be fine," I lied. Felix's beautiful face twisted into an expression that called me on my bullshit—one eyebrow raised.

"No it won't," he said. "It'll suck. The media will devour her. You have to keep her away from them, Lio. They'll call her all kinds of names. They hold her to a higher standard, and you know it. Try not to let her see it. No matter how strong you think you are, the poison still seeps in."

I thought about what it must be like to be the only son of a woman who's just as well known for her porn films as her box-office-smashing ones. The press must have been brutal when they learned she had a child with no father. I couldn't imagine what that had done to Felix's sense of self-worth.

"I'll try to protect her." As far as promises went, it was a lame one. "Why are you packing already?"

Felix looked down at his suitcase and up at me again with confusion clear on his face. "I'm leaving in twelve hours, Lio. When did you expect me to pack?"

"Twelve hours?" The panic in my gut reared its ugly head again and stole my breath. "What? What do you mean? I thought you were leaving tomorrow morning?"

Felix reached out a hand to cup the side of my face. Without realizing it, I closed my eyes against the familiar comfort of his touch and leaned into it.

"Lio, it's after seven. I leave at six thirty tomorrow morning."

"No," I breathed. "I'm not ready to say goodbye to you."

I moved forward into his arms and tucked my face into the side of his neck. The warm thrum of his pulse pushed against my cheek.

"Felix," I begged. "Please don't go yet."

# CHAPTER 24

## FELIX

The whimper against my skin almost brought me to my knees. If Lio had any idea how much I wanted to stay with him, he'd run screaming back home to take the throne with pleasure just to get away from his crazy stalker. It was already taking all of my self-control not to change my travel plans and stay longer.

But I'd heard through the castle grapevine that he was leaving the following day as well, so there was no point in me extending my stay. The man had important work to do, not to mention the incredible responsibility of taking the throne if what he'd implied was true. I couldn't even imagine what it would feel like to know it was almost your turn at bat in a position like that.

Liorland wasn't like some other monarchies. The sitting king had an active role in running the country. It wasn't just a figurehead position there. I'd learned over the past week that Lio had spent years of education and training preparing to lead the country after his dad's death, but I also knew he'd never in a million years thought that time would come so soon because of his father choosing to retire instead.

I couldn't imagine the heavy load of stress on his shoulders, and it was that thought that helped me realize what I needed to do.

"Come on. I want to go have a cup of tea in the treasury room," I said, gently extracting him from my embrace. "Will you join me?"

I saw a spark of interest in his eyes. "Of course. Can we stop by the kitchen for something sweet to take with us?"

How could I not laugh? The prince of Liorland had just asked me permission to grab some cookies from his own castle kitchens.

"Yes, Lio. You can have some cookies with your tea," I teased.

"Shut up. I didn't eat dinner," he said with a pout.

Once we had our snacks, I led Lio to the red salon and through the secret panel to his hideaway. As I knelt and pressed the stained glass crown jewel, I tried so hard not to think about the fact it would be the last time I'd ever get to do it.

Lio started the fire as I poured the tea, and by the time we were settled in the two armchairs, an awkward silence had descended between us again. I decided to address it head-on.

"Well, this isn't awkward, now is it?"

Lio smiled softly into his mug. "I hate this."

"Same here."

He looked up, deep furrows lining the space between his brows. "Can you come visit me sometime? In Monaco?"

I thought about it for a minute before answering. "I don't think so. How would you explain my presence there? Plus, you're going to be so busy. Once you get back to town, you won't even have time to remember me."

"Bullshit. You know that's a lie, and I could just tell people you're a good friend."

I felt a lump form in my throat and fought to speak past it. "I don't think I can pretend we're just friends, Lio."

His face fell as he set his mug down on a side table and dropped from the chair to his knees in front of me. His arms came around my waist, and he buried his face in my stomach.

"I'm so sorry," he whispered against my shirt. "I didn't mean for this to happen, Felix. I care about you so much. I wasn't expecting it."

I ran my fingers through his hair and closed my eyes to memorize the feel of it by touch alone. I could hear the familiar pop and crackle of the logs in the fire and smell a mix of nutmeg, Lio's shampoo, and woodsmoke. I knew without a shadow of a doubt any one of those smells would have the power to gut me in the future.

"I know. Me neither," I admitted, although he knew that already. Who in their right mind would have imagined meeting someone in the tiny unknown island in the North Sea?

Lio lifted his head with such wide eyes, I wondered what the hell was going to come out of his mouth.

"Come home with me, Felix. Can't we figure something out? We can—I know we can."

The desperation on his face and in his voice made my nose sting, and I wondered if I was actually going to tumble into an ugly cry right here in front of him.

I shook my head. "You know I can't do that. And anyway, you don't mean it. Let's just accept that you can care about someone without being able to be with them long-term, and enjoy our final night together. I brought you in here so we could spend it in my favorite spot."

"I thought the glassworks was your favorite spot." His mouth quirked up, letting me know he would let me drop the serious shit.

"Hmm, there are no cookies in the glassworks. And I can't get naked there," I mused.

Lio's eyes opened wide again as he tried to figure out if I was joking or suggesting.

"But you can get naked in here?" His eyes flicked to the doorway before he quickly stood and made his way over to lower the small latch lock on the back of the panel. By the time he turned back toward me, I'd closed the heavy curtains across the windows, despite them facing a private courtyard, and begun to remove my sweater.

Lio stared at me with his navy blue intensity. "Oh hell yes," he growled, stalking toward me. "Take it all off, Felix. Show me that gorgeous skin."

I thought about what I wanted from that night with him. I wanted so many things. For Lio to stop worrying and start having fun. For the two of us to create some hot memories to carry with us. For this to not be the last time enjoying each other's bodies, but if it was, I wanted it to be an epic last time.

"Watch me take off my clothes for you, Lio. I want your eyes on me the whole time. Every time you see my nipples harden or my cock jump, I want you to know you did that."

I pulled off the shirt I'd had on under my sweater, revealing my bare chest. Lio's eyes flicked down to gaze at my nipples, and just the thought of him staring at them made them tighten into hard nubs.

"That's it," I murmured. "Just watch. Sit down in that chair and get hard for me."

Lio's hand came down to palm himself through his pants before he sank down into the chair in front of the fire. I moved around to remain in front of him so he could watch in comfort.

I brought my hands slowly to the button of my pants and toyed with it, watching Lio's intense gaze focus on that spot. My hands rubbed up and down my torso before I tweaked my own nipple and groaned a little. It felt so good to have him watch me. I'd never understood how some people were confident enough to put on a show for someone else in the bedroom, but being with Lio made me want to try it.

Anything that dilated his pupils like that was worth any amount of embarrassment I may have felt stripping in front of him.

But I wasn't embarrassed. For some reason, I felt more empowered than anything else.

My fingers made quick work of the button and zipper at my fly before reaching into my underwear to stroke my cock.

"Oh god," I whimpered when I felt how hard it was and how good touching it felt.

"Jesus, Fee," Lio groaned. "You're making me crazy. Pull it out. Let me see that gorgeous cock, baby."

I closed my eyes and enjoyed a few more strokes, pulsing my hips forward and feeling my hard cock push through my fist.

"Gngh." I grunted and swallowed, noticing the wetness at my tip and bringing my hand out to taste it without thinking. When I realized what I was doing, my eyes flew open just in time to see Lio roar up out of his chair and practically slam me down onto the carpet.

After that, it was like being mauled by a lion dosed with extra-strength Viagra. I yelped as he tore my pants off and ripped my underwear down my legs, engulfing my cock in his throat and reaching up to tweak my nipples at the same time.

His muffled grunts and groans made me even harder, and I couldn't help but thrust up into his hot mouth over and over in desperation for more.

"Fuck, Lio, fuck! Please, baby. I need you inside me. Please," I begged. "Fuck me. Take me. I know you want to fuck me hard tonight, and I need it so badly. *Please.*"

His head came up, and dilated pupils pinned me where I lay. "How do you want it, Felix? Because I want to fuck you through the floor, and I'm not sure you're ready for that."

I let out a whine before he even finished his warning. "Oh god. Yes, that. That's what I want."

I scrambled up onto my knees and began tearing at his clothes, desperate to get him naked so he could fuck me.

As I was struggling to get his shirt off, I found myself nose-to-nose with him. Our eyes met, and there was an entire world of emotion exchanged in the glance.

When I spoke, my voice shook. My words came out so quietly, I was surprised he could hear them. It was my deepest desire confessed in a secret voice inside a hidden room.

"I want you to own me, Lio," I whispered. My whole body trembled with need and fear of his reaction. "I want you to hold me down and fuck me so hard, I can barely breathe without feeling your cock shove deeper inside me. I want you to make it hurt a little so I feel it for days and days. I want you to… I want to…" I sucked in a breath. "I don't know how to say it. I want you inside my body, and I don't ever want you to leave it, Lio. Make me yours in a way no one else can, okay?"

After that, we pretended not to see each other's glistening eyes. We pretended it was hard fucking instead of making love. But both of us knew the truth.

When he shoved his cock mercilessly in my ass with little to no prep, I heard the soft words of tender affection murmured into my ear.

When he rolled me over and fucked me face-first into the carpet, I felt every soft touch of his hands dancing along my skin.

When his strong hand pinned me to the floor by the back of the neck, his other one stroked my hip like I was a porcelain doll.

When his teeth bit into my skin, his sweet tongue came along right behind them to soothe the burn.

And when he roared his climax against the side of my face, I felt his arms tighten around me in a desperate clutch and his soft lips land on my hot skin, light as a feather.

But most of all, when I limped out of bed the next morning, I heard the quiet echo of his last words mumbled into my hair in the middle of the night.

*I'm not sure I can live without you.*

# CHAPTER 25

LIO

I took the coward's way out.

At one point we woke up in front of the fire and made our way upstairs to my room. Once we'd taken a sleepy shower, I led Felix to the bed and wrapped him up in my arms to sleep. He fell asleep almost instantly, but I lay there for hours unable to stop my head from spinning. I tried desperately to come up with a reality in which I could have it all—the man and the crown.

There was simply no way.

So I gently disengaged myself from him and got dressed, silently grabbing only the essentials before dropping a kiss on his forehead and sneaking out of the room like a jackass.

I didn't even try to find Jon. No part of me wanted to discover him sleeping in my sister's bed again, and it wasn't his shift anyway. He could get pissed at me later for fucking up our original plans. I needed out of there as soon as possible.

Once I was airborne on the private jet with Arthur and the skeleton crew of guards, I thanked my lucky stars I wasn't the king yet. I could still manage to pull off a move like my midnight escape without it being a massive strategic endeavor. As it was, several royal guards had been scrambled to see to my sudden change of plans, and the pilots had been summoned from a dead sleep to move the flight up several hours.

Throughout all of it, Arthur didn't said a word. From the look on his face, I could tell he knew exactly what was going on.

I'd needed off the island before I could grab on to Felix's ankle and beg.

According to the pilot, we had just passed over northern Liorland, the area between the Netherlands and Denmark, when a call came in from Henriette.

"Good morning," I said and tried to cut her off before the ranting and lecturing could begin. "Sorry to leave without you, but I—"

"It's no problem," she said in a calm voice. "Everything's fine."

"Wh-what?" Maybe she hadn't realized yet that I'd ducked out without saying a proper goodbye to Felix.

"It's fine. Felix and I had an early breakfast, and I just wanted to let you know I'll be staying a couple more days. I want to stay away from the paparazzi a little longer till the heat dies down."

"Wh-what?" I repeated, only having heard the part about Felix.

"Close your mouth lest the flies get in," she admonished.

I realized my jaw was hanging open. "What... I mean how..." I cleared my throat. "How was Felix?"

"Fine."

I waited for her to elaborate, but nothing came.

"Did he make it to the airport on time?" I was the stupidest idiot who ever spouted bullshit questions.

"I'm sure you'll be in touch with him at some point and you can ask him yourself." And there was the familiar holier-than-thou tone in my sister's voice. Stupid fucking sisters.

"But how did he seem? Okay? Upset?" I wanted to kick myself for sounding so desperate.

"Enough about Felix. Mother called late last night and told me they're preparing the big announcement the day after tomorrow," Hen said. "So the next couple of days are going to be crazy for you, not to mention Mother's big New Year's do."

I'd forgotten today was New Year's Eve. A day normally celebrated the world over for fresh starts and hope for a better life.

Fat fucking chance.

"Okay. Happy New Year, Hen," I muttered.

"You too, big brother. I have a feeling it's going to be a doozy."

I had a feeling she was right. The moment I touched down, my assistant, Lucas was on hand to notify me of all my upcoming obligations, including an official date with my mother's first-choice princess pick.

The woman had been foisted upon me several times previously by my meddling family. The daughter of a highly placed minister in my father's first cabinet, she was currently a professor of art history at a university in Paris. I hadn't seen her in many months due to her teaching schedule, but I assumed she was in town visiting family over the holiday.

I didn't have much time to worry about that, and I assumed it was just one of many official events I'd be dragged to against my will in the coming days and weeks. With the Felixmoon slipping too quickly into the past, all I was left with was a laser focus on what I had to do to take over the throne.

When Lucas said go, I went. When my mother said put this on, I put it on. When my father said read this, I read it. Arthur was the only person who saw how I really was because it was only when I fell into bed at night, exhausted and hollow, that I allowed myself to remember the comforting touch of the man who'd somehow grown roots around my heart.

But that man quickly became the man of my dreams only—not someone real. Not someone I'd ever be able to hold again in this life. My real life had no room for Felix Wilde in it. I had other more important things I needed to focus on.

I was to be king.

# CHAPTER 26

## FELIX

I knew before even falling asleep in Lio's bed that he'd chicken out of sticking around for the goodbye. And, honestly, I was relieved as all hell.

Neither one of us could handle it. Not with the way things had progressed so quickly between us. It wasn't normal. It was some aberration born of the singular situation from being practically stranded on a deserted island with each other. It wasn't real.

So I decided to take it with my chin up and squash down all the emotional shit until I could get home and find a nice little shady spot on Doc and Grandpa's ranch to curl up in the fetal position and lose my ever-loving shit.

Until then, I was the man of goddamned steel.

"Good morning, Hen," I said with surprise when I entered the kitchen in the still-dark early morning. "What are you doing up so early?"

"Couldn't sleep. I kept wondering what other private pictures that photographer might have gotten through the castle windows."

"Oh god. I hadn't even thought of that. Do they know? Do you have media relations people who can find out from the photographer somehow?" I poured myself some coffee and sat down next to her at the table.

"They're trying. And I've never gotten undressed without making sure all curtains are closed no matter how far removed a building is from public view. I heard a story once about journalists using drones, and it freaked me out. So even if there are more, they shouldn't be too bad. It's just the invasion of privacy, you know? Now knowing what personal moment could be made not quite so personal after all."

"I know exactly how you feel," I admitted. "My mom's famous, so I've been on the end of the lens before. Never as bad as that though. I'm so sorry that happened to you and Jon."

She sighed. "That's the other thing that pisses me off. It happened to Jon too, but no one seems to give a damn about him. It's all about how my privacy was invaded and my life is being turned upside down. Not one person has mentioned how this might be affecting Jon as well."

I reached my hand over to squeeze hers. "You're right. How's he handling it?"

She shrugged. "He's putting on a stoic face, but he barely slept a wink all night either. He only just fell asleep an hour ago. Good thing Lio left the island without him, or he would have been dead on his feet today."

I felt my heartbeat kick up. "Lio's gone back to Monaco."

Her eyes widened. "I thought you knew? Didn't he tell you? He flew out in the middle of the night."

I'd assumed he had, but hearing confirmation was still a kick in the teeth. It was so like him, I almost wanted to laugh. That cowardly motherfucker. He never wanted to get within punting distance of his feelings if he didn't have to.

"He didn't tell me, but I'm not surprised." Before Hen could go off on a rant against her brother, I stopped her. "It's okay, Hen. Honestly, I was relieved he wasn't there. I can't handle the goodbye any more than he could have. I just didn't realize he left the island altogether. I thought maybe he was hiding until after I left."

"He's halfway home by now," she said with a sigh. "And straight into the dragon's lair. I don't envy him the bullshit he has in store."

I thought about everything he'd told me about his father—how cold he was, how indifferent to Lio and Hen's emotions. Even his mother, while much better than his dad, wasn't the warmest person. According to his stories, she valued appearances because she'd been raised to do so. She'd grown up in one of Manhattan's old money families, and after meeting King Lior at a yachting regatta in the Hamptons one summer, she'd taken to her role as if born to be a queen.

"Does Lio have someone besides you in his corner? Someone he can confide in when he gets overwhelmed?"

Hen looked at me with sad eyes. "His best friend, Iggy, is an airhead player. I think Lio only keeps him around because he's been the only person Lio can trust with his secret besides Arthur."

"What secret?" I asked before I could think.

She rolled her eyes at me. "He's gay?" Then she snorted a little and winked at me. "You know, in case you didn't notice when you two were naked in bed together."

I felt my cheeks ignite. "Har har."

Hen leaned over and ruffled my hair. "I'm sorry, Felix. I know this can't be easy for you. I could tell the two of you were starting something special."

I flicked my eyes away from her as if that would help hide the massive heartbreak etched in them. "Yeah, well."

She pushed back her chair and pulled me into a tight hug. It was the kind of hug that came from family—the kind that said it knew you felt flayed open and gut shot and were currently held together with nothing more than spit and baling wire.

"Fuck," I whimpered before I could stop myself. "Fuck, Hen."

"I know, honey. It sucks. It's okay to let it out."

So I did. As if I could have held it back anyway. There was simply no way after that. She was too kind, too loving and understanding. Hen had been one of only a handful of people who'd seen the two of us together. And that somehow made it real—undeniable. It couldn't be a figment of my imagination because there had been witnesses.

I cried like a baby on her shoulder and didn't even slow down long enough to feel embarrassed about it.

"Why can't I fall for a regular guy?" I complained once I caught my breath and took the dish towel she offered me for my face. "I mean, a prince? Really? Jesus."

She laughed through her own tears, and I realized she'd been crying too.

"Why are you crying?"

She rolled her eyes again. "'Cause it sucks. I told you that. It's so unfair. It's not like we chose to be born into this family. We should be able to be with the people we love."

"You're not thinking about breaking up with Jon, are you?" I wondered whether her situation would allow her to date someone like a royal guard and whether things were serious enough between them to find out.

"Hell no. No. I love him, and he loves me. But I shouldn't get trashed in the media because of it."

"No. You shouldn't."

"I wish Lio would come out of the closet. That would take the heat off me quite nicely."

I stared at her in disbelief before noticing the teasing twinkle in her eye.

"Bitch," I muttered.

"Sucker," she quipped back.

We were both quiet while we took a moment to sip our coffee. Just before I opened my mouth to tell her I needed to finish packing my things, she turned to study me for a moment.

"What is it?"

She pursed her lips before speaking. "I just remembered Jon got a notice from Bert about the road to town being washed out."

"How can that be? It hasn't rained."

She shrugged. "He said something about a water pipe break. You know that bridge across the inlet leading to town?"

I nodded, picturing the narrow single lane structure that seemed to be on its last breath.

"It's totally wiped out. You won't be able to get to the airport until they've fixed it. And today's New Year's Eve. Tomorrow's New Year's Day."

"How did Lio get out?"

Hen paused, her face coloring with guilt. "It happened after he left. Like, just before you came down."

"You're a terrible liar."

"You can't go yet, Felix. I need your help."

"No, you don't," I said, standing up. "You want to find a way to make things happy ever after for your brother, and that can't involve me. I'm leaving this morning regardless of how awful I feel about it, Hen. There's nothing in Monaco for me. Please don't make me go there under the guise of some harebrained scheme to get the two of us together."

"You watch too many Hallmark movies," she muttered.

She wasn't wrong. "You know your brother watches them too."

She shrieked. "No! No way! Tell me everything. Every dirty little secret about that fucker." The evil glint in her eyes was 100 percent little sister. I'd seen it many times in my cousin Hallie's eyes when she teased her brothers.

I laughed as I rinsed out my mug. "Nope. Some secrets I will take to the grave. No one should know the royal prince cranks up Celine Dion when he thinks no one is around, he sips tea with his pinky out, or that he prefers purple socks."

Another shriek. "Oh my god, he's so gay!"

"I made up one of those things. Two truths and a lie is a staple in my family." I made my way over to her and drew her into a big hug. "Thank you for everything. Meeting you has been one of the joys of my life, Hen, and I will never forget it."

I heard her sniffle in my ear and mutter, "Goddammit. Don't make me cry again."

After extricating myself from the embrace, I made my excuses so I could take one last walk around my favorite spots around the castle. It was when I finally found the hidden entrance to the little private courtyard outside Lio's treasury room that I spotted the ancient grave marker and felt my heart stutter.

*Mon Etienne...*

# CHAPTER 27

## LIO

I spent New Year's Eve studying my ass off at the office. My father and his council members had gathered binders full of information I needed to review, and my mother kept interrupting to update me on plans for the coronation festivities the following week. Everything had been moved up in an effort to have me solidly on the throne before news of Eleanor and her pregnancy broke. By the time the clock chimed midnight, my head was pounding and all I could think about was how badly I wanted to talk to Felix.

Instead of succumbing to the temptation to call or text him, I forced myself to put in another hour of work before taking a hot shower and falling into bed. The following day was more of the same with a long break in the middle for a big formal meal with family and friends.

I wasn't at all surprised to find a myriad of women there whose sole purpose seemed to be luring me into asking them out on a date. My mother was pushing the princess plan hard.

It wasn't difficult for me to smile and make polite small talk. I'd been raised to excel at diplomacy after all, and it wasn't until my uncle Laurence grabbed one of them around the waist that I lost my composure.

"Excuse him," I barked, pulling her away from his grasp. "He's losing his balance as he ages."

The woman's eyes widened at my words, and I waited for the guilty conscience to hit me. It didn't. The man was a pig and deserved everything he got. I steered the woman over to an area with some seating where my friend Iggy was holding court. He raised his eyebrow at the tall blonde on my arm before rescuing me.

"Véronique, why don't you come tell me all about your visit to Florence. I heard it was insane."

I shot Iggy a grateful look before searching around for my mother. Did I dare request for her to hold off her pesky matchmaking until after the coronation?

Once I found her by the bar with the extensive wine selection on display, I noticed her face brighten as she reached for me.

"Lior, darling. Come here and meet Elise. She—"

"I'm sorry, Mother. I was just coming to give my apologies. Father is expecting my response to an urgent memo within the hour. I need to take a moment in the office." I nodded to the attractive young woman next to my mother before turning to make my way out of the room.

Later that night, Iggy texted to ask if he could sneak into my place and stay over. The cramp in my gut was an unnecessary message from my body. I already knew the answer was not only no, but hell no. There would be no more nights spent in bed with my old friend. Instead, I went to bed alone.

It was only the first day of the year, and it was crawling as slow as honey on a sloth. How in the hell was I going to make it to the coronation? And how soon after that could I sneak in a visit to a tiny town in Texas where a beautiful boy hid himself away behind colored glass and textbooks?

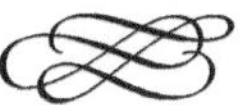



# CHAPTER 28

Spending New Year's in a hotel room by myself in Paris was less than thrilling. I tried my best to enjoy the City of Light on the night when it was illuminated by hundreds of fireworks. I'd eaten at a small cafe near my hotel and took my time walking back through the throngs of people in the streets. I spent much of that day and night thinking about what I wanted my life to be. Getting a taste of true happiness with Lio had woken up something inside of me, and I wondered if I'd have the guts to keep that part of me awake and alive when I returned home.

I thought about what I wanted to do next besides finding a teaching job for the following school year. Did I want to pursue glassmaking as an art more than just a hobby? Did I want to begin researching and writing another book about a different aspect of glassmaking or glass history? I couldn't imagine beginning another project like that right away, so I quickly moved on to other aspects of my life.

Before leaving Hobie, I'd struck up a new friendship with my cousin's boyfriend, Nico, and looked forward to spending more time helping him design his tattoo shop above the small bakery he owned. Grandpa and Doc had purchased the building the year before in an effort to preserve some of Main Street's historic properties in Hobie. I wondered if there were any other projects like that they needed help with. Regardless of what my job prospects were, I knew I'd need a side project to sink myself into for the coming months until I got over the current ache in my chest after leaving Lio.

When the day of my presentation arrived, one of the event sponsors picked me up to escort me to the museum where the symposium was taking place. The older woman was friendly and bubbling with enthusiasm when she introduced herself as the head of operations for a local glass-restoration company. Her English was flawless, and she thanked me profusely for taking Ruth's place with short notice.

"Everyone is so very grateful to hear what you have to teach us about Etienne DesMarais. I know your presentation will be something no one at the symposium has heard before."

If only she'd known how much extra time I'd spent perfecting it as an excuse to keep my mind off of Lio.

As I entered the Louvre, I was struck silent by the reality of visiting as a presenter. I'd spent a few hours there the afternoon I'd arrived in town, but it hadn't been nearly enough to see everything I'd wanted to see. Now, I saw it not as a tourist, but as a member of the art history academic community. I was overwhelmed with gratitude for the journey my life had taken to lead me here.

I owed Doc and Grandpa everything for their encouragement, their financial contributions, and most of all their encouragement of my studies and my visit to Gadleigh. Their solid support had led to my standing in front of a crowd of curators, preservation experts, students, and professors in the Louvre in Paris. It was beyond my wildest dreams.

Once the sponsor had introduced me, I took the podium in front of a packed room and began my presentation.

"Thank you so much for having me. As Madame LaPièce mentioned, my mentor and friend, Ruth Lawson, was so sorry to miss being here. I'm sure she would have loved going on and on about her beloved William Morris. But since she is not here, I shall, instead, go on and on about my beloved subject: Etienne DesMarais."

The crowd chuckled softly, and I saw several people smiling in anticipation.

"I have spent extensive time researching the mysterious and exquisite glass found in the castle on the remote island of Gadleigh. As any scholar of stained glass can tell you, Gadleigh is like Disney World for glass enthusiasts. Or the Louvre for da Vinci enthusiasts."

More chuckles.

"I was lucky enough to spend the holidays at Gadleigh Castle and studied under the current Gadleigh glass master, Calum Grier. Not only did I learn what their current program entails, but I also saw the historic glass of the unnamed artist from the 1500s."

I took a moment to look around the room, wondering how many people knew much about stained glass.

"As many of you know, the extensive works of the unknown artist were originally credited to a glass artisan who was popular during that era, Gian Antonio da Lodi. But in the early 1970s, a scholar found evidence that da Lodi had never been to Gadleigh. That discovery prompted further testing, which determined the glass was made almost sixty years after da Lodi's death."

After a pause to give myself a mini pep talk, I continued.

"It is my theory that the reason the credit was given to da Lodi in the first place was to hide the identity of the real glass master of Gadleigh. Through my research, I've discovered that there was an unknown glass master in residence during the time all of the glass was created. It was the reign of Liorland's King Gabriel IV, and the artisan was a man by the name of Etienne DesMarais.

"There is no official record of Etienne visiting Gadleigh despite his being one of King Gabriel's inner circle. But I found evidence in the journal kept by another glassmaker in nearby Nice who specifically mentions a man named Etienne DesMarais escalating his glassmaking talents to the point of regional fame. Upon further research, I began to see implications that the king and DesMarais were in a secret relationship."

I paused to test the audience's reaction. It wasn't every day an academic made accusations of homosexuality about a royal personage in front of a renowned group of art history buffs. When I'd mentioned my theory to Lio, I'd been terrified of offending him. But that had been stupid. Lio himself was gay, so learning one of his ancestors was gay hadn't been a huge shock. He'd found it fascinating instead. And sad.

We'd discussed at length how awful it must have been for the king and DesMarais to have to hide their relationship, but after knowing the story, anyone with eyes could see the love that had been put into every glass installment around Gadleigh.

"When I visited the castle, I was struck by how extensive the glass installations were. There are details as major as the main rosette window in the royal chapel and as minor as the handle of a garden water pump that have been lovingly crafted from stained glass made with sand collected on Gadleigh's own beaches.

"It is the work of a lifetime. The work of love and dedication to a place that meant everything to the artisan. While I was there, I attempted to count each individual work of handmade glass around Gadleigh Castle. I stopped counting after eight hundred. This wasn't a visiting artist. It wasn't a world-renowned maker or a neophyte attempting to learn the ropes. It was a focused, dedicated master, honing his art in the process of expressing a lifetime's worth of love in the place of his heart."

I stopped to take a sip of water to wash away the lump in my throat as I thought about Etienne and Gabriel hiding away at Gadleigh in order to find each other away from real life. The similarity to mine and Lio's situation was excruciating. The fact that in five hundred years, nothing had fucking changed.

"So one of the greatest glass masters of all time was never named. He never came forward and claimed his due—never received recognition for his amazing life's work at Gadleigh. Instead, he went down in history as a courtesan, a hanger-on to one of Monaco's brightest kings during the time of the late renaissance and England's King Henry VII."

I looked around the room and decided to say one more thing before moving on to the technical part of the presentation.

"The intersection between art and recognition has always been fascinating to me. Is the art less valuable because we didn't know who created it? Is it more interesting to us now that we may know who's responsible for it? If DesMarais had been credited with the glass all along, would people have revered him, studied his work, had their own art influenced by his styles and techniques? Would he have had an impact on the future of glassmaking? We'll never know. Had it been acceptable then to out himself as the king's lover, he might have left an incredible legacy like da Vinci did. Instead, he left the glass at Gadleigh and a simple gravestone marker in an enclosed courtyard on the estate."

I advanced the slide deck on my laptop to show the photograph I'd taken outside of the treasury room at Gadleigh when I'd discovered the tiny, almost hidden stone marker.

I had translated it from the French:

*My Etienne - whose heart shined like colored glass in the sun.*

THE FOLLOWING DAY, I had to admit to myself I wasn't ready to go home yet. I wanted to stay longer in Paris, maybe even visit the stained glass I'd studied in textbooks. I thought about the stained glass at nearby Chartres Cathedral, and I realized it was a shame to be so close to some of the most famous glass in the world and not get to see it. Paris was the city of art, after all, and art was what restored me.

After an overly vague call to Doc and Grandpa about taking some extra time in Paris, I extended my hotel reservation. But instead of getting out and seeing glass, I spent the next forty-eight hours drowning my sorrows in French wine and baguettes and watching stupid French-dubbed American movies in my hotel room.

Clearly I wanted to keep hiding—keep avoiding my real life. The one without Lio.

It only took two days of wallowing in self-pity before I opened the door of the hotel room one morning and saw Doc and Grandpa in the hallway.

They'd come to knock some sense into me.

LIO

By the time the official announcement of my father's retirement came, I'd begun to feel like maybe I could do this. I'd gotten a handle on the most pressing issues that would need my attention when I took my new position, and the idea of being the king was beginning to sink in. If this was what I was born to do, I would embrace it with my full focus, including allowing my parents to help me select a wife.

That attitude lasted a good four or five days until my date with Sabine.

Jon and I picked her up from her parents' house and drove her to the Salle des Etoiles for the Save the Children Winter Gala. The event was one of my favorites because it raised significant money for youth aid programs around the world. I had spent two months during high school working on one of their volunteer projects in Indonesia to help register some of the thousands of children displaced by the tsunami there. Ever since, it had been a charity I volunteered for and donated to as often as I could.

Sabine was breathtaking in a royal blue ball gown that seemed to float in the night air. Sparkling jewelry winked from her ears and throat, and her dark hair was swept up, leaving only a few curled tendrils to fall along her slender neck. I was taken aback by how regal and elegant she looked. I'd always known she was beautiful and grace-ful, but there was something about her demeanor that night that instantly affirmed why my parents had given me such pressure to give her a chance.

She would make a lovely queen.

I kissed her on the cheeks and offered her my arm. "Thank you so much for agreeing to come with me tonight," I said politely.

"It's my pleasure. I've really been looking forward to it, Lior," she said with a bright smile.

"Ah. It's taking me some time to get used to the new name," I admitted. Even though the news was out about my father stepping down, I couldn't get used to the new deference in public just yet.

We made our way in the town car to the event venue and entered along a red carpet through throngs of photographers. Luckily, the truth about the reason for my father's retirement hadn't come out yet. He had given the press a half-truth, saying only that he and my mother were divorcing and he'd decided that it would be a good time to transition the throne to me so that the focus could remain on Lior-land's strong future rather than the personal life of the king and queen.

No one believed it, but so far the speculation seemed to remain on concerns over his health. It was only a matter of time before the truth about Eleanor and her pregnancy came to light. In the meantime, she'd been tucked away in a country home owned by one of my father's closest confidants and was told to stay out of the way until he was free to join her.

How in the world she put up with the bastard was beyond me.

But the news had caused intense media focus on me, of course, and the photographers went wild snapping pictures of me with Sabine on my arm. Questions were shouted about who she was and what our relationship was, and I took a moment to be grateful Sabine had been prepared ahead of time by my mother's assistant.

Regardless of her prep, when we got inside the ballroom, Sabine's eyes were wide and a little freaked-out.

"Are you okay?" I murmured, leaning in close so no one else could hear.

"Yes, I just… that's… how do you get used to so many photographers and reporters in your face?"

I shrugged and gave her my most confident smile. "I don't know any different, but I can tell you from personal experience that it gets a little easier after a glass of wine."

Her face relaxed into a smile of gratitude as we made our way toward the closest drinks server. Once we had wine in hand, I began to introduce her around until it was time to take our seats for the formal dinner.

Sabine was charming and poised; she had a natural ability to set people at ease and seemed to connect easily with everyone she spoke to. I wanted to kick myself for having such a bad attitude about this date. She was proving to be smart, funny, sincere, and compassionate. She asked questions about the charity projects Save the Children was currently focused on and expressed genuine interest in getting involved herself. Even Hen leaned over to me at one point during dinner and remarked on it.

"She's the total package, isn't she?"

Despite her public smile, my sister's sarcasm bit into me with a direct hit.

"Yes, she is. Mother chose well," I said, trying my hardest to mean it.

Her face turned serious. "How are you holding up? I haven't seen you much since you've been so busy."

"Busy is good, Hen. Less time to wallow." My tone was light, but she heard the truth of it.

"Have you talked to him?"

I looked around quickly and noticed Sabine had turned away from me to engage in a conversation with the person on her opposite side.

"No," I said firmly before clearing my throat. "I dare not. At the sound of his hello, I'd fucking lose my shit, dear one."

"Oh, Lio," she said, and the pity in her voice was suffocating. I looked around the large ballroom, eager to find someone I could excuse myself to talk to. Unfortunately, every face I saw was someone who'd want to chat me up about my new role, and I was losing my ability to fake enthusiasm. I turned back to Hen when she spoke again.

"Have you thought about inviting him here as a friend?" Her suggestion sparked a tiny jolt of excitement in my heart until I remembered how much he despised the press.

"Believe me, I tried that, but I can't beg him to come to paparazzi central, Hen. He hates the media, and that's my life right now. Even if we were able to be just friends, he'd hate the scrutiny involved in being friends with the royal family."

"Why not let him decide?"

I shook my head. "No. He'd agree. He's sweet and selfless like that. If he thought I needed him, he'd drop everything and fly back over here."

"He's still in France," she said quietly. "He decided to stay a little while after his presentation in Paris. Says he wanted to see some sights. You should reach out to him."

The thought of Felix within a six-hour train ride from me made my throat constrict.

*Why the hell does the thought of him get such a strong reaction out of me, dammit?*

"I can't," I breathed before excusing myself and quickly striding toward the men's room.

The rest of the night passed easily because something splintered inside of me on my way to the bathroom. It was like I became two different people. One was Lior, the smiling diplomat who was preparing to become the king and graciously responded to the well-wishes of his peers. The other was Lio, the gay man who pined for a shy Texan. That part of me hid away safely in my heart, reliving memories of touch and taste, laughter and lingering conversation by the fire. Lio was untouchable. He lived inside and stayed in a happy bubble meant only for him. Lior, on the other hand, was everything his parents had always dreamed of.

Over the coming days, Lior would surprise everyone with how

adept he was at preparing to be king. He took Sabine out for lunch at a popular restaurant in town, held her hand as they window-shopped in front of the paparazzi, and laughed at her soft jokes. Lior made my father proud and my mother giddy.

Lio only surfaced late at night. When the lights were out and the doors were closed, and the feel of the cool, soft sheets slid across his legs as he imagined Felix's tight warm channel clasped around his cock. As the scream of his climax went straight into the thick down pillows with someone else's royal crest embroidered on the case. As the hot splash of his tears could evaporate before morning when Lior would rise again and take charge of the day.

# CHAPTER 30

FELIX

It didn't take much for Grandpa and Doc to get the truth out of me. With the exception of Lio's identity anyway. There was no way I was taking the chance of saying anything that could result in outing a damned king.

My cousin Otto had come with them, no doubt using the trip as an excuse to avoid settling back down in Hobie. I knew he had to be restless going from a career traveling the world in the military to coming home to our sleepy, tiny town. Regardless of the reason, I was glad he'd come with them to see me. Otto's big muscular presence made me feel safe, and his strong but silent vibe made for good company when I wasn't in the mood for idle chitchat. I didn't feel pressured to fill the silence when I was around Otto.

The four of us were sitting around a dining table with a million-dollar view of the Eiffel Tower. We'd ventured out to an Italian restaurant for dinner, and Otto was currently stealing everyone's remaining pasta to fill his bottomless gut.

"Jesus, man," I teased. "Where the hell are you putting all of that?"

"Going sightseeing tomorrow," he grunted. "Carbo loading."

I made eye contact with Grandpa, who shook his head before muttering, "The kid hasn't stopped moving since he got home."

Otto swallowed his last bite and wiped his mouth with a napkin before speaking. "I'm not passing up an opportunity to see Versailles for fuck's sake, old man. And you're coming with me whether you like it or not. You can get a cup of coffee in the cafe and park yourself on a bench somewhere while I explore. We're here and we're going to have an experience."

Doc laughed and squeezed Grandpa's shoulder. "He's right. I'd love to see the fountains even if we have to bundle up to do it. Let's all go. Maybe Felix could stand a little exercise and fresh air."

So the following day Otto dragged me around the extensive palace and grounds, exhausting me to the point my legs and feet were complaining, when my cousin suggested taking a break to grab a bite to eat in the restaurant where Doc and Grandpa were relaxing by a nice big fire.

Once seated, the claws came out.

"You should go to Monaco," Doc began.

"Don't start," I mumbled into my cup of coffee.

"Hear him out," Grandpa chastised. "The man knows what he's talking about. He's somewhat intelligent if you didn't know that already."

I tried not to roll my eyes, but I noticed Otto snicker into his own coffee.

"I'm just saying that maybe you could let him know how you feel about him. Give him a chance to pick you over whatever the hell that job is that he thinks is more important than coming out." Doc's words were well-intentioned, but he couldn't understand that sometimes there were jobs you could neither avoid nor come out for.

I sighed. "Doc, let's just say… he's taking over the family business. It's a long-standing traditional company with superconservative employees and coworkers."

Doc opened his mouth as if to say something, but Otto beat him to the punch.

"What about just being friends with the guy? You said the two of you could talk for hours, right? If he's going through a stressful time taking over his dad's business, he could probably use a friend."

Otto was right about Lio needing a friend, but I wasn't sure I was strong or selfless enough to be Lio's friend without wanting, aching, for more.

"Friends, hm?" Doc and Grandpa exchanged a meaningful look before looking at Otto with accusation.

"Keep it to yourself. I know what you're thinking," my cousin growled.

"Hypocrisy," Grandpa mused. "How interesting. Pot, this is kettle, you're black."

Otto sighed and excused himself to get some more coffee. I turned to my grandparents and quirked an eyebrow.

"What was that about?"

"Walker."

Walker and Otto had been best friends practically from the womb. Growing up, where Walker was, Otto hadn't been far behind. All of that changed when Otto followed his brother Saint into the Navy and Walker left to go into law enforcement. I hadn't put two and two together that they were both back in Hobie now.

"What's going on between Otto and Walker?" I dove onto the opportunity to shift the attention off me.

"Otto's avoiding him," Grandpa explained. "Which is awkward as hell considering Walker is the sheriff and Otto got a job at the firehouse."

I opened my mouth to ask more about it when Grandpa held up a hand to keep me from speaking.

"Later. Right now we're still talking about your new man."

"He's not my new man, Grandpa. He's… he's…" I gave up trying to define what Lio was to me. A dream? A memory? Fuck. Either way it was depressing as hell.

"A nice man in need of a friend?" Grandpa's words were gentle, as usual, and it made my chest tight. "Because, honestly Felix, I think you're one too. And I think letting this guy in could be good for you."

"Why are you two pushing this so much?"

The two of them exchanged looks again before focusing back on me. It was Doc who spoke next.

"Because without your grandfather, I wouldn't have survived losing my wife and raising our children. That friendship saved me, Felix."

I noticed Grandpa's eyes fill as he reached for Doc's hand and looked away. Doc continued.

"Even if nothing else had happened between us, knowing there was one person, one heart, on this earth who saw and understood the real me, who stood behind me no matter what, made all the difference in the damned world. It sounds like this guy could use someone like that. Someone like *you* in his corner."

Grandpa leaned over and kissed Doc's cheek, causing Doc to turn and bury his face in Grandpa's neck. I heard them exchange murmured I love you's and Grandpa's strong arms came around to squeeze Doc tight.

The lump in my throat grew so big at the sight of the two men who were essentially my parents exchanging a love that had survived so much adversity through the years. These two men inspired me. They modeled the kind of relationship I wanted, and I knew it would be hard settling for anything less than what they'd found with each other.

"I'll think about it," I said just before Otto dropped down in the seat next to me again.

"Enough of this feelings bullshit. Felix is coming with me to the far fountain again. I forgot to take some pictures for my parents."

I'd never expected to be so relieved to leave the warm comfort of the fire to venture out into the cold again.

I'D THOUGHT about my grandfather's words the rest of the afternoon and through dinner at a nice restaurant near the hotel. My three companions seemed to be having a wonderful vacation in Paris while I quietly contemplated my entire fucking life.

So by the time Hen's call came that night, I was wound up as tightly as a bowstring.

"Henriette," I said, trying desperately to sound happy and carefree. "So good to hear from you."

"Cut the shit, Felix. My brother needs you."

My stomach launched itself into my throat. "What's wrong? Is he okay? Did something happen?"

"Oh, honey, no. I'm sorry. He's fine. Well, I mean… clearly he's not fine. The stress is burying him. He's become some kind of automaton. It's like he's slipped on this fake mask of cordiality and there's no one beneath it. It's super creepy."

"I'm sure he's just trying to navigate the demands of his new role," I said, wondering if I was reading from some kind of corporate teleprompter.

"No. He's freaking the fuck out. And now he's gone away somewhere in his head, Felix. Which is causing me to freak the fuck out. And that means Jon is—"

"I get it," I interjected. "But I don't understand what you think I can do about it."

"You told me you were in Paris."

"I am."

"Well, on your way home I was hoping you'd just stop in for a few days to maybe talk to him. Calm him down. Figure out where his head is with all of this. It's like he's being pulled in a million different directions, and I'm afraid he's going to snap. The coronation is in just a few days, and he could really use a friend right now."

"Hen—"

Her voice started to tremble, and I didn't know her well enough to decide whether it was put on or not. "I'm worried, Felix. This is serious. It's not okay. Can't you just come for the ceremony? He could use some moral support. Or… hell. Come see me. Come talk *me* down from the ledge. The stress of this coronation shit is getting to me too. And Jon is trying his hardest to be the perfect royal guard, which means I get to see him approximately never, and then there are the demands of my parents—"

"Fine. I'll come for *you*. But I'm not staying longer than it takes for him to go through the ceremonies. And you have to remember Lio and I… we're just friends. He made his decision, and we're going to respect that. Don't think this is more than it is, because we both know it can't be. And I'll be damned if I'm going to cause him to feel even more torn in different directions than he already is. Promise me, Hen."

There was silence on the other end, and I worried that our call had been cut off somehow. When she finally spoke, her voice was soft but sincere.

"Thank you, Felix. From the bottom of my heart. Lio is a good man, and he deserves a… friend… like you."

This time her raw emotion was definitely real, and I steeled my jaw against it.

"I might be bringing along some family baggage," I warned her. "Prepare yourself."

I wasn't off the phone ten minutes before the phone rang again with another call from Monaco. This time, it was Arthur.

"If you don't get your scrawny ass down here, I'm quitting the royal service and he can dress himself. I'd be just as happy dressing the rich and famous at Hermès."

"Arthur?" I bit my upper lip to keep from laughing. "You'd hate all that pretentious bullshit, and you know it. You'd be dressing more than Monaco's hoi polloi. You'd be dressing their purse dogs with thousand-dollar silk scarves while offering them Evian in a silver bowl and calling them Madame Buttercup."

I could hear his wince across the miles. "You might have a point. But it just goes to show how dire things have become here that I'm even voicing the thought. Our young prince has lost his marbles and become some kind of robot prince. Fix it, Felix. Fix it *now*."

"I can't fix it, Arthur," I said on a sigh. "I wish I could."

"Please," he begged. "Come to Monaco, Felix. We need you here."

"I'm on my way," I promised.

Silence.

"Well," he muttered. "That was easier than I expected."

# CHAPTER 31

LIO

I was in a late-night meeting with my father and his closest council members when I spotted Felix Wilde in the palace. The day had been interminable, and I was at my wits' end with some of the nonsense my father was pulling in an effort to be done with his responsibilities as soon as possible.

When I saw him wander past the open door of the conference room, looking lost, I blinked. Had my daydreams become hallucinations? Was I seeing things?

I excused myself and bolted out of the room. I had to determine if it was really him. As soon as my steps thundered onto the hardwood floor of the corridor, Felix spun around to face me.

It really was him: my Felix, there in the royal palace.

The sound I made was a cross between a garbled shout of surprise and a strange kind of relieved sob. Felix's eyes shot wide when he realized it was me, and I immediately noticed how intimidated he looked. I wanted to engulf him in my arms—more than that, I wanted to absorb the man into my body.

"Felix," I whispered. "*Felix.*"

His eyes immediately filled and threatened to spill over. Just the sight of him, scared and emotional, made me want to burst into angry tears. Why was he here? Clearly he wasn't happy about it.

"Lio." His voice sounded shaky and small. "I'm sorry. I didn't mean to interrupt you. Hen told me to come find her when I got here."

My hands still held his upper arms, and I squeezed them to keep from hauling him into my chest there in the public hallways of the royal palace.

"Hen? I don't understand. Why are you here? What's going on? Is everything okay?"

Felix looked around as if expecting to be caught doing something wrong.

"I should let you go back to your meeting. I need to find Hen," he said. He sounded tired and looked as exhausted as I felt.

I couldn't help but cup his cheek with one hand. "Please tell me what's going on," I said in a more gentle voice. My thumb smoothed across the pink apple of his cheek, and his eyelashes fluttered closed at the touch. "Felix, sweetheart, you have no idea how good it is to see your beautiful face," I whispered.

His eyes opened wide again, as if searching to see if I'd meant what I said. My body ached to hold him, to comfort him, to curl around him and finally sleep the deep sleep that had eluded me since returning to Monaco. But I needed to know why he was here.

A throat cleared behind me, and I jumped apart from Felix. Thank god, it was only Jon, but his presence reminded me I couldn't touch Felix like that in view of anyone in the palace.

"Come here," I said, guiding him to my office which was back the way I'd come, past the conference room where my father and his group still convened. Jon followed quietly and remained outside in the hallway while I steered Felix toward my inner office. I was surprised to see Lucas still at his desk.

"Is the meeting over?" he asked, flicking his eyes to Felix and back to me. "I was just leaving you a note about tomorrow. You have an eight-o'clock breakfast with Milane, several phone calls throughout the morning, lunch with your mother and Sabine, a press briefing midafternoon to discuss the additions to the foundation's new charity distributions, and of course coronation dress rehearsal tomorrow evening—"

I held up my hand to stop him.

"Please cancel or move everything through lunchtime. I'll be back by the press briefing." I made sure to say it in such a way that he knew not to argue with me, but he certainly knew something was up. Another glance toward Felix before he gathered his belongings and shut down his computer.

"Yes, sir. Good night."

"Good night, Lucas," I said before gesturing Felix through the door to my private office and closing the door behind us. I made sure to flick the lock closed as silently as I could before turning to face him.

Before I could open my mouth to ask him yet again why he was there, he launched himself at me, wrapping his arms so tightly around my neck, I could hardly breathe. It took me all of a microsecond before my arms came just as tightly around his waist, and I pulled him against me with everything I had.

"Oh my fucking god, you feel so good," I moaned into his neck. I breathed him in as deeply as I could, reacquainting my senses with his smell and feel. It was at once familiar and foreign, comforting and exciting.

"I shouldn't be here," he mumbled against my shoulder. "I tried not to come, but Hen told me I had to. I didn't want to. I shouldn't have. I'm so sorry, Lio. I should have stayed away. This is awful. It's just so wron—"

I couldn't let him continue berating himself for coming, especially if he'd been expertly played by my sister. And I sure as hell didn't want him calling something that felt so perfect, wrong.

"Shhh, it's okay. I can't even tell you how good it is to see you," I assured him. "I'm so glad you're here."

"Just don't let go for a minute, please," Felix said into the damp fabric of my shirt. "Please."

I cupped the back of his head and pulled back just enough to look him in the eyes. They were wet and worried, and I wanted to see them sparkling and happy again, the way they'd been with me at Gadleigh.

When I leaned in to kiss him, it seemed to happen in slow motion. Perhaps part of me was trying to give him a chance to stop me. Or maybe my conscience was at war with my heart and wanted to stop my body before I took advantage of the sweet, sweet man in my arms.

But I couldn't stop. There was no way in hell I was going to keep myself from kissing him when his delicious mouth was this close.

His lips were as soft and sweet as I remembered. It had been at least ten days since I'd tasted him, since I'd left him there, asleep in my bed in the castle. Ten days that seemed like a lifetime. Ten days that had shot me out of that dreamscape with the rocket fuel of reality here at home.

Our mouths danced lightly together and apart, the slightest brushing against each other until Felix pressed in and took what he wanted from me. His kiss was insistent and frantic, growing in aggression as his body remembered mine and he realized I wasn't going to stop him.

My hands lowered into the back of his pants to cup his ass over the smooth fabric of his boxer briefs, and I lifted him up so he could wrap his legs around my waist. I turned until I could press his back against the wall before I moved my mouth to trail eager kisses along his jaw and down his neck.

Felix was panting hot breaths by then, and his hips tilted to thrust his erection into my lower belly. With his upper back against the wall and his hips pushing forward into me, I was free to fondle his perfect, rounded ass cheeks. I squeezed before running greedy fingers down his crease. I felt the heat rolling off his body, and I wanted inside of him so badly, I thought I would come just from touching the warm sensitive skin of his rim. The small sounds he made drove me wild, and I couldn't help but push my own cock up against his ass in desperation.

This was getting out of control, but it was a freight train with broken brakes.

There was no way in hell I was letting him go until I wiped the fear from his face and replaced it with the blissed-out splendor of his climax.

Suddenly his wiggling turned to thrashing until he wrenched himself off me and stumbled to the nearby sofa and collapsed onto it, burying his face in his hands and mumbling something I couldn't catch.

I slowly approached him and knelt down on the floor in front of him, reaching out to grab his wrists and pull his hands into mine.

"Talk to me," I said softly. "Whatever it is, it's okay. Take a deep breath. We don't have to do anything you don't want to do. I'm sorry if I did something wrong. I just... I was so happy to see you. I wasn't expecting you. I didn't stop and think; I shouldn't have assumed it was okay to kiss you like that."

Felix's sudden laugh shocked me.

"Are you kidding? It is more than okay for you to kiss me like that. Lio, if it was up to me, you'd kiss me like that every day, all day. It's not me I'm worried about. It's *you*."

I was the reason he was so upset. Well, *fuck*.

"Why don't you let me worry about me?"

"You didn't ask for me to come here. I was foisted upon you by a wicked witch," he muttered, pulling his hands out of my grasp to wipe his face with his palms. Felix sighed before continuing. "Believe it or not, I didn't come here to attach myself to your face, Lio. I came to be your friend. That's all. Just friends, okay? We've already agreed that's all it is. Let me be your friend."

I realized I was in the midst of a bad dream. A nightmare of my own making.

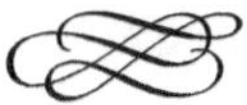

# CHAPTER 32

FELIX

I actually felt sorry for Lio then. In addition to the responsibilities being handed to him each day, he had to deal with this shit. Why the hell had I agreed to come here?

Lio sat down next to me and reached for my hand.

"Okay. Let's just take a breath. Why don't you tell me how you ended up here?"

So I told him. I explained about giving the presentation in Paris and deciding to stay after that. About my family showing up because they were worried about me. I told him about Hen's call asking for me to come as a friend.

"She really shouldn't have done that," Lio said.

"I'm sorry. I didn't mean to impose. I know you're busy."

He pulled my face into the crook of his neck and wrapped his arms around my back.

"Dammit, Fee. I'm the one who's sorry. I'm so sorry about all of this. My life is just… fucked-up. Hen shouldn't have brought you into this mess."

As hard as it was to pull away from his touch, I forced myself to do it. I was keenly aware of the fact that just down the hall were all sorts of governmental officials and most likely even the king himself.

"It's been a long day, and I know my grandfathers are probably wondering what the hell happened to me. So I'm going to go back to my room." I stood up, intending to make my way back to the guest suite Hen had so graciously arranged for my family.

Lio let out a choking sound. "No, wait. Wait. Just… just wait, okay? Will you please stay for the coronation and the ball?"

"Well, I told Hen I would but… I don't think it's a good—"

"Please. I need you there, Felix. *Please.*"

There was silence in the room while his panicked plea echoed around us.

How could I say no to him when he asked me with so much emotion in his voice and looked into my fucking soul with those cobalt eyes?

"If Hen can still hook me up with a tux, I will come as a *friend*," I said reluctantly.

Lio cleared his throat and seemed to gather his composure.

"Friends. Yes," he murmured, and then his eyes brightened with an idea. "Doc and Grandpa are here? I'd love to meet them. Can we go grab them for a beer or something? I have some in my apartment. Arthur can help us if not."

I was tempted to introduce him to my beloved grandfathers. I wanted them to know what a good man Lio was, and I wanted Lio to see what wonderful parents I had. But I knew I'd make an idiot out of myself and accidentally touch him or gush over him or look at him like a lovesick fool in front of my grandfathers. That was not the action of a *friend*.

"Ah, no. No, thank you. I don't think that's a good idea, Lio. They don't know who you are to me, and if they see us together, they'll figure out the truth. Plus, you have a big day coming up, and apparently your sister has signed me up for some kind of comportment lessons tomorrow. If I want to be at the coronation events, I must know how to properly address royalty, dance a waltz, and…anyway. Goodnight." I clenched my teeth to stop myself from babbling even more and stood up, carefully avoiding touching Lio before making my way toward the exit of his office suite.

I could sense him shifting as if to call me back or grab me or follow me, but I kept walking.

When he didn't come after me, I sent up a silent prayer of thanks. Had he tried to stop me, I would have folded like a cheap house of cards. I wanted him desperately, but that was the problem.

If he got near me just then, I'd throw myself at him again. And this situation was no joking matter. I couldn't be the one to put his coronation at risk. One hint of impropriety on his part could bring the entire thing tumbling down into more of a hot scandal than his family already had brewing. I would not be the person to put any of that in jeopardy.

When I reached the private sanctuary of our suite of rooms, I was trembling with the effort of keeping myself together. I knew that I just needed a hot shower and sleep to gather my mental fortitude for the following day. Just forty-eight more hours and I'd be on my way home for good. I simply had to make it through the ceremony and ball. The coronation.

When Lio would become the king of Liorland.

I could do this. I could be Lio's friend for as long as it took to get him through the upcoming festivities. According to Hen, the coronation was heavy shit—a ceremony in full regalia followed by a massive ball at the palace. Her hope had been for me to be there in case he needed some moral support behind the scenes. Hen had sworn she was just looking out for her brother's mental health.

It was bullshit, of course. Her real hope was for him to see me and decide to throw up a big middle finger to the world and announce me as his boyfriend. But that was never going to happen. Now that I was here, in Monaco, I could understand. Everything was so formal and traditional. Monarchies were practically defined by their conservative histories. I couldn't even imagine walking through the impressive portrait gallery and seeing a royal portrait of a king and his male consort. The idea of it was laughable.

When Doc and Grandpa realized I was back, I could tell from their faces they knew something was wrong. I tried playing the exhaustion card, but they didn't buy it.

"We didn't just come here for your new friend, Hen, did we?" Doc asked gently.

I shook my head and tried blinking back tears. "No, sir."

"The man you told us about is here too, isn't he?" Grandpa's eyes sought the truth in mine and must have found it there.

I nodded.

Grandpa pulled me into a tight hug. "It's okay, Fee. You don't have to tell us about it now, but just know we're here for you. We love you."

I could tell it was hard for them to let me go without a more detailed debrief, but they must have known I really needed time to myself.

When I crawled into bed still damp from the shower, the memory of Lio's hands and lips on my skin earlier that night carried me off to sleep.

# CHAPTER 33

## LIO

*Friends.*

He was right. I couldn't ask more of him, especially if I wasn't willing to follow through. He'd set clear boundaries with me, and I had to respect them.

But good god, they hurt.

I couldn't sleep at all that night and was embarrassed to find myself trolling the corridors of the palace near the guest wing in the middle of the night on the off chance I ran into an equally insomnia-riddled Felix. No luck, but I did run into an older gentleman I'd never met before and quickly realized he was either Felix's Doc or Grandpa.

"Mr. Wilde?" I asked hesitantly. "I'm Lio. Can I help you find something?"

We were standing near one of the exits leading to the palace court-yard, and I had the sense he'd just returned from a midnight stroll.

When he learned who I was, his face lifted in recognition of my name.

"*Prince* Lio, heir to the throne of Liorland?"

Fuck.

"Yes, sir. I'm a friend of your grandson's," I said, as if I somehow had a kind of claim on Felix. I didn't. Of course I didn't. Especially compared to one of the men who raised him. "Are you Doc or Grandpa?"

His face transformed into a mischievous smile. "Should I make you guess? What if I promised to answer one question? Could you figure out who I am that way? It just can't be the obvious choice of what my name is."

I couldn't help but laugh. "Your name wouldn't help. I still wouldn't know which one you were. But I already know what question I would want to ask. Why does Felix love stained glass?"

His face fell. Clearly he'd assumed the question would be one to help me identify which grandfather he was, but I didn't need to know that nearly as much as I needed to know Felix's heart. And when I'd asked him several times at Gadleigh what had given him such a visceral connection to the art, he'd blown off the question. Who better to ask than one of the two closest people to him?

I could tell he didn't want to answer.

"You promised to answer one question," I said quietly.

"And so I shall, Lio. But first, what about showing an old man to the coffee maker? My husband won't let me have any, so I have to sneak it when he's not around."

I hid my grin as I turned to lead him to a nearby lounge where breakfast would be served in a few hours for any guests of the palace. There was always coffee, water, tea, and simple snacks available.

Once we were settled with coffee at a small table, Mr. Wilde studied me.

"Do you know about his mother? Our daughter, Jackie, wasn't the best parent to Felix…"

"I know. He told me. You were lucky to raise him," I said.

His eyes snapped up to mine in surprise, and his mouth widened into a bright smile. "You're the first person who's gotten it right in all these years, son. *We* were the lucky ones. Everyone tells Felix he was lucky to have *us*, but they have it upside down and backwards."

I nodded. "So, what happened?"

"When he was eight, his mother dropped him off at the Mountain

View Mausoleum and told him to go inside until she returned to get him. She didn't return."

I sucked in a breath and felt my heart trip over itself. "A child left *in a mausoleum?* Why in the hell did she do that?"

He sighed. "She swore later she'd thought it was a church. She'd had an important rehearsal. Mind you, all auditions and rehearsals were important to her back then. According to Jackie, it was 'a once in a lifetime' role. She didn't have childcare for Felix, so she decided to have him sit quietly in the church building until she returned. Well, by the time the cemetery closed for the day, she still hadn't returned. The authorities were called. They tried reaching Jackie, but she didn't answer, so they called me. Luckily, I was on the emergency contact form at the school. You can't even imagine how it felt to be so far away from him when I got that call."

Even after twenty years, I could see the toll the memory took on him. I reached out to squeeze his hand.

"What did he do all day? He didn't find an adult and ask for help?"

"She'd told him to be quiet and try not to be seen. I guess she pictured him reading a book quietly in a back pew of a nice church. But when he went inside, it was all marble internment boxes and stained glass. Thank god Felix didn't know what the place was. He just thought it was a strange kind of church with the most exquisite stained glass windows he'd ever seen. After he finished the library book he'd brought, there was absolutely nothing else for him to do but study the windows all day, so he sat and sketched in his notebook and thought up ideas for his own designs."

He took a deep breath before continuing. "Unfortunately, in the process of trying to find the boy's mother, the police discovered she had a record for public indecency. Once they figured that out, they booked her on child neglect and held Felix until we arrived to take him. Of course, someone in central booking recognized her from an adult film and leaked it to the press. The media swarmed the station and screamed questions at us while we tried getting Felix out of there. It was awful, and he always associated the press with fear and anger after that."

"Rightly so." I seethed. "I can't believe they didn't have the decency to give a child more privacy than that."

Mr. Wilde blew out a breath. "It was clear they were trying to get a salacious story about a porn star who was in the process of making it onto the big screen. At that point she'd already landed a role in her first feature-length film, so it was bigger news than it would have been if it had happened six months before."

"What happened with Felix after that?"

"We told her we were taking him. She had to choose Felix or her acting career because it was obvious she couldn't manage both."

I let out a heartbroken sigh. "She chose the career." I wanted to say more, but I remembered we were talking about this man's daughter.

"Yes. Poor Felix. He was so loving and innocent. The kid hadn't even realized what a mausoleum was, thank god. He discovered later that the mausoleum's architect had been interred in there and insisted we go back before leaving Los Angeles for good so he could say thanks to the man for designing such a beautiful, peaceful place."

I didn't even know what to think. The idea of Felix, a knock-kneed quiet nerdy boy of only eight, alone and afraid in a cold marble death chamber made me want to run at top speed upstairs to where he slept and gather him up to keep him safe. So he knew he'd always be warm and never be alone again.

"That sounds like him," I murmured, toying with the flimsy wooden stir stick left over from my coffee. "Thinking of the positive, the peace and beauty rather than the death and loneliness."

"He's an amazing man," Grandpa Wilde said. "The biggest heart of anyone I know, but the one most fragile too."

He looked at me then with an assessing, almost accusatory glance. I didn't blame him. His goal was to look out for the ones he loved, and I'd set Felix up for a fall.

"I really care about him, Grandpa Wilde," I said quietly. "When I left him at Gadleigh, it was like I left one of my lungs there too. I can hardly breathe."

His smile was old and knowing. "How did you know which one I was?"

I gestured to his mug. "Doc doesn't let you have coffee. He worries about your health. He and Felix strategize behind your back ways to keep you alive as long as possible."

"They think I don't know they've swapped out all the good stuff at the ranch with crappy knockoffs. Who the hell wants light butter? Or fat-free sour cream? Jesus. It's like I might as well already be dead." He stood up to pour himself a second cup of coffee, and I thought about what Felix would say if he knew.

"No way to the second cup. Not under my roof. If Felix wants to keep you alive, then that's what I want too," I said. "I'll get you a bottle of water instead. You should try and get some more sleep anyway."

He lifted his eyebrow at me. "Tell you what. I'll let you boss me around about the coffee if you tell me about Felix."

*Well, shit. That's what I get for interfering.*

I retrieved two bottles from the small glass-fronted refrigerator in the corner of the room and sat back down, passing one to Grandpa Wilde.

"You already know everything there is to know about him," I tried.

"Pfft. Horseshit. I clearly didn't know that the man he'd fallen in… something… with was the future goddamned king of wherever."

"Well, Felix didn't either. At first. When I realized he didn't recognize me, I felt like for once in my life I could be someone other than William Triannon Frederik Harald Christien Grimaldi of Liorland—Duke, Marquis, Count, Baron, and Seigneur of all kinds of shit. But with Felix, I was just Lio—the guy he met on vacation. It was fun and free. We talked and laughed and touched. It was so damned right, you know? It was everything."

"How did he find out who you were?"

I cracked open my water and took a deep draw. "There was a security alert of some kind in the middle of the night at Gadleigh. My guards came into the bedroom like a SWAT team and scared the living hell out of the poor man. Felix thought they were kidnapping me. Before I had a chance to explain to him what was going on, I'd been removed and secured without him. The guards took him to a separate room where he met my sister. After that, of course, the jig was up."

"He must have been angry."

I felt my heart grip in my chest. "No. Mostly sad. I think he under-stood where I was coming from. At least that's the way he made it sound. Because of his mom. He gets the pressure from the media and the reason I didn't want to risk him knowing. I explained that once I had feelings for him, I wanted to tell him. But that's when he wound up telling me about Jackie. After that… well, I knew I would be ten times worse in terms of bringing the heat down on him. So I couldn't do it."

He seemed to study me again, causing me to feel like a restless bug under glass. When he finally spoke, I felt like I was talking to the stern father of my prom date.

"You departed Gadleigh as friends."

"Yes, sir."

"And? What are your intentions now?"

I wasn't quite sure how to answer that. "I didn't know he was coming here. My sister convinced him to come."

He nodded. "She told him you needed him. Is that true?"

I blew out a breath. "God yes. More than you could ever know."

"Why him? If the world knew you were attracted to men, you could have any gay or bi man on earth. Why Felix Wilde?"

I felt my cheeks pull wide as the feeling of happiness spread through my chest. "God, that's an easy question. He's gorgeous, inside and out. The man would carry a dying elephant up a mountain if that's where the elephant's favorite pillow was. He knows all the lyrics to 'Manic Monday' but won't sing them any other day of the week because he's afraid it will lessen his enjoyment of belting it out on Monday mornings. He'll drink unlimited cups of hot tea even though he hates it because he thinks it would hurt my feelings if he admitted to not liking it. He calls himself a scientist or a professor because he's afraid he's not good enough to call himself an artist. He… he once realized I'd left the castle building without protection, and he ran inside to tattle on me to the guards because he cares more about my safety than wounding my pride. When my sister and her boyfriend were outed in the press, he put on his rattiest sweats before snuggling

Hen on the sofa and watching Jane Austen movies with her all afternoon so she wouldn't feel so alone. Where was I? On the phone freaking out about the fallout in the media. But Felix? Felix was freaking out about the fallout in my sister's heart."

I stopped ranting long enough to catch my breath. Why hadn't he stopped me before I turned into a raving lunatic?

"He's such a good fucking human being, you know?" I added in a rough voice. "So beautiful. His heart is so pure. He deserves *so much*."

I looked down and realized I was gripping Grandpa Wilde's hand.

"You should tell him all those things," he said lightly.

"I can't. I can't be what he needs. What he deserves."

He gave me a look like I was a simpleton who needed the Cliff Notes version of life's lessons.

"You already *are* what he needs and what he deserves, and from that little outburst I can tell he's what you need and deserve too. What's stopping you?"

"Are you kidding?" I gestured around me at the ornate furniture and the palace beyond the lounge doors. "The entire fucking universe and their goddamned expectations. A thousand years of history and tradition."

Grandpa Wilde's eyes brightened. "Felix told me the guy he met at Gadleigh shared his love of artichokes."

I stared at him. Felix hadn't mentioned his grandfather suffering from dementia, but now I wondered.

"Yes, sir."

"I'm surprised. It would seem from your attitude about Felix that you'd walk right past a good-looking artichoke for fear you'd get pricked."

He stood up and pushed in his chair. "Imagine if someone somewhere along the line hadn't had the guts to work their way past the prickly outer bits of one of those things to find that glorious heart in the center. None of the rest of us would have known how good those damned things were. But it took one brave soul to try it first. And after that, people could look at that artichoke pioneer and model their actions. 'If they can do it, so can I,' they'd say. And after a while, eating artichokes became so commonplace, no one thought the prickly bits were anything to worry about. Ignore them, or snip them off and move along."

I tried to get his metaphor straight in my mind. "I get that having Felix is the heart, but what are the prickly bits? There's nothing remotely prickly about that man."

He took one last look back at me before walking out of the room.

"Homophobes and the godawful bloodsucking tabloid press. The best part of life is waiting for you, Lio. All you have to do is get past the bullshit and claim it. You might get poked, and the damned things might draw a little blood, but isn't it worth it? I'll answer that for you from personal experience. It's worth every single thorn you come across. When you meet my husband someday, you'll see. He lights my life on fire, and seeing his beautiful face every morning when I wake up is worth every bit of bullshit I went through to claim him. Good night, son."

I was left with a lump in my throat the size of Texas, and the realization that fire spreads. Grandpa Wilde's passion for Doc was enough to set my heart ablaze with thoughts of what it would be like to wake up beside Felix every morning. What it would be like if I was strong enough to fight through the bullshit and claim what was mine?

## CHAPTER 34

### FELIX

The following day was like one of those silly princess makeover montages from a teen rom-com movie. Hen convinced Arthur to drag me to some kind of high-end tailor's shop to have me fitted for a tuxedo, and the staff of the place bent over backward to accommodate such a good friend of the prince and princess. For a split second, I wondered what princess they were referring to. Henriette had never seemed princessy, especially when she'd been sobbing and slobbering all over my shirt while we gorged ourselves on caramel popcorn Mari had made us the day the photo came out of Hen and Jon.

Doc and Grandpa came with me to ooh and ahh over the fancy clothes at the custom boutique, but they'd declined the invitation to attend the coronation themselves, claiming they'd rather stay back in their pajamas and eat some of the pastries they'd picked up at a nearby bakery. Otto hadn't come with us to Monaco, preferring instead to sneak off somewhere in Spain to visit friends on leave from a naval base there.

Once back at the palace, Hen dropped me off in what appeared to be a formal music room for royal etiquette lessons. As soon as I entered, I met Jeanette, the woman teaching us, as well as two fellow students, Eleanor and Sabine. It turned out that Sabine taught art history in Paris and had heard about my presentation at the symposium from a colleague.

"I didn't know you had a connection to the royal family, Felix! What a lovely surprise. Wait until you see the palace all decorated for the event. It's unlike anything you've ever seen before," Sabine said after we met one another.

Both Sabine and Eleanor were close friends of the royal family and told me that there was no such thing as too much preparation for an event of that nature. Sabine wasn't able to stop gushing.

"It took me ages to learn the rules about how to properly greet a royal person and the order in which people are to be seated at dinner. Not to mention the basics of table place settings and—"

"I'm going to stop you right there," I said with my hand up. "I'm already way past overwhelmed and bordering on slightly panicked. And I'm just a spectator."

Her slender hand reached for mine. "It's going to be okay, Felix. But you at least need to meet the prince while you're here. He's gorgeous and funny. You'll love him. Just remember to call him 'Your Royal Highness' or 'sir' since it's a formal event."

My eyes jerked around, frantically searching for an exit or at the very least a men's room. The very idea of calling Lio, *my* Lio, "sir" made me want to hurl or at least cackle maniacally with laughter. But this was no joke. He actually was His Royal Highness, soon to be His Majesty.

Sabine continued gushing about royal manners.

"Do not extend your hand for a handshake. If he extends his to you, you may shake it, but don't forget to remove your dress gloves first." She must have noticed me on the verge of losing my lunch because she smiled to reassure me. "Don't worry, he's super nice, so even if you mess up, I'm sure he won't hold it against you."

"You know him?" I'd coughed to try and cover my squeaky voice, but Sabine had been too far gone with her swoony crush-on-the-prince face to notice.

"We're dating."

I stood there staring at the beautiful woman in front of me while my heart winged its way out of my chest and fell with a splat on the intricate inlaid flooring.

"You're…" I tried to clear my throat. "You're dating Prince Lio?"

She blushed prettily and looked at her clasped hands held gracefully in front of her. "Well, it's not official yet, but…"

I wondered if my abhorrence of the media included the comprehensive coverage that would surely follow the cold-blooded murder of a lovely art history professor in the music room of the royal palace in Monaco.

"Oh. That's… oh. Good for you." I thought I might choke on the words. "How exciting that must be. To be dating a prince, I mean. I can't even imagine… He must be very special."

The hours since seeing Lio the night before had already been spent in a perpetual state of nausea and second-guessing. I'd wanted to fall into him and get lost in his body for the rest of the night. But I'd known it was impossible. He was clearly well on his way to having the stand-up, presentable life he'd been raised for, and I had to admit part of me admired him for his family loyalty and sense of responsibility to his country and its traditions.

Of course, the selfish part of me wanted to claw at my chest in the town square and scream to the entire country that it was all bullshit pomp and circumstance obscuring the real Lio. The man who needed true love, not the fairy-tale fake love, and who needed to live a life with meaning regardless of what others thought.

Would he have that with Sabine?

I had to get out of my head and focus on what I was doing. I turned to the other woman in the room. She'd been introduced to me as Eleanor. I wasn't sure what her role was, so I made a joke to break the tension I felt.

"And you? Are you also dating a royal?"

Silence fell like ghostly fog around the room.

*Oh god,* I groaned to myself when I realized exactly who Eleanor was. Lio had never told me the name of the woman his father had dallied with, but I noticed her slight baby bump when she turned to face me.

After a brief pause of surprise, she raised an eyebrow at me. "I guess you could say that. What about you, Felix? Are *you* dating a royal?"

I shook my head violently and stammered my way through the remainder of the class like an idiot.

I had to admit both Eleanor and Sabine were beautiful, smart, charming and capable. Either one of them would make an amazing queen, which sucked for me. I'd wanted to hate them. I'd resented the hell out of Eleanor contributing to the reason the throne was foisted on Lio so soon, and of course I wanted to hate Sabine for getting the happy ever after with the man I thought of as my very own Prince Charming. But, try as I might, I couldn't hate these two complex and sincere women.

As I said my polite thanks to the instructor and my two companions, I left the music room to go on to another appointment at the salon with my thoughts reeling. The next thing I knew, Grandpa was trying to get my attention.

"Are you listening to me, Felix?"

I turned my head and focused on him. He was in the stylist's chair next to me at the salon. Arthur had herded us there for a haircut and shave, mumbling something to the stylist that sounded suspiciously like "eyebrow wax." At this point, I was beyond caring. Whatever he wanted was fine with me. I'd begun a silent countdown in my head until our return flight home. I needed to keep reminding myself this was all a weird time out of time, that my real life waited for me back in Texas.

"I'm listening, Grandpa. What is it?"

"I met your young man last night."

I began to swivel my head to him, but the stylist's strong hands held my head in place.

"You did?" I asked in surprise. "When? Where? What did he say?"

Grandpa paused for a moment, and I noticed Doc watching him from his seat on the other side of Grandpa.

"I like him, Felix. He's a good man."

"Yeah," I agreed quietly. "He is."

"That doesn't mean I agree with what he's doing, mind you."

"No, sir," I said automatically.

"But I'm not so sure he agrees with it either. He seemed awfully torn up inside," Grandpa said gently. "I can tell he cares about you very much."

"Mm," I mumbled, when what I really wanted to say was *pfft*.

"I ran into him in the hallway. I couldn't sleep, and apparently, neither could he."

"Mm," I said again, thinking about Lio restless in a bed, thrashing in the sheets and frustrated. I remembered miles of Lio skin, warm and sleep-scented in bed with me at Gadleigh. The memory of his naked body washed over me with such clarity, it left me feeling tight-skinned and antsy.

"Felix?"

"Huh?"

Grandpa's smile was devilish, and I could see Doc chortling out of the edge of my vision.

"Is your mind wandering, son? Care to share?"

"Shut up," I muttered. "At least now you know how freakishly good-looking he is."

Doc's laugh was boisterous, booming his joy throughout the small salon and making the stylists snicker. I couldn't help my own smile even while sending up a mental thanks for Arthur's recent departure to grab us some hot drinks from a nearby cafe.

Once we were done at the salon, we returned to our guest suite to relax.

Or so I thought.

# CHAPTER 35

## LIO

Felix was avoiding me.

I'd tried to get him to introduce me to his family the night before, but was rejected. I'd tried joining him for breakfast, but found he'd gotten up and out the door early to be primped by Hen's minions. I'd even been hoping to meet him somewhere for lunch, but Hen had informed me he was at some damned spa being pampered with massages and whatnot. I didn't find out until later that it was actually Arthur taking care of them and making sure they had everything they needed not to feel out of place at the events the following day and night.

By the time Jon did as I'd asked and informed me of Felix's return to the palace, I was vibrating in my office chair. I needed to see him with my own eyes again, even if only for a minute.

I'd just finished the press briefing and didn't have anything else important on my schedule until it was time for the rehearsals that evening. Sabine would be joining me to go over her role as my date for the ball. Thinking of her reminded me that I needed to talk to Felix about her, but what exactly was I going to say?

*Yes, we're dating because, if I can't have you, what does it matter?*

*Don't worry, baby. When I kiss her good night, I pretend it's your soft lips instead of hers.*

I was sure those would go over really well with him. It wasn't exactly like he and I were in a relationship, one in which either of us could expect fidelity. We'd already agreed there was no future there, but was that what I really wanted? Could I really do that—live my entire life without loving the person I truly wanted to be with?

Fuck.

I bolted out of my office in the direction of the guest wing when I almost ran right over my mother.

"Mom!" I blurted. "Sorry, I didn't see you there."

"Lior, I came to talk to you for a few minutes before things get crazy around here this evening."

"Sure. What is it?"

She looked from me to our surroundings in the very public palace corridor before gesturing me back toward the privacy of my office. I tried not to clench my teeth at the frustration of being thwarted yet again at seeing Felix.

Once we were seated on the sofa, she turned to me with concern.

"I was trying to keep this from you because I didn't want you to get hurt, but I'm afraid you're going to find out anyway. Sabine has... ah... been spending time with a gentleman, and I've just learned he'll be at tomorrow's events."

I had a feeling I knew where this was going, and I had a hard time holding back a smirk.

"Oh really? Who is it?"

"An American friend of hers named Felix Wilde. She had the audacity to use him as her dance partner in the lessons with Jeanette," she sniffed. "Ungrateful thing."

"There's nothing between them, Mom. Felix is gay," I said, hoping to put her mind at ease that she could safely put Sabine back on her princess pedestal.

"Oh thank god. You should have seen them dancing together. He's a very nice-looking young man, you know, but now that you mention it..." She trailed off.

"Now that I mention it…"

"I guess I can see how he's gay. He's kind of pretty in a way," she said.

"Mother, you cannot tell someone is gay just by looking at them. There are plenty of pretty men who are straight as an arrow, believe me."

Her eyes narrowed at me. "Is that right, Lior? I don't even want to know how you know such a thing. I've heard the rumors about you and Ignatius. I hope for your sake that nonsense is out of your system now that you have Sabine and are taking the throne. Surely you understand you can't get away with that playboy act any longer. You need to settle down and consider starting a family for the sake of this monarchy. You'll need an heir."

If only she knew how close I was to wanting to dedicate myself to one person and one person only for the rest of my life.

"I understand. It is not my intention to bring more scandal to this house, I can assure you," I said coldly. "So spare me the lectures, please."

She sniffed and looked away with a melodramatic sigh. "You know I just want you to be happy, Lior."

I noticed she was deriving great enjoyment out of using my new moniker.

"Do you, Mom? What if my being happy required something that upset the apple cart? What if it meant I'd have to shake some things up around here?"

She thought for a moment before responding, her pale hands smoothing out the navy wool of her skirt out of habit. "If you'd asked me that six months ago, Lio, I might have given you a different answer. But after trying to keep up appearances since your father announced our divorce and we had to start holding our breath waiting for the dirty secret to come out… well, I can understand how difficult it is to pretend you're okay while the whole world is watching. Sometimes I wonder if it's worth it. Surely the people of this country can handle the reality of a royal affair without the world crashing down around us. Maybe we don't give our citizens enough credit."

Her words stuck with me long after I kissed her cheek and escorted her back to the residence entrance. I made my way toward the guest wing feeling lighter than I'd felt since leaving Gadleigh.

If even my mother could admit that the people of Liorland could handle scandal, then maybe they could handle a gay king. It wasn't something I could spring on them right away, of course, but it was something I could at least consider down the road.

I needed to stop stringing Sabine along. It wasn't fair to offer her half a life. I wasn't sure it would have ever gotten that far between us, but realizing I couldn't live my entire life without a true love connection brought home the realization that I couldn't ask that of her either.

When I got to the Wildes' suite, a man I hadn't seen before answered the door.

"May I help you?" he asked.

"You must be Dr. Wilde," I said, holding out my hand to shake. "I'm Lio. Felix has told me so much about you."

Doc's face broke into a pleasant smile as he greeted me.

"Felix," he called over his shoulder. "Someone here to see you."

The other Mr. Wilde popped his head out of another room and gave me a wave. "Nice to see you, Lio. Well done on the charity announcement. I just saw it on television. Your foundation seems to be doing good work with children."

"Thank you, sir. I'm looking forward to getting more involved. Felix encouraged me to use my upcoming role to do good things in the world."

"That kid is pretty smart," Doc said with a wink. "We must have done something right."

"You did quite a few things right," I said in agreement. "He's a good man."

Felix walked out, and I could tell by the flush coloring his neck and cheeks that he'd heard our words of praise.

"Hi," I said, suddenly unsure of what I wanted to tell him.

"Hey."

*Awkward.*

"Can we... uh, can we talk?" My eyes lifted to his beautiful face. "Oh. You look really nice. Did you get a haircut?"

He patted his hair self-consciously. "Yes. Your lord and master frog-marched me down to the little town and forced some man named Milo to do intimate things to my personal style," he muttered. "Your valet is a bossy little thing. At first I thought it was your sister's doing, but now I'm not so sure."

I laughed. "I think you're right." I shortened the distance between us and ran my fingers through his newly shorn hair. "I miss your waves," I murmured.

Felix shuddered a little under my touch, and I realized how close we were standing. I turned back to see if Doc and Grandpa Wilde had noticed, but they were gone.

"Want to sit down in my room?" Felix asked.

We entered his room and closed the door behind us. I wanted to pull him into my arms once we were alone, but Felix's body language was screaming at me to stay away. His arms were crossed in front of his chest, and the skin around his lips was tight.

"Are you okay? I'm sorry about Arthur dragging you around today," I began.

"It's fine. I just felt... I don't know. Weird. Out of place. I'm not sure what I'm doing here since you and I can't really be together. I don't really understand how to support you, you know? What can I do to help you relax?"

Of course my stupid, lusty brain zinged in a million dirty directions, but I knew that wasn't what he'd meant.

"I couldn't sleep last night," I admitted.

"I know. Grandpa told me. I'm sorry."

The concern in his face made me feel warm inside. He cared about how I'd slept and how I was dealing with everything in my life right now.

I cleared my throat. "Is there... is there any chance you'd let me take a nap in here for a couple of hours? With you, I mean?"

His eyes widened.

"No," I rushed to add. "Nothing like that. Actual sleep, Fee. I'm really tired, and tonight's going to be a late night followed by an insane day tomorrow."

Felix's face softened, and he gestured toward the bed in the center of the room. It was made up with the most luxurious bedding the palace offered, and the idea of curling up in that bed with Felix's body next to mine was irresistible. The palace around me could burn for all I cared, as long as I could nap in that fucking bed with this kind and beautiful man.

I kicked off my shoes and slipped off my tie and dress shirt before stripping down to my undershirt and boxer briefs. I carefully laid my clothes over a nearby chair so they wouldn't wrinkle. Out of the corner of my eye, I saw Felix do the same with his sweater and khaki pants.

By the time I slid between the cool crisp sheets, I was trembling with the need to touch him.

"C'mere," I murmured. "Want to hold you."

He eyed me suspiciously.

"Baby, please. I promise not to touch your dick, okay? Just let me wrap my arms around you for a little while."

He crawled in close and rested his head on my chest, resting one arm on my front with his index finger near the divot between my collarbones. The pad of that finger toyed with my skin so lightly, I felt goose bumps prickle all over my body.

I had one arm wrapped around him under his back, and my other hand was sifting through his hair.

"Thank you," I said softly. "Maybe now I can sleep."

"What if I *want* you to touch my dick?" I could hear the teasing in his voice.

"Don't start with me," I grumbled. "I'm like a hair trigger for you right now. You don't even know."

I tried not to notice his breathing pick up, but I couldn't ignore the thunder of his pulse against my rib cage.

"Stop thinking and go to sleep, Felix Wilde," I said with a yawn. "No hanky-panky."

I must have fallen asleep quickly because the next thing I knew, the weak winter sunlight had moved across the room and there was a warm wet mouth on the inside of my thigh, trailing slowly up toward my cock.

"Mppfh!" I practically jackknifed up in bed and stared down at his sleep-rumpled hair. The carefully styled look had been obliterated, and his thick dark hair stood up everywhere in product-stiffened spikes. When he looked up at me, his cheeks were flushed and his eyes were bright.

"Oh god, baby," I moaned, staring at Felix's wet, red lips. "Please don't stop."

# CHAPTER 36

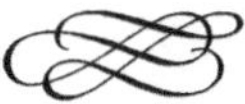

## FELIX

All of my self-discipline went out the window the minute I woke up and found myself rutting against Lio's hip. My dick was so hard, I thought I might die of blue balls if I didn't get off, and his perfect body was right there for the taking.

I wanted to taste him.

After slipping beneath the covers and sliding Lio's black underwear down his muscled thighs, I stared at the semihard cock left behind. God, it was so nice. The surrounding patch of dark curls lay tidy and neat, and as the warmth of my breath landed on his exposed skin, Lio's cock twitched. I ghosted my palm down the length of his cock, the head still hidden from view inside its soft sheath. It filled and expanded under my touch, and I moved my hand over to push one of his thighs open before dropping a trail of wet kisses up the inside of it.

That woke him up.

After begging me to keep going, Lio threaded his gentle fingers into my hair and cradled my head while I sucked along his length. He smelled amazing and tasted even better. I ran my tongue around the sensitive ridge of his cockhead until he was whimpering and begging me to take it all the way down.

Finally I did as he asked and began to deep-throat him as well as I could. I wasn't very good at it, but god, I wanted to make him feel amazing.

"That's… *oh god…* that's perfect, baby. Just like that, *fuck.*" Lio's words babbled out, and his fingers shook in my hair as his cock hardened more and more against my tongue. I ran my hands down to play with his balls and felt them draw up tight and wrinkled against his body.

"Fee," he hissed, trying to pull my head away. "Baby, gonna—"

One of his hands tore out of my hair and flew to his mouth to muffle his cry as his hot release spurted against the back of my throat and on my tongue. I was practically fucking the mattress between Lio's legs but suddenly found myself on my back with Lio's tongue down my throat.

"Oh my fucking god," he panted against my lips between pulls on my tongue. "That was amazing, Felix." He drank from my mouth like it held the only air he could breathe, and then he shimmied down my body to lay claim to my own aching dick.

His mouth was so hot and wet, his lips practically dripping with spit, that I damned near came on the first pass. I arched my back and reached for the headboard for leverage before thrusting up into that sucking heat.

"Ungh," I cried in a high keen. One of Lio's large hands came down on my mouth to stifle my cries as his mouth took no mercy on my body. Within seconds I was screaming into his palm and trying to blink away black spots in my vision. Through it all, Lio's talented tongue caressed and cleaned me.

My chest was still heaving when he pulled away, and my brain didn't have nearly enough blood supply to put words together. I thought maybe if we hadn't just taken a nap, I could have fallen asleep and slept like the dead. For the first time in over ten days, I felt completely at ease and sated.

Lio nudged us both back under the warm covers and pulled me into a spoon with our heads on the same pillow and his lips next to my ear.

"I want to come out, Felix," he said carefully. "Publicly."

I froze, sure the words had gotten jumbled up in my brain.

"Huh?"

"I was a fool to think I could spend the entire rest of my life living a secret. What, was I just not going to ever have satisfying sex again? Never give another person a blow job again? Never make the kind of connection that you and I have made in such a short time? Now that I know what it's like, how can I even consider spending the next fifty years without it? I have to just tell the truth and let the chips fall. Either the people will cry for a change in royal leadership, or they'll get over it."

My brain scrambled to think of something to say while my heart scrambled to decide how the hell I felt about what he'd said.

Soft lips grazed the shell of my ears. "Say something, please. You're making me nervous. I didn't mean for my declaration to make you feel pressure. It's not really about you."

I took a deep breath, but he spoke again before I could.

"I mean, I'd like it to be about you," he added quickly. "But it doesn't have to be. If... if that's not what you want."

He sounded nervous, and I turned in his arms to face him. Deep lines scored worry between his eyebrows.

"I think that's amazing, Lio. My heart broke at the thought of you denying this part of yourself for the rest of your life. I'm so fucking proud of you."

My heart was thundering with a cross between excitement and dread. This decision carried the mother lode of pros and cons—too many to list. I tried giving him my most supportive smile.

"You look like you just swallowed a slug," he said.

I lifted the covers and glanced down at his shriveled cock, resting limply against one thigh, before I looked back up at him with a raised eyebrow.

His bark of laughter made me indescribably happy, but he quickly settled down and poked me lightly in the chest with his finger.

"Talk to me, Felix. Tell me what you're really thinking."

His eyes were pools of deep blue. They searched me for any hint of reaction.

"I think I love you, and it scares me," I blurted, feeling suddenly so light-headed at the realization of what I'd done, I thought I might actually black out. "Oh god."

Lio's face lit up like the brightest sun. Eyes sparkling and bright, smile wide and sweet, and excited hope written all over the fucking place.

He leaned in to kiss me then, starting with the most tender press of lips and ramping up into a fever pitch before pulling away abruptly.

"I think I love you too, Felix. Pretty sure about it actually. I've never felt this way before. I want to tell the whole fucking world how amazing you are, and the very thought of denying those feelings has been making me sick."

"It's too soon," I said before he could continue. "You can't. *We* can't. This isn't the time. With everything else going on, I think you need to focus on you right now—the coronation and your new duties. There's the thing with Hen and Jon, and your dad and Eleanor. I know the last thing you want is to be part of a trifecta of royal sex scandals. And I don't think this country deserves that either."

I could see his disappointment, but I could also see the part of him that agreed with me, that knew waiting was the right thing to do.

Lio placed his palm on my bare chest and held it there.

"You're freaking out. I can feel your heart trying to beat out of your chest."

"I don't quite know if I can handle being part of all this," I admitted in a whisper. "It terrifies me."

He gathered me against his chest and wrapped both arms around me. "Me too, but isn't it so much better being terrified together? I'm so damned lucky I met you."

"I just don't see how it'll work. Even if we wait," I began, but he cut me off.

"No way. You do not get to decide it's not going to work before you've even given it a try. No. Forget it. We are going to talk it through while we wait for this other shit to settle down. We'll come up with a plan, okay? Something that works for both of us. Just don't... please don't give up on me before we have a chance to think it through together, okay? You can't break up with someone you're not even dating yet. Promise me."

I reached my hand up and ran a fingertip along his jaw. "I promise."

There was no way for me to know by the end of the following night, I'd break my promise and run home to Texas.

# CHAPTER 37

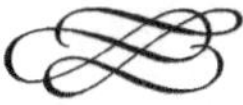

## LIO

Walking into my coronation ball the following night, I felt ten feet tall and bulletproof. I had the love of the one person on earth I cared about most of all, and I could for once in my life envision having everything I'd ever wanted.

The ceremony itself had gone through as smoothly as I could have hoped. There was something about an official royal ceremony that brought the hairs up on your skin and a swell to your chest. The import of the moment was not lost on me. I was taking my place in a thousand-year-old line of rulers, all of whom shared a part of my DNA.

As I'd stood at the front of Saint Nicholas Cathedral for the mass led by the archbishop, I thought of the many coronation masses that had come before mine. I had studied them in great detail as part of my education, but the only one I'd attended, of course, had been my father's.

When my beloved grandfather had passed away, my father had officially mourned for three months before his own investiture ceremonies. Even when it had been time for his coronation, I'd been so overwhelmed with sadness upon losing my hero, I'd spent the festivities in a fog. I'd been eighteen at the time and had been flown home from boarding school in the States to attend his funeral and subsequent official ceremonies to seat my father on the throne.

I remembered everyone greeting me with sadness and pity in their eyes. It had been no secret how much my grandfather had meant to me. He'd been kind and loving, funny and irreverent. But most of all, he'd seen me—the real me. He'd reminded me as often as possible to be myself and let my heart shine through to the people of Liorland.

He'd said, "All they want is a leader to look up to. It is our job to model genuine goodness. To set the example of what it means to help others, to accept people's differences, to allow our strengths to complement others' weaknesses, but more than that... it is our job to recognize when others can lend their strength to complement our own weaknesses. No one wants perfection, Lio. They want real, fallible leadership. They want to know they are not alone and that when we fall, we dust ourselves off and stand again. It is our job to show others how to handle hard times with grace. And when it is your turn on the chair, you will promise to do your best. You will not promise to be perfect. You will promise to live truthfully and with great heart and a strong spirit, yes? If you do this, they will follow you with their whole hearts, Lior."

It was the only time he'd ever called me Lior. I laughed now, remembering how he'd only ever referred to the throne as "that chair," as if it was just a regular thing. It was nothing special, just the place where the man sat. Remembering his words as I spotted the throne at the front of the ballroom, I realized he'd been giving me the right words for this very moment in time.

He'd told me to be a leader who lived his truth, trusted his heart, and remained strong through adversity.

I'd walked into the cathedral a prince, a child. When I'd walked out of it, everything had changed.

I was the king, and it was time to act like it.

With one foot in front of the other and medals clinking on the front of my formal dress, I strode into the room with confidence.

~

It wasn't until after my speech and the sit-down dinner that I saw Felix for the first time that day. I'd known in theory he was at the coronation mass, but with everything going on, I hadn't actually seen him. The crowd was massive, and, knowing him, he'd hidden in the very back so as not to attract attention. I could only hope he hadn't somehow missed seeing it.

I was dancing with Sabine on the wide wooden dance floor when her face lit up. "Oh! There's my new friend Felix. I can't wait to introduce him to you. He's the sweetest thing."

My heart jumped into my throat when I turned to follow her gaze.

There, in one of the arched doorways of the ballroom, stood the most gorgeous man to ever enter a room.

He was dressed in a form-fitting, custom-tailored tuxedo. His face was clean shaven, and his hair was styled like a movie star's. As he entered the room, I felt like all the oxygen was sucked out of the building. I couldn't breathe. I couldn't look away. His eyes were bright and sparkling as he laughed at something my sister had whispered in his ear. The sight of him happy and relaxed caught me around the ribs like a boa constrictor.

That was my heart right there, and it was walking around free as if it didn't belong in the center of my chest.

Out of the corner of my eye, I saw a trio of young women staring at him in obvious enthrallment. I wondered if I was just one of a hundred people in that ballroom who wanted him. Once my eyes caught sight of the stunning man, they couldn't stop tracking him if I'd wanted them to.

"Lior?" Sabine asked, dragging my attention back to her earlier words.

"We've met, actually," I said as calmly as I could. "At Gadleigh. He was there over Christmas."

She was clearly surprised. "I knew he met Hen there, but he never mentioned meeting you as well. It's not every day you meet a prince. You'd think he would have said something to me when he found out you and I were... I mean when he found out you and I knew each other."

I ignored the attempt to define our relationship. "I believe it was common knowledge I was hiding away from the media. Maybe he was deliberately valuing my privacy."

"Hm. That makes sense. He seems like a quiet sort anyway. But really lovely. Did you have a chance to get to know him at all? He said he spent lots of time in the glassmaking studio while he was there."

I noticed Hen whisper in his ear again. His head tilted back to laugh, exposing part of his creamy-skinned throat.

"I'm sorry, what?" I asked. I was fairly sure Sabine had asked me another question.

Her eyes flicked from Felix back to me. "He came to some dance lessons with me here and mentioned having gotten to know Hen while he was at Gadleigh. They must have become quite close for your sister to have invited him here, especially for the coronation ball."

"Felix is her escort for the ball tonight, I believe. Jon is working, and our public relations people weren't keen on the optics of him escorting her to an official event this soon anyway," I said without thinking. My eyes were still tracking Felix as he pulled Hen out onto the dance floor. Had this been a movie, I would have excused myself from Sabine and tapped my sister's shoulder to cut in.

How I would've loved to pull Felix into my arms and dance with him.

"Shall we switch?" Sabine asked.

I snapped my eyes back to hers. How the hell had she been able to read my mind so easily. "What? Jesus, no."

"Why not? Felix promised me a dance tonight. Surely you don't mind dancing with your sister," she said with a teasing glint in her eye. "She may be your sister, but she doesn't have cooties, Lior."

I swallowed my embarrassment for being so obtuse before casting her a smile. "Yes, of course. Let's switch."

We danced over to where they spun in each other's arms, and instead of tapping Felix's shoulder, I placed my hand on it and gently squeezed.

"May I cut in?" I murmured as close to his ear as I could get without drawing attention.

# CHAPTER 38

FELIX

That deep, familiar voice next to my ear dripped sex straight down into my cock. Great, now I had a goddamned boner at the ball. I shuddered and clenched my teeth to hold back the undignified whimper that threatened to escape. After clearing my throat, I mumbled something suave like, "Uh, sure."

I gave Hen a smile before turning to greet Sabine and give Lio a nod. But when I saw him up close, I almost swallowed my tongue.

He was magnificent.

The man in front of me was not the Lio I'd met a few weeks ago. He was poised and upright in full formal regalia. Polished medals, smooth ribbons, countless insignia, and even a silk sash all declared him to be someone of great power and accomplishment. I'd learned from our discussions at Gadleigh that he'd spent a few years in the French army, but now I saw evidence of his service on his chest along with who knew how many additional honors and awards.

This man in front of me was a king.

A *king,* and the reality of his situation came down on me like an imploding super dome, leaving me crushed under the dusty rubble. I was nothing. I was no one of importance. The bastard son of a selfish fame whore. A man so scared of his own shadow, I'd barely left the comforting scent of textbooks and Bunsen burners in the past decade.

"Felix," the king said, his tone flush with meaning.

"Your Majesty," I choked out before bobbing my head the way I'd seen everyone else do all evening and the way the etiquette teacher had instilled in me the day before.

I quickly turned and pulled Sabine into my arms and twirled her away to the other side of the dance floor. I hadn't even looked back to see his face. There was no way I was taking the chance of someone, even the king himself, seeing me so overwhelmed by the day's reality crashing in on me.

"Felix, are you okay?" Sabine asked sweetly. Concern wrinkled her brow enough to cause me to slow down and focus on her.

"I'm sorry. Yes. It's just… well, I guess I'm just a bit overwhelmed. I feel… out of my depth, to be honest," I admitted. "I left my hometown a few weeks ago to study glass, and now here I am at a royal coronation ball."

While it was the truth, it clearly wasn't the real reason I was so upset. The real reason was knowing, without a shadow of a doubt, that I didn't belong in this place. I didn't know the first thing about politics, diplomacy, or any of the other issues a royal family would have to deal with on a daily basis. What in hell had I been thinking? Daydreaming of a future with Lio had just been that—daydreaming. I couldn't possibly contribute anything of value to this world.

It was a fairy tale only. It had all been just a damned fairy tale—the stuff of children's dreams and young women's fantasies. I was an imbecile.

While leading Sabine around the throngs of dancers in their formal finery, I tried my hardest to fake friendly interest in her chatter. She told me about the dates she and "Lior" had been on and how she couldn't believe she was dating an actual king. She gushed about how sweet he was, how courteous he acted toward her. She even made a half joke about him being too gentlemanly at times, "If you know what I mean, Felix."

Were the tears in my eyes ones of relief or unmanageable jealous rage? Hard to tell.

I'd been the one to encourage Lio to put off his difficult discussion with Sabine until after the coronation. There was no sense in dashing her hopes before giving her the night of her dreams. But now I was having a hard time with seeing her on his arm.

When the song ended, I practically chucked the poor woman back at her table before striding as quickly as possible for the door. I needed to go home. Now.

As soon as I exited the ballroom into the vast corridor, I spotted a door to the wide balcony and knew that's what I wanted. Fresh air and solitude.

I crashed through the double doors, and by the time I hit the balcony railing with my palms out, I was heaving in breaths, trying not to freak out.

"Come with me," a steady voice said from behind me. Arthur grabbed my elbow and steered me through a side door, down what looked to be a service corridor, and into a small sitting room.

Where sat the king of Liorland.

My panic disappeared at the sight of him in the stately chair with ornate carved wooden handles and gold and burgundy upholstery. Suddenly, I knew exactly what I wanted to do. I crossed the room and knelt at his feet.

His eyes widened as he looked down at me.

"Felix, baby, did something happen?"

I stared up at him in all of his royal regalia. Finally, I managed to suck in enough breath to answer him.

"Yes, dammit. You became a king! I… I… I mean, Your Majesty…"

My words echoed in the small room as his eyes widened. But when he spoke, his voice was eerily calm.

"Yes, Felix. I did become a king. And I'm not going to apologize for it. But if you ever call me 'Your Majesty' again we will have to explore a spanking kink. Your pale ass might look nice with a bit of pink on it in the shape of my hand."

His eyes were intense as he leaned back in the chair. The power emanated from him in heady waves, making my cock hard and hidden confidence simmer under my skin.

I wanted to show him how strong I was so when I was no longer here tomorrow, he'd know I would be okay.

Without moving my eyes from his, I reached out and unfastened the lower buttons of his coat before opening his belt and pants. I heard the sharp intake of his breath and saw his eyes dilate.

Lio's fingers came up to slide my glasses off before placing them on a side table. As soon as my mouth dropped into his lap, his fingers returned to fist in my hair. It was quick and dirty. Part of me wanted him to go back into his formal coronation ball with my spit dripping along his skin like a brand. So he would know that beneath the clinking medals and the royal sash, he was still mine.

And when we couldn't dance together in front of a thousand witnesses, I'd still have the taste of his climax on my tongue.

There was no sound other than the muffled moans and gasps coming from both of us. His were noises of pleasure while mine were sounds of goodbye. If I was going to leave him, I wanted one last taste of him. One last moment of being completely his. A final acknowledgement that the man in front of me was the king I wanted to serve for the rest of my life.

When it was done, and I'd returned his clothing to its proper readiness, I stood up and walked over to a corner of the room, stupidly wedging myself face-first into the silky wallpaper there as if the silly gesture would hide me from his intense gaze and my own sadness.

He came up behind me then and pressed his warm, strong frame against my back. His arms slid around my front, and he tucked his nose into the side of my neck. "I'm still your Lio," he whispered in a strained voice.

I turned in his arms and buried my face in his chest, trying very hard not to interfere with the hardware there. "I'm so sorry, Lio," I breathed. "I didn't mean to pull you out of the dance. I just needed some fresh air."

"You must be joking. First of all, that was amazing. Second, I've been counting down the moments since I saw you in the ballroom, desperate for an excuse to touch you. And when I danced the first dance with Sabine earlier, all I could think was that I wished it was you instead. It should have been you, Felix."

We looked at each other then, so many words unspoken.

Lio reached out his hand to me, white gloved and steady.

"Felix Wilde, may I have this dance?"

There stood William Triannon Frederik Harald Christien Grimaldi, Crown Prince of Monaco and King Lior IX of Liorland, in all of his glory. And he wanted to dance with *me*.

"I'd be honored," I said with a shaky smile, reaching out to take his hand. With no way to hear the music from the tiny, enclosed room, we just swayed together in each other's arms for several long minutes. I ran my hands up and down the luxurious fabric of his coat and nuzzled my nose into his Lio-scented skin.

He whispered words of love and devotion into my ear—enough to thicken my throat and tighten my arms around him. The moment was magical… no, it was *majestic*.

But it had to end.

I pulled back from his embrace. "You need to go back in there," I said with as bright a smile as I could fake. "There are hordes of people waiting for an audience with the new king. You are going to be the most amazing king Liorland has ever known."

"Where are you going? Can I come to your room after the night is over?"

I thought about how I wanted to leave things with him, how I wanted him to feel once I was gone. He needed to be able to focus on the job ahead of him without the distraction of someone five thousand miles away. If I told him I was departing for home right after I left him there, he would beg me to stay. The ensuing argument would interfere with his evening even more than my presence already had. If I didn't tell him I was leaving, he'd be pissed at me for lying. But at least he'd manage to get through this important evening before discovering my absence.

"Yes. Now go have fun. I'm going to leave the ball early so I don't shoot puppy eyes at you across the crowd all night, okay?"

His own dark blue eyes bore into me. "I love you," he said. "Of all the vows I spoke during my coronation mass and all the promises I made to the people of Liorland in my speech, do not doubt that those three words I say to you now are the most important ones I said today. Do you understand?"

My chin trembled as I nodded.

"Say it, baby," he breathed. "Tell me you understand how important this is to me. How important *you* are to me. Please."

"You love me," I repeated. "But you have to understand I feel the same way about you."

"I do. I know how much you love me, Felix. That's what I'm afraid of."

Before I could ask him what he meant by that or even steal a final kiss from him, there was a commotion outside the door. Jon cracked it open just enough for us to hear him tell Lio's mother the king would be out momentarily.

"See you soon," Lio said with a grin before dropping a quick kiss on my forehead and sliding out the door.

I waited at least fifteen minutes to ensure the coast was clear before sneaking out into the hallway and finding my way back to the guest suite where Grandpa and Doc were packed and waiting.

"How did you know?" I asked, pulling off my clothes as quickly as I could before slipping on comfortable sweats for the long flights home. I left the custom-fitted tuxedo laid out on my bed and turned to my grandfathers. It was impossible to ignore the looks of pity etched in both of their faces.

"We raised you, son," Grandpa said in a quiet voice. "Of course we knew. Let's get you home."

I didn't say a word as we snuck out of the palace, out of Lio's home.

And I tried not to feel as though I was closing the book forever on my real-life fairy tale.

# CHAPTER 39

## LIO

"That fucking coward!" I hissed the words at my sister before slinging my phone across the room toward the sofa. It missed by a mile, clattering to the ground and sliding to a stop under an antique blanket chest my sister had stolen from my mother's apartment after she moved into her house in town. I'd asked her to stay as long as she wanted to at the palace, but she'd declined. It had taken me a few weeks after the coronation to figure out that she was relieved to have a break from everything Grimaldi for a while.

I could hardly blame her.

My father had retreated to the house in Grasse and was secretly ensconced in the countryside with Eleanor. I'd begged him to go public with his situation so that our public relations people could manage the fallout our way, rather than being responsive when it inevitably came out anyway. Despite Eleanor's begging him to do it too, he'd refused. While I was still supremely pissed at my father, I was secretly a little happy for Eleanor finally at least getting his full attention. I'd hated seeing her exhaustion and sadness that day at the palace.

I'd tried for the millionth time to reach Felix, but he wasn't answering the damned phone.

"Lior," Hen said to get my attention. "Can't you see Felix is trying to do the right thing? He's trying to give you some space while you get your legs under you in your new job."

"It's been three months since he fucked on out of here, Hen! And he sends me another fucking text asking for more time? What the hell? He can't just talk to me on the damned phone for five minutes? We had a deal. What if something's wrong with him? What if he's not okay?" The very idea he could be sick or hurt—

"He's fine. I talked to him last night. Stop being melodramatic."

I snapped my head around to glare at her. "What? He talks to you?"

"Not willingly. I have to call Doc and get him to force the phone into Felix's hand."

I couldn't believe what she was saying. "What? You can do that? How did you get Doc's number?"

She stared at me. "My brother is the leader of an entire freaking country. I can find out the phone number of a man named Dr. Wilde in Hobie, Texas, for god's sake. I think it took all of two seconds on Google."

"Dammit!" I paced back and forth in my sister's cozy family room. Jon had moved in with her quietly about a month ago and was sitting in a chair in the corner of the room, dozing off in front of the television. At my shouted curse, he jumped awake.

"What the hell?" In true royal guard fashion, he came fully alert in half a second, ready for action.

Hen laughed at him. "Stand down, sweetheart. It's just Lio bitching about Felix again."

Jon rolled his eyes before closing them again. "Wake me when something new happens."

"What did he say?" The question was directed at my sister, and she knew I was asking about Felix.

"The usual. That he's trying to give you space to get accustomed to your new role. But the truth is, he's feeling unworthy, brother. I think he's scared."

I knew she was right. I'd seen it in his face that last night before he bolted. The coronation had overwhelmed him, leaving us in a stalemate.

He was avoiding me because he worried about not being good enough to be the king's partner, and I was hesitant to push him because I worried about forcing him into a life under the microscope.

Which meant we were right back where we started, except we'd switched sides. Now it was Felix who feared tarnishing the monarchy, and me who feared attracting the tabloid press.

"I have to do something," I roared. "This is bullshit. I've spent three months with my head down proving I know what I'm doing, when all the while I feel like I don't know what the hell I'm doing! It's like I can run a fucking country, but I can't get one damned glassmaker to return a freaking phone call!"

Hen's eyes sparkled at me, and I could tell she was trying her best to hide a smug grin.

"Stop being a pest," I grumbled. "You don't understand what it's like not to have the person you love in the same continent as you."

"Why do you think I came to Gadleigh for Christmas," she teased.

I looked over at Jon and saw him gazing at her with a stupid love-struck puppy face.

"Don't make me puke," I warned them both. "Help me solve this, dammit."

This time, it was Jon who spoke up. "Why don't we just fly over there and get him?"

I opened my mouth to tell him how ridiculous that was when I realized he had a point.

"No," Hen said firmly. "You need to come out first. I think half his fear is ruining things for you here. He feels responsible for messing up the plans you had for taking the throne and marrying Sabine like a good little king. He needs to know that you coming out to the country is for you, not because of him."

"But it is because of him," I argued. "If not for him, I would have never even considered it. He needs to know it's because of him, I realized it's worth it."

"What if he rejected you now? Would you stay in the closet forever?"

Her question made me stop and think. "No. I don't think I could pretend again the way I tried to with Sabine. Knowing there is someone out there who makes me feel the way Felix does... no. I think I need to come out regardless of what Felix decides to do."

"So, you see," Hen said proudly, "I was right. You need to come out. Prove to him this is the right thing for you, regardless of what he decides. It might take some pressure off him to be worth it all the time. Does that make sense? What if you came out 'for him' but then things didn't work out? If he felt like he was the reason you came out, he might feel pressured to stay."

The thought of things not working out made my stomach turn. Regardless, Hen was right.

"Okay. Yes. As much as it pains me to admit, dear one, you are right. I'm going to talk to Milane." I turned to walk to the door of her apartment when she stopped me and threw herself into my arms.

"I'm so proud of you, Lio," she said thickly into my necktie. "I love you. When you're ready to fly to Texas, I'm there."

"Thank you for helping me see reason, Hen. He needs to know how much I love him, but he doesn't need to feel responsible for what's going to happen when I come out."

After dropping a kiss in her coconut-scented hair, I turned and left her residence, making my way down the long halls until I arrived at my own office. I'd learned early on that the king did not just turn up in his employees' offices unannounced without causing massive stress and chaos.

"Oh good, Lucas, you're still here. Please ask Milane to come see me as soon as she's free, and when she arrives, come in with her. It's going to be a long night."

I didn't wait for an answer before striding through to my private office. Lucas had made it very clear that for this first year of my reign, his time was mine, however much I needed it to be. We both knew that the long nights and weekend work would be frequent, and I'd be lying if I said I wasn't glad he was single. I didn't feel quite so guilty about keeping him at the office so late.

Once both of them were seated comfortably across the desk from me, I began.

# CHAPTER 40

## FELIX

Once I returned home to Hobie, I hid myself away in the glass workshop on the ranch. Whenever one of my family members expressed concern about my solitude, I explained I was practicing the new techniques I'd learned at Gadleigh.

And that was the truth.

But not all of it. Mostly, I wanted to be alone with my thoughts so I could feel sorry for myself in private. I spent hours reliving my time at Gadleigh with Lio. Every touch, every kiss, every shared childhood story or debated item in the news played back through my mind like a highlight reel of our time together.

When I wasn't remembering Lio, I was concentrating on creating the most beautiful, unique glass I could. I wanted to show my grandfathers that I'd done my time at Gadleigh proud, that the money they'd invested to enrich my education specialty had helped me come away a better glassmaker than I'd left here.

I perfected the technique used in making the knotted puzzle ornaments and created a stash to save for special occasions in the coming year. Once finished with that, I played around with some of the other advanced maneuvers to work on my own original pieces. I was proud of the work I was doing even though my dedication to the studio was keeping me away from my family.

Finally my cousin Saint called me on it one Sunday morning just before lunchtime. It was early spring, and the day was warm with a cool breeze blowing across the ranch.

"Get the fuck in the house, we're here for an intervention," he barked. I could immediately see how he'd succeeded as a Navy SEAL and wondered if maybe they wanted him back. We needed another bossy Wilde man around the ranch like a hole in the head.

"West says Wildes don't do interventions," I snapped. "Which means it's a love posse. Which is like fifty thousand times worse."

"Yeah, well, whatever it is, it's happening. Get your ass in the house."

I reluctantly turned off the gas to the furnace and tidied up my studio before closing it down for the day. There was no doubt that if the Wildes had come to have words, I would not be returning to my hiding place anytime soon.

After trudging across the narrow gravel lane toward the old farmhouse, I noticed the familiar vehicles of more than just the Hobie Wildes. The Dallas Wildes were there too, which meant this really was a love posse.

I hated those fuckers and their stupid-assed unconditional love. Every once in a while it would be nice to be neglected and ignored. Left to rot out in some shed somewhere with only a fire to keep me warm and bits of broken glass littering the floor...

I sighed. I wouldn't make a good Oliver Twist.

As I entered the house and made a beeline toward the big farmhouse sink in the kitchen, I ignored the loud hubbub of the extended family. Two of my aunts were there and what seemed like all ten of what we called the "Canadian" siblings—Hudson, West, Saint, et al. Even Winnie was there and she hated emotional shit.

Grandpa tried to make sympathetic eye contact with me, but I shot him daggers. Hallie screeched when she saw me and tackled me with an enormous, boob-filled hug.

"Jesus, woman, get those things out of my face," I bitched. "I turned gay to get away from that shit."

"You will let us love you, Felix," she warned. "You know the drill."

"I hate the drill."

"Here," a voice said before a cold drink was shoved in my hand. I turned and flashed a grateful smile at my cousin MJ, one of the only sane Wildes.

"Thank you. Did I ever tell you you're my fave?" I took a sip of the drink and discovered it was a Jack and Coke. Perfect. I wasn't usually a drinker unless this crowd was involved.

"Brace yourself," MJ warned. "According to Twitter, your mom is engaged to that talking-head jackass."

The room seemed to silence like the scratch of a needle on vinyl.

"Fuck," I whispered as I felt the blood drain from my face.

"Yep. Sucks to be you right now. The hordes are going to want your take on Psycho Stepdaddy, especially if they find out you're gay," she said before turning and plopping down on one of the huge sofas in the TV room.

I couldn't help but look around the room for Doc and found him walking toward me with his arms outstretched. I rushed into them and let him hug me tightly.

"It's okay, Fee," he muttered into my hair. "You don't have to talk to anyone if you don't want to. We don't even have to let them onto the ranch. You know that."

Grandpa appeared and wrapped his strong arms around us both. Even though he'd been retired for years, I could feel the rancher's callused grip on my shoulder.

"We love you, son. Whatever you need, you'll have it," Grandpa added.

"I need Lio," I said before I could stop myself. I cleared my throat. "But that's not happening, so maybe that means I need to man up."

"I hate that expression," Doc grumbled.

"Fine," I snapped. "Then maybe I need to woman up. Regardless, it's time the reporters remember I'm not a part of her life anymore. Maybe then even *she* will get the hint."

My cousin Max started a round of applause from where he sat in an overstuffed chair by the sofa. "Hell yeah, Fee. You tell her."

"Is that why you're all here? So when I lose my shit about my mother, you can all get me drunk to help me forget about it? Hell, is it even noon yet?"

I was kidding. Sort of. The last time I'd gotten drunk was the night before leaving for Gadleigh. It had been at the family holiday bonfire after my mother had tried to arrange a "small favor" by telling her then new boyfriend, Chris Corbin, he could have an exclusive sit-down interview with me. When his people had called to pin me down on a date, I'd been mortified. It had taken me every bit of self-control to decline politely rather than rant about what a homophobic, bigoted asshole their boss was. But, of course, that would have just created an even bigger scandal than me denying the promised interview.

Instead of calling Chris Corbin out on his bullshit and calling my mother to rage at her for putting me in the situation in the first place, I'd gotten rip-roaring drunk and propositioned the older woman who delivered our mail. Thankfully, she'd thought I was joking around and went on about how cute and funny I was.

I'd felt thoroughly rejected at the time until I'd fallen into bed and remembered the one tiny detail that had made it a lucky near miss: her lack of dick.

Was I willing to get heterosexual-drunk again today? Mm, I wasn't so sure. Not enough time had passed to erase the memory of the hangover yet.

My cousin West's boyfriend, Nico, sidled up to me and put his inked arm around my shoulders. "No, Felix. Last time you got drunk was so special, I'm afraid trying to repeat it would just end up in disappointment. No way you'd be nearly as adorable this time around. You're too maudlin tonight. Plus, I think the real reason you're here is because the king of Liorland is going to be on television in a minute. Some big sit-down interview."

My stomach lurched and my eyes jumped over to the large flat-screen mounted above the fireplace. The channel showed a news desk with a banner across the bottom indicating the king of Liorland was making a special announcement at seven in the evening local time. Which meant noon our time.

"Shit," I breathed. "Do they know what it is?"

I wondered if the story had finally broken about his dad and Eleanor. Lio had been trying to get a hold of me, but I'd ignored his calls. Had he needed to talk to someone about some shit going down with his dad? If so, I felt all kinds of fool. What if he'd needed me and I'd ignored him? How selfish could I possibly be? No, surely Hen would have told me if something was wrong.

When I'd returned to Hobie and gotten his angry messages about me running away from Monaco without saying goodbye, I couldn't help but call and explain myself. I'd told him it was for the best, we'd already agreed we couldn't be together right away, and I explained that even attempting a long-distance relationship was being "together." He'd asked me to put a timeline on it.

"Felix, baby, if you're going to refuse to answer my calls while we let time pass, at least tell me how much time needs to pass," he'd insisted. The frustration in his voice had made me nervous and fidgety.

"I don't know, Lio. At least a few months, okay? I can't... I can't do this halfway."

He'd yelled into the phone then, his frustration bubbling over from anger and fear. "I'm not asking you to, dammit! I want *all* the way, the *whole* way. I don't want halfway. *You're* the one insisting on halfway."

"Please don't yell at me," I'd begged in a shaky voice. "I can't—"

"Fuck," he'd said, interrupting me. "I'm sorry, baby. I'm so sorry. I didn't mean to yell at you, I just miss you so much, and I'm scared you're going to change your mind. I don't want to spend a few months without knowing how you're doing and talking to you before I fall asleep at night."

"I know. But I don't have all the answers. I just know if I come there now while you're working your ass off to prove yourself to the people, I'll either throw you off your game or you'll work your ass off and leave me home alone, you know? Either way isn't okay with me."

I'd known he agreed with me then even before he'd admitted it, but it had still been practically impossible to deny his attempts to reach me. In the beginning, I'd thought something was wrong.

"Lio! Is everything okay?" I'd answer in a terrified gasp.

"Yes, of course. I just needed to hear your voice. It was a hard day."

"Lio, we agreed we weren't going to do the long-distance thing," I'd remind him, grinding my teeth to swallow back the words I really wanted to say.

*I needed to hear your voice too. It was a hard day for me too. I love you and miss you so much. I think I might be dying of heartbreak not being able to hold you after you've had a bad day.*

So I'd begun ignoring his calls and texts for my own sanity. Otherwise, I would have broken, right there on the other end of the line from him. I would have asked something stupid like, "Is tomorrow a good time for me to arrive in Monaco and never leave your side again? Okay, see you then."

But now I wondered if I'd done the right thing. Because there on the screen was my beloved Lio, sitting across from a lovely news anchor dressed in a sharp light blue skirt suit.

"Good evening, Your Majesty," she said with a flirty but professional smile.

"Lior, please. And it's nice to see you again, Valerie," he said in that deep, familiar voice that wrapped around my heart like baling wire and pulled tight.

"Oh god," I murmured, falling onto the arm of the sofa and staring dumbly at the screen. The entire room had gone silent when the interview began.

"Congratulations on a successful first quarter as the king. According to the polls, the people of Monaco and Liorland as a whole think you're doing a wonderful job. How does it feel to be sitting on your father's throne?"

His eyes bore into hers with leonine authority despite the warm, friendly smile on his face.

"I like to think of it as my throne now, Valerie. And it's beginning to feel more comfortable as each day passes."

"Yes, that's good to hear," she said, clearing her throat. "Despite a rocky start with the news of your parents' divorce as well as the unexpected exposure of your sister's secret relationship with a member of your personal guard, you have managed to accomplish quite a few things in your first few months. Is there anything in particular you're especially proud of?"

He smiled and crossed his legs comfortably, oozing royal poise and presence like he'd been born into it. Which, of course, he had.

My young cousin Cal sighed. "That man is hot as fuck," he said.

Several of my male and female cousins tutted their agreements.

Lio answered the question. "Yes. I would have to say signing the Global Health Security Agenda was a significant step for Liorland's efforts to join the world's leaders in preventing pandemic outbreaks as well as properly training personnel in particularly vulnerable populations to react swiftly in the case of disease outbreaks. In addition to the GHSA, we were also able to approve greater funding for our commitment to the UN Children's Fund earmarked for helping the children of Syria. On the home front, the Monaco football club stands a chance at a European title for the first time in… oh, let's just say *ever*. Can I take credit for that?"

Well, wasn't the fucker just goddamned adorable?

*Jesus.*

Hallie elbowed me. "He's so fucking hot—all confident and shit. Like an alpha male. I'll bet he has a big dick."

I choked on my own saliva and began a coughing fit. West banged me violently on the back, which was surprising, considering he was a medical professional.

"Dude, really?" I squawked at him. "Glass of water, maybe?"

"Nah, you're fine," he said as he continued pounding my back while his daughter, Pippa, giggled from where she perched on his hip.

"Not you too, Pipsqueak," I accused. "Your daddy is a meanie."

"Shh!" my aunt Gina hissed. "He's saying something."

We all shut up and focused back on the screen.

Lio's face had turned serious. "Well, one of the things my grandfather used to lecture me on was honesty. In the process of ascending the throne, you can imagine I've spent many hours remembering the lessons I learned from both my father and his father. Grandpa spoke of leading by example. Of earning people's trust. I've decided to do just that, but I can't begin to build trust until I prove to the people of Liorland that I am trustworthy.

"There are two pieces of personal information I'd like to share with you tonight in an effort to start my reign with the honesty my grandfather held so dear. The first is not my story to tell, but I have been given permission to tell it anyway."

Lio pursed his lips before looking directly at the news anchor and continuing.

"My father is expecting a child with a dear family friend of ours, Eleanor Wu. They are scheduled to be married as soon as my parents' divorce is final. I ask that the public and the press please respect their request for privacy. And the request includes, of course, my mother. That is all I have to say about that."

The news reporter must have been warned not to ask follow-up questions because she only said, "What is the second item?"

Lio swallowed and looked unsure of himself for the first time since appearing on screen. My stomach lurched and roiled as if I'd swallowed a healthy dose of glass dust in the studio.

"Well, the good news is that the second item will help the press quickly forget about the first," he said with a cheeky wink. "I'm gay."

It felt like the entire universe held its collective breath.

Even the woman interviewing him looked shocked. "Excuse me. Did you say you're gay?"

Lio actually laughed at her. "Yes, Valerie. I did. Whew. It actually feels nice having gotten that off my chest. Been a long time coming, honestly."

I knew he didn't feel nearly as cavalier as he was acting even though I'm sure his words held some truth.

"Damn," Otto swore under his breath.

"No shit," Saint said with a nod. "Ballsy fucker."

A laugh bubbled up in my throat and spilled over. "Oh my god, he did it," I said with a giggle. I couldn't help it. The man was unbelievably brave. I just stared at him while he sat in front of an international audience and made being a gay king sound absolutely goddamned normal.

"He sure did," Grandpa said with a wide grin as he reached out to squeeze my shoulder.

"Atta boy, Lior," Doc murmured at the television from behind Grandpa. I saw his hand resting on Grandpa's hip and took a moment to enjoy the visual sign of their connection. They'd always been the living proof that modeling truth helped others live their own.

I looked around the room at the gay men and women among us and knew without a shadow of a doubt many of us would have never had the guts to live out and proud in our tiny Texas town without seeing Grandpa and Doc do it first.

And now Lio was doing it on an international stage for all to witness.

"I have to call him," I said, standing up suddenly. "I have to tell him how proud I am of him."

I turned to run for the door so I could step outside into the mild spring weather and make the call in private. Before I even turned fully around, I heard his deep, familiar voice again and looked back at the screen. Except it was playing a commercial.

"Wha?" I asked like an idiot.

"I said, you can tell me in person."

I turned around to see Lio standing there, tall and proud and exhausted and nervous all at once. But none of those things mattered. The only part of his appearance that mattered was the location of it.

In Hobie, Texas. There, in front of me.

# CHAPTER 41

LIO

It had been a long, hellish week. After coming up with a strategy with Milane, it had taken an army to put it into action and prepare for the fallout. My only consolation was knowing I was going to fly to Texas the minute I was done. The network only landed the interview after agreeing to embargo the information between taping and airing. I needed a chance to get to Felix and be there when he heard the news. Milane had insisted I stay and make myself available for the local press after the interview aired, but I'd remained strong, convincing her the local press could allow me a few days to myself after such a big announcement before pouncing on me.

Arthur had lectured me for half the flight.

"You can't just show up there unannounced."

"Watch me," I'd grumbled from the seat next to his before taking a sip of orange juice.

"What if the media catches wind of our arrival? It's not exactly like we're traveling incognito in this thing." He'd gestured to the private jet that was emblazoned with everything royal.

"I already told you. There's a global affairs summit in Dallas this week. It's public knowledge that someone from my office is attending. Why do you think we brought Martin?" I had glanced toward the back of the plane where one of our environmental specialists had been snoring and drooling in his seat. The poor guy had gotten only a few hours' notice before having to meet us at the helipad.

"I still think you should have gotten a wig. I've been dying to see you as a blond. Ever since that photoshop prank when you were at Georgetown, I've thought—"

"Arthur, stop. You're making me even more nervous than I already am." I'd begun drumming my fingers on the armrest without realizing it. Arthur reached out and placed his hand over mine to stop it.

"He loves you, Lior," he'd said quietly. "It will be okay, I promise. Felix is a good man."

I'd looked over at him with gratitude before he rolled his eyes and forced a sleeping pill on me. "So help me god, if you don't pass out for the next ten hours, I'll have to toss you out the escape hatch," he'd muttered. "Think of it as resting up before the sexfest."

But now we were finally there, standing in Doc and Grandpa's farmhouse in tiny Hobie, Texas.

As soon as Felix saw me, I had my arms full of him, squeezing him to me for all I was worth.

"*Felix.*" I breathed in his familiar scent, brushing my lips against the warm skin under his ear. "Oh god, you feel so good."

His entire body was trembling against mine, and when I realized it, I pulled back and looked at him. "You okay?"

His brown eyes were shining as he gazed at me like I wasn't real. "Are you kidding? I've never been better. I'm so proud of you, Lio. I can't believe you just did that. Are *you* okay?"

"I am now."

I brushed my fingers along one of his cheeks before leaning down and kissing the hell out of him. He tasted so fucking good, I could have gotten lost in his kiss for hours.

If only the air hadn't split open with catcalls.

*"Go get it, boy!"*

*"Show us some skin!"*

*"Felix gettin' naughty with Prince Charming."*

*"What do you call french kissing in French? Is it just kissing? That's boring."*

*"I call dibs next!"*

*"Introduce us to your boy toy, Felix."*

I pulled back and stared at a room full of people I could have sworn hadn't been there a moment before. At least fifteen people in their twenties and thirties grinned at us from various seats and perches around the big kitchen and family room combo. Were they having a party?

When I glanced back at Felix, I saw his face ignite with embarrassment. "Dammit," he muttered under his breath. "Prepare yourself. We're called Wilde for a reason."

Doc and Grandpa Wilde stepped forth from the throng and welcomed me to their home. I slid a possessive arm around Felix's waist with absolutely no intention of letting him go anytime soon. His body melted against mine in response.

"Everybody," Felix said loudly enough to carry across the group. "This is William Triannon Frederik Harald Christien Grimaldi, Prince of Monaco and King of Liorland. He prefers it if you bow deeply and kiss his ring, but—"

I interrupted, feeling a blush steal across my own face as I barked out a laugh. "Shut the hell up. Leave my ring alone, but you can kiss something else, smartass. How did you even remember all that?" I looked at the collection of Felix's extended family. "Please call me Lior," I said. It had taken me a while to accept the new version of my name, but I'd finally done it. Now, when Felix called me Lio, it was like staking a claim on me not many people were close enough to have.

As Felix walked me around, introducing me to everyone, I noticed how happy and relaxed he was. Seeing him ensconced in the house he grew up in surrounded by so many people who obviously loved him made me feel warm and full. I felt especially thankful to Doc and Grandpa Wilde for giving him the life he deserved, and I wondered, not for the first time, about whether or not it was fair to drag him away from the people and place he loved so much.

After an hour of getting to know his family and being teased for the lovesick way I stared at Felix and kept a tight grip on his hand, I heard him tell Doc he was taking me home.

"I thought you lived here on the ranch," I said as he extricated me from his cousin Hallie's tight hug.

"I do, but not in the main house. I have my own cabin just behind the first pasture," Felix said with a blush. I heard a muffled laugh behind me and caught Arthur winking at Grandpa Wilde.

"We're going to Felix's house," I told him, trying to reclaim my professional air.

"No, sir. Just you. The rest of us are being put up at the bunkhouse out back. These gentlemen have graciously offered to entertain us in your absence," he said with a smirk.

I swallowed an audible sigh of relief and nodded my thanks to Doc and Grandpa Wilde.

Once we said our goodbyes and promised to return for a late dinner, Felix led me down a gravel path to a narrow space between two long fences. The early-spring grass was green and young, trampled from what was most likely daily foot traffic between Felix's cabin and the main farmhouse.

"It's so peaceful out here," I said to Felix's back. The narrow passageway between the two fenced pastures didn't allow us to walk side by side. "You must love it. How often do you go into the town itself? Hobie is charming, by the way. You described it perfectly. I even saw the bakery and the old theater."

"I'm not sure I've heard your nervous chatter before," he said with a grin over his shoulder.

Felix was right—my stomach felt like there were a thousand angry bees swarming around in it, and my skin itched like I'd rolled in nettles.

"All I can think about is getting you alone," I admitted. "My hands are shaking with it."

Felix turned around and grabbed my face, crashing his lips into mine and smiling against my mouth.

"Mpfh, you taste good," he mumbled. "I want to get you naked and suck hickeys into your skin. And then I want to lick your cock before riding it. And then I want to—"

It was my turn to attack, and I did. My tongue thrust into his mouth, surprising a squeak out of him. I walked him backward, hands roaming all over his back and ass before he finally dislodged himself from my person and took off running toward the tiny cabin in the distance.

I raced after him. Once we were through the door to the place, he slammed and bolted it. His clothes were off in a blink, and I stood there staring like a fool at his slender, fit body.

"Christ, you're beautiful," I murmured, stalking closer to him. "I want to eat you for dinner."

His grin was playful, but his eyes were intense.

"Only if you ask nicely," he teased, stepping backward toward what I assumed was a bedroom. "Take off your clothes, *Your Highness.*"

*If you insist.*

# CHAPTER 42

## FELIX

I felt like I'd just sucked in three helium balloons and could fly. But the reality was, I only got the squeaky voice.

When Lio stripped and threw me down on my bed, I squealed like a little kid being tickled to death. Lio teased me mercilessly.

"What's with the giggles, giggler?" he asked, hands roaming over my ribs, which only made it worse.

"I'm just so freaking happy to see you, to touch you, hopefully to fuck you," I admitted with glee. "I feel like... my fairy tale is coming true."

Lio was lying on top of me, his naked body bringing up all kinds of feelings against my own bare skin. His gaze turned from playful to intense.

"Do you have any idea how much I missed you, Felix?"

I swallowed a lump in my throat. "If it's anything like what I felt for you, I'm sorry."

His hand came up to brush the hair from my face. "I don't want to be apart from you anymore, Fee. Will you come home with me? I know it's asking a lot. I know you'd have to put up with the media and leaving your family and—"

"Yes," I breathed, feeling the tangle of emotions that word entailed.

Lio squeezed his eyes closed in relief and dropped his forehead onto my chest. "Thank god. I hate to even ask you this in case the answer is no, but are you sure?"

"Babe, I don't really have a choice," I said, bringing my legs around to cross ankles behind him. "My heart's already decided. It's picked you. I didn't really have a say in it."

He lifted his head. "And if you had?"

I shrugged. "Meh. You don't seem all that worth the trouble you bring. I was hoping to find a nice ranch hand here in Texas. You know, someone who could support me in the manner to which I've become accustomed." I gestured toward the window where we could see a barren pasture with some abandoned, half-rotten hay bales next to a broken-down tractor. It was a fairly normal part of living on a giant ranch but looked pretty pathetic compared to the opulence of his life in Monaco.

He laughed. "Baby, what if I promised to have the palace staff chuck some straw piles haphazardly here and there around the court-yard? We could even bring in some chickens to peck around at the roses in the gardens."

I pretended to think about it for a moment. "Hmm, that sounds lovely. Add in a farting cow or twelve and we have ourselves a deal."

I shrieked when he rolled me around on the bed, biting at my neck and digging fingertips into my ribs to get a rise out of me. And rise, I did. Or, rather, a certain desperate dick did.

"Fuck me," I gasped before I lost all ability to speak. "Please stop goofing around and get inside me, Lio. I need you."

He stopped tickling and met my eyes. "I was sort of hoping you might want to top me this time."

My heart rate skipped up, and my dick jumped. "Oh hell yes. You sure? Never mind. I don't care if you're sure. Move over and let me grab what we need."

When I stretched for my bedside table drawer, I felt Lio's palm come down with a smack on my right ass cheek.

"Yikes! What was that for?" I asked, turning back around with the condom and lube bottle.

"Your ass is fucking perfection. I think I changed my mind about bottoming."

"Too late. Your ass is mine. We can switch later."

We started kissing again, and I forgot all about the lube and condom. Our hard cocks slid against each other with the slick from our precum, and I wondered idly if we were even going to get to anything more than a good frot.

Honestly, I didn't care either way. I had Lio naked in bed with me, and I was going to make him feel good. That's all I could ask for.

After sucking a spot on my collarbone and thrusting his hips into me, Lio gasped. "If you don't fuck me soon, I'm going to come all over your stomach."

I finally grabbed the lube and slicked up my fingers before reaching down to find his entrance. "You're going to come all over my stomach anyway," I said with a smirk, teasing the rim of his hole with the pad of one finger. I felt his body react to my touch, and it only made my cock harder.

"More," he grunted. "C'mon baby, please."

I captured his mouth with mine before sliding the first slick finger through his tight ring of muscles into the warmth of his body.

*Oh god.*

"Ngh," he moaned. "More."

"Bossy fucker," I muttered, twisting and pulsing my finger before adding another. "You're so damned tight, babe. Have you bottomed before?"

"Yes, but only a couple of times and not with something like that," he said, reaching for my cock. "It's looking bigger and bigger every second."

I pulled my fingers back. "We don't have to—"

His eyes flashed wide with frustration before he scrambled for the condom and thrust it at me. "Stop talking, Fee. Please."

As I opened and rolled the condom on with shaking hands, I muttered, "Give a guy a bejeweled crown and a shiny new chair and he thinks he owns the fucking place. Bossy mother —*jesusfuckingchrist!*"

Lio's slick finger hit the hot skin of my own hole and pushed right in before pulling back out again just as quickly. I whined at the loss of it and noticed him shoot me a look of satisfaction.

"Quit your muttering and fuck me."

"Sure thing, Your Majesty," I snapped before slathering my cock with lube and positioning it at his entrance. His knees were pulled back against his sides, and his eyes were wild. "Permission to invade, sir," I said with a snort. The man looked about as faraway from a royal leader as he could possibly get, and I couldn't help but tease him.

I was just so goddamned happy.

Before I could snicker, Lio tossed me over on my back and shoved himself down hard on my cock.

His body thrust up and down with desperate abandon, but his eyes were smiling. Between heaving breaths he was able to tease me back.

"Such a fucking smartass. You need a gag and restraints."

The tight squeeze of his body on my cock was too much. I didn't stand a chance at responding to him with words.

"Unh!"

My hips canted up into him as he slammed down on me.

"Ffft," I tried, gasping for breath and clutching his ass like it was my last tenuous hold on this life.

"Fuck, Felix, baby. You feel so good. You feel so good inside me—god!" He seemed to lose his rhythm then, and I instinctively took over. After pushing him off me, I pressed him face-first into the mattress and pulled his hips back until his poor abused hole was in front of me. I slid home again and rocked into him over and over while he whimpered and begged underneath me.

"Fee, *Fee*," he chanted. "I can't…" The final whimper was followed by the tight clasp of his body and the cry of his release. Neither one of us was touching his cock, and the realization that he'd been turned on enough to come hands-free brought me to my knees. I collapsed onto his back with one final thrust deep inside him. My release shot off with rapid pulses from my cock and tingles up and down my groin. I sunk my teeth into his shoulder as I gasped through the orgasm, and when I was done, we both lay in a sweaty heap, sucking in breaths like we'd just finished a sprint.

After I pulled out to dispose of the condom, Lio rolled over and quirked his lip up.

"Go again?"

I burst out laughing as I stumbled to the bathroom on noodle legs.

"You're a king, not a superhero," I called over my shoulder.

When I crawled back onto the bed with a warm wet washcloth to clean him up, Lio grinned at me.

"What if I feel like a superhero?"

"Smug bastard," I murmured before tossing the cloth away and snuggling against him. "You may feel like a superhero, but I feel like I'm about three months out of shape. I'm going to have to go back to bottoming if fucking you leaves me this winded."

He ran his fingers through my hair. "Why haven't you been exercising since you got home?"

I shrugged. "Feeling too sorry for myself, I guess. I've been hiding away in my glass workshop."

His hand stopped carding through my hair before he shifted so he could look me in the face. The concern he had for me was apparent, and it made me feel warm inside.

"I'm sorry, Felix," he said sincerely. "I should have come out sooner."

My jaw dropped. "No you shouldn't have. You did things exactly the way you needed to do them. I should have gotten off my ass sooner. Stop blaming yourself! I'm the one who insisted we not talk to each other, so it was my own damned fault."

Lio sighed. "Well, it's done. We'll go home and start exercising together. How does that sound? I'll have to find us some horses to ride or something since that seems to be what you're used to."

I pictured the Lipizzaner Stallions marching daintily in the forecourt of the royal palace while Lio looked excitedly at me. The laugh bubbled out before I could stop it.

"Jogging in a park is just fine, babe."

Lio's face darkened. "Well, you know you'll have royal guards, right? I mean, I wish I could say you didn't have to but…"

My stomach flipped a little with nerves. "Yeah. I guess you're right. The treadmill it is, then. That… that's going to take some getting used to."

We lay quietly after that, just touching each other softly and exchanging kisses here and there. After a while, I realized Lio had fallen asleep. I finally realized the low-level intermittent buzzing I was hearing was the silent ringer of his phone.

I slipped out of his arms to retrieve it from the other room where it lay abandoned in his trouser pocket. Twenty-three missed calls. No doubt his office's public relations people were working overtime to deal with the media fallout from the interview.

I wandered back into the bedroom and set his phone on the table next to the side of the bed he was using. Lio's face looked so relaxed in sleep, I didn't dare wake him. Instead, I slid between the covers and nudged him onto his side so I could spoon him.

As I curled my body around his, my entire soul seemed to let out a sigh of relief. Lio Grimaldi was in my bed. My Lio was safe in my arms in tiny Hobie, Texas, and for at least the next couple of days, we could hide out from prying eyes and relax.

But of course that's not what happened, because fate was an asshole like that.

And so was my mother.

# CHAPTER 43

## LIO

During a huge Wilde family dinner that night and the bonfire that followed, I was treated to a healthy number of adorable Felix stories as I got to know many of his cousins. The beer consumption matched my Texas-sized expectations, and only two of Felix's cousins kept offering me something prissy instead. I guessed they assumed someone from Monte Carlo couldn't stomach something as plebeian as a simple beer.

"Are you sure you wouldn't like a cosmopolitan?" Hallie asked while batting her eyelashes. "I hear they're all the rage in Monte Carlo."

Felix rolled his eyes. "So is drag racing, but he doesn't do that either."

I smirked at him, and he rolled his eyes a second time. "Let me guess," he said. "You do, in fact, drive a race car."

"No, baby, but the royal family never misses a final in our local Grand Prix," I added. "You'll have to learn the difference between Formula One and drag racing though. One is what we do in Monaco, the other is for street thugs."

A little while later, Felix's cousin Hudson wandered over with his girlfriend, Darci. He handed me a drink that seemed an overly vibrant shade of green.

"What's this?" I asked.

"Appletini shooter," Darci said with an excited grin. "Otto said it's the only thing you guys drink back home."

Hudson looked like he was going to wet his pants laughing while Otto snickered from the other side of the bonfire. I took the glass and lifted it in tribute to both of them before tossing it back.

"Now can someone please get me a goddamned beer?" I asked after swallowing the tart shot.

The crowd around the fire roared with laughter, and I noticed Arthur enjoying himself with Grandpa and Doc's only great-grand-child, Pippa. She was sitting on his lap while he tried blowing bubbles from a cheap bottle of bubble soap into the night air.

The Texas weather was mild, and the bonfire chased away any lingering evening chill. I looked around at the casual interactions of the Wilde family, hoping it was the first of many to come. Felix and I would have to find a way to stay close to these wonderful people despite the distance between our homes.

"You're thinking awfully hard over there," Felix said softly beside me.

"You have a wonderful family, Fee. I just hope I can offer you enough to make it worth moving so far away from them," I admitted. "I see now why you never really left."

He looked around at his family and took his time answering.

"No. I never really left because I was scared. I grew up thinking the media would take advantage of me. I thought there was nothing redeeming about them."

"I can definitely understand why you thought that," I said gently. I wasn't sure if he knew Grandpa Wilde had told me the story of how he came to leave his mom.

"But I'm beginning to see it a little differently now, Lio," he said, looking up at me in the firelight. The golden tones danced with shadows on his face, and it made my heart thump in a goofy rhythm. "When I saw you on television, I thought about how you were using the power of the press to control your story. To take charge of your public perception and make sure the people who matter, the people of Liorland who count on you, know the real you. They can see you speaking on that screen and know your truth. That's powerful, Lio. And I never realized that part of it before."

I tightened the arm I held around his shoulders and squeezed him tighter to me. "I'm starting to realize that also, baby. It's up to us to control the narrative. So much of leadership these days is setting a good example and a good tone for the country. Lead by example. It will make all the difference if the people can hear it directly from me."

"Did I tell you how proud I am of you, Lio?" His eyes shined in the light from the bonfire.

"You did. But without you, I would have still been trying to stick to my stupid plan of being something other than myself."

He leaned in for a kiss, the lightest brush of lips against mine before there were catcalls again.

"*Get a room!*" The shout permeated the night.

"*Get the video camera!*"

"Get used to it," Felix shouted back with a laugh.

Everyone was having a good time until I noticed Grandpa Wilde straighten up and reach for Doc's hand. One by one, everyone seemed to stop laughing and turn toward the house. It wasn't until Felix went completely stiff in my arms that I turned to see what it was.

The infamous Jacqueline Wilde.

I didn't even realize I'd attempted to turn Felix into my chest until I felt him resist me.

"It's okay, Lio," he said quietly. "She's my mother."

Doc spoke up. "Felix, why don't you take Lio and—"

"It's fine, Doc," Felix said with determination.

"But she might tip off the press about Lio being here," he warned.

I could see the blood drain from Felix's face. "Oh shit," he said, glancing up at me. "He's right, go back to my place. Otto can show you how to get there in the dark."

Otto moved around to lead me off, but I stayed where I was. "I'm not hiding anymore where Felix is concerned. If Jackie chooses to make a big thing of it, Felix and I will deal with it. Together."

Felix began to shake his head in disagreement, but I stopped him with both hands on his shoulders.

"Look at me. We are together now. Please don't send me away because you think you know what's best for me. What's best for me is being with you. Do you understand that? I want to *be with you*. That starts now."

"Fine. Don't say I didn't warn you," he muttered, pulling me toward the farmhouse.

I sensed my bodyguard, Marco, follow us at a distance. Jon had stayed behind in Monaco to celebrate the arrival of his brother's new baby.

When we met up with Jackie on the path, I recognized Felix's warm brown eyes in her face right away.

"Jackie, what are you doing here?" Felix's voice was sunshine over steel. I hadn't realized he called her by her first name.

"Felix, sweetheart! There you are. Let me have a look at you." She cooed over him like he was a little boy in his first church suit. "Don't you look well! And who is this now? Aren't you a handsome one. You look familiar. Have we met before? You have to excuse my memory, it's just that I know so many people."

"No ma'am, we've never met before," I said, feeling Felix shift closer to me.

"Jackie, this is…" He stopped and looked up at me like he had no idea how to introduce me.

"Lior," I said.

"Lior… that's unusual. Are you a friend of Felix's?"

"You could say that," I said with a smile. "I'm his boyfriend."

Felix's jaw dropped at my casual admission of our relationship. I turned to him with a grin. "What? Aren't I? Or are you dumping me so soon?"

"Dude," he mumbled. "Don't be a smartass."

"Felix, that's no way to speak to your young man here," Jackie scolded. "Lior, where do you live? Here in Hobie? You don't seem like a small-town Texan."

She seemed to be eyeing my clothes as if judging from the wrinkled button-down and ripped blue jeans I had on. Part of me wished I'd been wearing the Hermès yachting clothes I'd been given after attending a regatta last summer.

"I live in Monte Carlo, ma'am."

Her eyes grew hungry. "Is that right? And what do you do there?"

"I work for the government."

I wasn't sure if Felix snickered or rolled his eyes, but anything to keep him from being stressed was a bonus as far as I was concerned.

"What do you need, Jackie?" Felix asked.

"Well, I came by to see how you were doing, darling. We haven't seen each other for so long, and I wanted to find out what you've been up to. I didn't even know you had a boyfriend. How did you two meet?"

I knew neither one of us was going to tell her the truth and risk her getting a personal story she could use in the media.

"Strip club," I said at the same time Felix said, "Rodeo."

I heard a bark of laughter behind us and turned to see Doc and Grandpa approaching.

"It was a naked rodeo, Jackie," Grandpa Wilde said. "Texas has gotten more risqué since you lived here."

"Dad, Pop," she said, stepping forward to give them each a brief kiss on the cheek.

"I guess you'd better come on in, then," Doc said. "There's at least some banana pudding left over from dinner. I know you used to like Pop's banana pudding back in the day."

Jackie looked at Grandpa Wilde with something close to a wistful smile. "Still do, I'm sure."

Once we were all settled in the kitchen with thick bowls full of the soft dessert, Doc got right to the point.

"So what brings you out to this old place, Jackie?"

"I wanted to talk to Felix about something." She turned to her son with exaggerated puppy eyes, and I couldn't help but notice the sliver of hope that entered his expression at the idea his mother wanted something to do with him. "My fiancé's daughter is trying to get into the arts school at UT, and I'd like you to write a letter of recommendation for her. Will you do that, sweetheart?"

The hope disappeared in a puff of smoke, leaving Felix's beautiful brown eyes sad and resigned. I'd never wanted to kill someone the way I wanted to murder my lover's mother right then. How dare she.

Before I could butt in and demand she leave the premises, Felix spoke up.

"Do I know her?"

"No, of course not. She lives in California," Jackie said, missing his point.

"Then how the hell do you expect me to recommend her? I don't even know her qualifications, or *her name.*"

"I need you to do this for me, darling," she pleaded in a grating tone. "Chris really wants her to get out of California and go to school somewhere more... family-oriented."

Felix snorted. "UT is home to fifty thousand college students living in the most liberal population in all of Texas. If he wants her to move somewhere more conservative than California, he picked the wrong place."

She sighed. "He hears the word Texas and assumes it means good old boys. But Chris isn't the only one begging me for your help. Chelsea really wants to go there, and it will take some pull to make it happen. Please do this for me, Felix. You owe me."

I noticed Grandpa's face get dangerously red, to the point Doc reached over and placed his hand on the back of Grandpa's neck to calm him. They exchanged a look but didn't open their mouths.

Hell, if they weren't going to stand up and put a stop to this, then I was.

"Like hell he does," I snarled.

# CHAPTER 44

FELIX

I reached for Lio's balled fist while swallowing back a laugh. Seeing him go into protective mode made me feel lighter than air.

"He's right. I don't owe you anything, but I'm willing to give the young woman a chance if she wants to come meet me and tell me why UT is the right place for her."

"I can't ask her to come to Hobie, Texas, just to have a chat with you about this. Why are you making this difficult, Felix? It's just a simple recommendation for god's sake," my mother scoffed.

I shrugged. "If she doesn't want it badly enough, that tells me all I need to know. But just be aware that I'm good friends with the head of the fine arts department, the art history department, and every professor that young woman would dream of working with."

Jackie rolled her eyes as if she was disappointed in me but not at all surprised I was being belligerent. "Fine," she said. "I'll let her know. I have to run though. Chris is waiting for me at the hotel."

She bolted out of there with barely another breath taken. When she was gone, everyone stood around staring at the door.

"Typical," Doc muttered and turned into Grandpa's arms. Grandpa hugged him tightly and kissed the side of his head.

"Sweetheart, stop blaming yourself for another adult's behavior,"

Grandpa said quietly into Doc's hair.

"How do you know I'm blaming myself?" Doc grumbled into Grandpa's neck.

"I've known you for a thousand years, babe," he murmured. "And you've always blamed yourself for Jackie's selfish behavior."

"If she hadn't lost her mother so young. If I hadn't—"

"Stop," Grandpa warned. "Or I'm going to get upset, and the next thing I know, you'll be whipping out the blood pressure cuff."

"What would you rather me whip out, old man?" Doc teased.

"Oh hell no," a voice growled from the back door. This time it was Saint shuddering with fake revulsion over accidentally hearing Doc's sexual innuendo. The rest of the family followed him into the room, chattering at top volume.

While I watched my grandfathers flirt and my cousins gripe about it, Lio put his arm around me and asked if I was all right.

"Yes," I admitted, turning to him with a smile. "So fucking all right, I can't stand it. Thank you for being here. And thank you for standing up for me."

Standing there in the heart of the old farmhouse with all my family there and Lio's strong arm around me, I felt like my life, my *real* life, was finally beginning.

And it was going to be amazing.

THE FOLLOWING MORNING, however, the amazing feeling wore off as quickly as it had come. My mother showed back up at the ranch after breakfast and brought company this time.

"Felix, this is my fiancé, Chris Corbin. Chris, this is my son, Felix Wilde," she said in her perfect Hollywood way.

"Nice to meet you, Felix," Chris said with a nod. I held out a hand to shake but he ignored it. If I hadn't felt Lio stiffen beside me, I would have thought it was an oversight rather than a slight.

Jackass piece of shit.

"And this is Felix's friend, the one I told you about," Jackie said in an overly cheerful voice. She turned to me with sparkling eyes. "You didn't tell me you were dating *the king of Liorland!*"

My heart sank and I felt my cheeks ignite with embarrassment. I knew that look. It was the same look a hungry lion gave a weak gazelle before culling it from the herd.

Chris beamed at Lio and thrust out his hand for a shake. "Chris Corbin. It's nice to meet you…"

"Your Majesty," Lio supplied, unable to help himself.

I stifled a laugh before cutting in.

"He goes by Lior, even though he's right. 'Your Majesty' is, in fact, the correct way to greet him in polite company," I said, enjoying the shocked look on my mother's face.

Her eyes widened before her smile did, and she did a slow pan from Lio to me and back again. "Chris tried to tell me you'd introduced me to the king, but I thought he must be joking. Surely this is some kind of prank, darling."

"On the contrary," Lio corrected with more false manners. "It's no prank. I'm the real thing. Flesh and blood and whatnot. Royal Scout's honor," he said, holding up three fingers, making sure one of them held the ancient ring his grandfather had given him with the royal crest on it.

Then Lio turned to me. "Tell them, sweetheart. You managed to turn the king of Liorland gay. Your mother should be proud."

This time I really did laugh, startling the two people staring wide-eyed at Lio and me.

Chris must have put two and two together that he was standing in the company of actual *practicing gays*, because his eyes widened comically and he retracted his hand as if bitten.

"I see my reputation precedes me," Lio drawled. "Nice to know where we stand. I caught it from him, you know," he said idly, pointing his thumb at me before leaning toward Chris and stage-whispering. "It's filthy contagious. Like genital warts. But with much better aesthetics."

"Jackie," I asked my mother as calmly as I could. "What do you want?"

# CHAPTER 45

LIO

I knew they were there to ask another favor of Felix, and from the look on Jackie and Chris's faces, I was fairly sure I knew what it was.

Jackie seemed to become flustered for the first time since arriving. "Let's… let's go sit down and have a chat, shall we?"

Felix gestured for us to take a seat at the kitchen island before turning to his mother.

"Why are you here?" he asked again.

Jackie's eyes shifted nervously. "Aren't you going to offer us a drink, sweetheart?"

Her fake affection grated on me. Felix wasn't her sweetheart; he was mine.

"I'm afraid we're all out," I said. "Will water do?"

Felix's jaw tightened, but he let me flit about the kitchen in my arrogance and make four glasses of plain tap water.

"Et voilà," I said, setting them down on the counter with a flourish. "Sorry it's not fancier than this. I'm afraid I left the champagne in my other mausoleum, I mean, pants."

Felix sucked in a breath and shot me a wounded glance. Fuck. He hadn't known I knew the story after all. I palmed the back of his head and pressed my forehead to his.

"I'm sorry," I murmured. "Fee, I'm—"

"I understand what you're doing, Lio, but it's not helping," he said just as softly.

Jackie leaned over to Felix with a concerned brow and reached out a hand to cup his face, forcing me away. "What's wrong, darling? Is he upsetting you? Who is this man to you, exactly? Are you two really dating?"

I couldn't hold back the snort, but before I could snap a snarky response, Felix answered her. "Lio is my heart," he said simply. "That's all you need to know."

My heart seemed ready to explode out of my chest, but apparently I was the only one who thought Felix's words were amazing.

Chris seemed to make a gagging sound in his throat before turning away and helping himself to the Wildes' kitchen cabinet stock. There was no doubt in my mind he was looking for the hard liquor.

Jackie stood up to get a good look at me. Now that she knew Felix was really dating a royal, she seemed to be assessing my worth.

"Christ Almighty, you really are that new king, aren't you?"

"Indeed, I am," I said with a sniff. Arthur called it my annoying imperious tone. I didn't pull it out often, but when I did, I was able to channel a thousand years of royal ego and prestige.

"What are you doing with my son?" The question was asked with suspicion like I would only be with him to take advantage of him in some way.

"Whatever he will let me, madam. As long as we're both naked, I don't much care what we do—*oof*!"

Felix elbowed me in the gut.

"Cut that out and behave like a fucking adult," he chastised. "You can either pull the imperious king crap or act like a petty child, but trying to do both at once is pushing it."

This time, it was Doc's voice that spoke. "Oh, I don't know. I rather like seeing him do both at the same time. Keeps us entertained."

"Dad!" Jackie's exclamation came out before she could control it, and for a microsecond, I saw the young girl she must have been years ago. The one who loved her fathers and would have been happy to see them. But just that quickly, she was gone. Jaqueline Wilde the actress was in her place, smoothing her hair before sliding her manicured hand through Chris's arm. "I'd like you to meet Chris Corbin, my fiancé."

Chris reached out a hand reluctantly, and I couldn't help but lean forward to remind him of something. "Oh hells bells, there's another one. Told you—*contagious.*"

Chris's jaw tightened, but he ignored me and shook Doc's hand before reaching past him to shake Grandpa Wilde's as well.

But that was apparently as far as he was willing to take it.

"Jackie, dear, shall we get to the reason we're here?"

Felix's grandfathers busied themselves making coffee and pretending not to listen. Everyone in that room knew they were listening.

"Felix, Chris has an exciting offer for you and Lior. Tell them honey," Jackie said excitedly.

"My network has agreed to let me interview you two during a prime-time spot," Chris said, leaning forward like he was offering us the moon.

I blinked at him.

"And?" Felix asked.

"And what, Felix?" Jackie said testily. "He's offering you two a chance to tell your story. He wants to interview you on television!"

Felix looked at me in surprise. "Is she serious?"

"I believe so," I said with a smirk.

Chris interjected. "Listen, if it's flexibility on the date you need... or if you have certain demands of the setup..."

"Are you serious?" Felix asked him with a louder exasperation than before. "What in the world makes you think we'd want to be interviewed by a conservative talk show host on a bigoted network?"

Jackie sucked in a breath. "Felix! You will speak to Chris with respect!"

"Come here, baby," I said to Felix with a grin. "Come sit a little closer. I think we should consider it."

Felix looked at me like I was crazy before quickly catching on.

"But, Lio," he whined while moving over to perch on my lap. I couldn't miss the look of disgust on Chris's face. "I only want to do the interview if I can sit on your lap and snuggle you."

After dropping a kiss on his nose, I turned to Chris. "Surely Chris wouldn't mind a little PDA on camera. Would you?"

Chris cleared his throat but couldn't bring himself to respond.

I ran my hand up the side of Felix's neck and into his hair. "I love you."

Felix shifted until he was straddling me on the barstool. His arms were wrapped loosely around my neck, and his eyes were twinkling.

"I love you too."

We leaned toward each other and kissed slowly, taking our time to nip and tease before going in for the good stuff. By the time we pulled back, Doc and Grandpa were holding up scores scribbled on the back of envelopes.

"Perfect ten!" Doc cried. "Encore!"

Grandpa just giggled and waved the envelope around gaily.

Chris Corbin's face was purple, Jackie's was resigned, and Felix's was enraptured.

I turned to the talk show host. "If you think there isn't a network on this earth who wouldn't offer us the world for an exclusive sit-down interview with our choice of reporters," I explained calmly, "then you're mistaken."

Jackie sighed and looked at her fiancé. "I told you Felix doesn't like reporters."

Felix climbed down off my lap and kissed his mother's cheek.

"That's not it. I'm actually looking forward to Lio's and my first interview on television. I want the world to know how lucky I am that he's mine. But it's not going to be done with someone who can't stand the sight of us together. And the fact that you're tying yourself with someone like that for the rest of your life speaks volumes to how you feel about me. We're done here, Jackie. I won't let you claim me as your son anymore."

He gestured to Grandpa and Doc. "I'm *their* son, and have been for twenty years. Thank you for giving birth to me, Jackie. More than that, thank you for gifting me with the two best dads I could have ever asked for. But please understand that I'm done being Jacqueline Wilde's son. I thought maybe when you showed up here, you wanted to see me. But you just wanted to use me, yet again. It's about what's best for Jacqueline Wilde. Well, from now on, I'm all about what's best for me. And you're definitely not part of that."

Felix turned to Chris Corbin. "And you're so far from what's best for me, I can't even believe you're standing here. Do you have any idea how many gay people are at this ranch right now? There's the four of us and a good six or seven of my cousins still asleep in the bunkhouse out back. All gay. So unless you want to be associated with the queerest family in Texas, you should probably take this opportunity to skedaddle."

Jackie mumbled something about coming back another time when peoples' "dander" wasn't up. After she pulled her bigoted partner out of the house, I turned to Felix and lifted a brow.

"Skedaddle?"

The corner of Felix's mouth twitched up. "I'm from Texas, sugar lips. Get used to it."

"You keep talking like that, and you're fixing to rile me up right quick," I said with an exaggerated drawl.

Felix wrapped his arms around me and kissed me full on the mouth.

"Next time try not pronouncing the *g* sound at the end of those words, hotshot," he teased against my mouth. "Or I'll have to find one of Grandpa's old lassos and teach you a lesson."

# EPILOGUE

## FELIX - THE FOLLOWING DECEMBER

"I'm sitting here with King Lior and his partner, American stained glass artisan Felix Wilde," Valerie said into the camera.

We were sitting in the Great Room at Gadleigh in front of a blazing fire in the enormous stone fireplace. It was the closest we could come to recreating the feel of the treasury room without letting anyone into our most private sanctuary. Lio had been adamant that I feel comfortable for our first in-depth interview on camera.

"I'm going to stop you right there, Valerie," Lio interjected with a sheepish grin. "I believe instead of partner, you'll want to refer to him as king consort from now on."

Valerie froze for a moment before catching on.

"Sir, do you have some news for us?" she asked with an excited gleam in her eye. A royal scoop was quite a coup.

Lio looked at me. "Felix?"

"I thought we agreed on the term 'queen,'" I teased. Lio's face flushed with a laugh before he turned back to Valerie.

"He's joking. I married a jokester," Lio said.

"You're married!" Valerie exclaimed. "Tell us more. How? When? You married in secret?"

"In *private*," he corrected gently. "We were married here in the

Gadleigh chapel last Saturday, just before Christmas. It was the anniversary and location of our first meeting, so you can imagine it holds special memories for the two of us. I wanted our wedding to represent a promise I made to Felix from early on in our relationship." He gazed back at me with the love in his heart as clear as day all over his face.

Valerie prompted him. "And what was that?"

"He comes first. Felix is my heart. Being the king of Liorland is amazing and wonderful and important. It's a big part of who I am and what I do, but my relationship with Felix is too. It's all those things. And just because I am a king does not mean I owe the people of Liorland access to my most private moments. Marrying Felix was beautiful and special. I want the people to celebrate with us, which is why we will hold a formal gala when we return home. But the ceremony itself…" He looked over at me. "That was for us."

Valerie smiled sincerely and turned to me. "He's awfully romantic, isn't he?"

"He's just trying to embarrass me by making me cry like a baby in front of the whole world," I said.

"What do you have to say about marrying into royalty, King Consort Felix?"

I wrinkled my nose. "I'm not sure about that new title. Just Felix is fine for now. As for marrying into royalty… I'm not sure I think of it that way. I mean, of course there are many rules and traditions to learn. I've been up to my eyeballs this year in Grimaldi history, but really I think of it as marrying the love of my life. Who, oh by the way, happens to be a king."

"That's sweet. What's your favorite thing about King Lior?"

I turned and studied him for a moment. He took the opportunity to wink at me, which did stupid things to my stomach even after a year of being with him.

"His big, generous heart. His sense of humor. His love of family. The way he takes care of me. When he lets me win at chess. The way he looks when he—"

Lio cut in. "One, she said. One!"

We'd been holding hands during the entire interview, and I lifted them up to drop a kiss on the back of his with a grin.

"And what about you, Sir?" she asked Lio. "What do you love about your new husband?"

"Husband," he said slowly and deliberately. "I like the way that sounds. What do I like about my new *husband*... Well, when he gets particularly angry, this adorable Texas twang comes out."

"Oh my gosh, stop," I said with a laugh. "That's unfair."

"And he's carrying on a family tradition by making the most beautiful stained glass. Have you seen his work?"

I felt my face ignite as Valerie nodded and gushed over a small show I'd had recently with some other artisans in Monte Carlo.

"And he laughs at all my jokes, which is unusual and a little crazy. But I guess I'd have to say what I love about him the most is his bravery."

Valerie's head tilted in question. "Tell us what you mean by bravery."

"He's been hounded by the paparazzi off and on his whole life, and yet he's still willing to be with someone whose very identity requires constant press attention. Instead of running away or chickening out when I asked him to drop everything and come be with me, he walked into this life with the utmost bravery. I'm in awe of his strength and grace. Whenever I wobble in my own convictions, I just have to look at my best friend to see the best example of constancy, love, and devotion."

Dammit. Now he really was going to make me cry.

"That's right," Valerie continued. "Your mother is Jacqueline Wilde, the actress."

I cut her off. "No. I was raised by my grandfathers in Texas. I don't have a relationship with Jacqueline Wilde."

She blinked at me and got the message.

"All right. Moving on, then... There's been plenty of speculation about the two of you making it official. Some of the concerns with a same-sex royal couple are, of course, related to the succession of the monarchy. Do you have an idea whether or not you'd like to start a family? Would you consider non-blood-related children to be eligible for the throne?"

Lio and I had prepared for many of the questions we expected her to ask once we made our announcement. He squeezed my hand before answering.

"Felix and I would love to consider having children one day, but we are both still young. In the meantime, my sister and her husband announced a couple of months ago they're expecting twins. I would love to see one of Henriette's children in line for the throne, especially if I'm around to show them all the tricks of the trade before then. In the meantime, according to Hen, the babies are actively competing to see who gets to come into the world first."

Valerie chuckled before turning to face the camera. "We're going to take a short break, but we'll be back with more questions for King Lior and King Consort Felix here at Gadleigh Castle. In the meantime, I hope to convince them to share a snapshot from their wedding day. Stay tuned."

When the cameras were off, Valerie and the crew scrambled to congratulate us on our big news before setting up for the next segment.

Lio turned and nuzzled into my neck before whispering in my ear. "Tell me something, anything, to get the image of you across that end table last night out of my mind. All I could see when I looked past Valerie during that segment was your gorgeous—"

"Zzzt!" I blurted before he could continue that description. "You're wearing a microphone, dumbass."

My face felt like it was on fire. The night before, he'd rimmed the hell out of me while I lay bent over that table begging for it. He'd said all kinds of dirty things about my ass when he was licking and sucking it, and now I wasn't going to be able to get the memory out of my head either. Bastard.

His deep, warm laughter vibrated through his chest where it leaned against my side. "I took the microphone off, baby. Even unplugged yours from the battery pack too. I've heard too many horror stories to get fooled by a hot mic."

At least my heart rate could come down from the stratosphere.

"Regardless, please save it for later. Now I'm not going to be able to think of anything else for the rest of the day," I grumbled.

"Good," he said with evil eyes. "Then you'll be primed and ready for what I have planned later, dear husband."

I couldn't help but shudder from the top of my head down to the tips of my toes.

I wanted it to be later right now.

# EPILOGUE CONTINUED

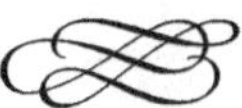

## LIO

Later that night, after stuffing his bright pink hat on his head, I blind-folded Felix and led him out to the dovecote. Arthur had helped me get everything ready for the surprise even though he'd griped the entire time about always being the bridesmaid and never the bride.

Thankfully, this time I'd thought to have our royal guard plan ahead and set up a small security van nearby so they could keep an eye on the dovecote from the comfort of a heated vehicle. The other benefit to the plan was soundproofing. They wouldn't be able to hear us from inside the van. Not that we had much privacy left from our personal guards... but still.

Once we approached the dovecote and stepped over the threshold, I pulled off his blindfold.

"Oh my god," he breathed. "Oh my god."

The entire circular space was filled with candles. A fire blazed in the large stone fireplace at one end, and a four-poster bed stood right in front of it, made with the finest royal linens from the castle. To one side was a picnic table covered in white cloth and laid out with all sorts of Felix's favorite treats.

He turned to me and hopped into my arms, squeezing me around the neck with his arms and around the waist with his legs.

"How did you do this? Please tell me you didn't send Bert off to set it up with a team of under gardeners."

"I beg your pardon," I said with a sniff. "I'll have you know I carried the pillows."

Felix laughed, the best sound in the entire world. As long as Felix Wilde—Felix Grimaldi—was laughing, all was right in my world.

"Thank you for doing this, Lio," he said with a shy smile. "You didn't have to. I would have been just as happy in our room in the house."

Ever since he'd moved in with me, he hadn't been able to admit to living in a palace or a castle. It was cute as hell. Every time he tried to refer to our home in Monaco, he called it the house. And when he referred to Gadleigh, he called it the Gadleigh… house.

"Have our royal residences become so commonplace to you now that you just see them as any old house now?"

Felix's eyes sparked at me as he immediately began undressing where he stood. "This is my real-life fairy tale, and I'm afraid it will all end at midnight. So quit teasing me and get naked. *Husband.*"

The word started my engine, and I nudged him toward the large chair I'd had placed by the fire. His pants were still on, but he was naked from the waist up.

"As you wish, *husband*. But just so you know, it's going to last way past midnight."

"Prove it, big talker," Felix teased. His bare skin was glowing golden in the candle and firelight. I couldn't resist taking in my fill of the view for a beat.

"I got you something," I murmured, reaching around for the wooden box I'd stashed there earlier.

Felix's eyes lit up. "What is it?"

He pulled the lid open to find the colorful hourglass nestled inside. His eyes flashed up to mine. "It's gorgeous!"

I pointed out the stained glass ornamentation along the delicate wooden frame of the hourglass.

"Calum made it to my specifications," I explained. "It is actually calibrated to take an hour to empty and the most important part is what's inside. Gadleigh sand."

Felix's eyes shimmered in the firelight. "Oh my god, Lio. You have no idea how much this means to me. That's magical sand for glassmakers."

"I know, baby. And it's yours. You are now listed as the official royal resident of Gadleigh. That means you're in charge of it as much as you want to be. Obviously your assistant or Mari and Bert can handle anything you don't want to bother with, but to the extent you want to have a say in the glassworks or the property itself, consider it yours."

He stared at the hourglass and then up at me again. "But Gadleigh's your favorite."

I felt light and joyful in a way I never had before meeting Felix Wilde.

"No. You're my favorite. Wherever you are is my favorite. And the fact that Gadleigh's history means so much to you, means a lot to me. I can't wait to make more memories here with you. You taught me that Gadleigh glass is special because of the sand. Likewise, I feel like my life is now going to shine because of you."

After carefully setting the hourglass down and flipping it over, he reached for my face to kiss me thoroughly.

"You ready to start making those memories now?" Felix's tease came through in the twinkle of his eyes.

"Huh?" I asked, dazed from the scorching kiss. I remembered what I wanted to do to him and quickly fumbled my fingers at his waist until his pants were open and his breathing hitched.

"What are you doing to me?" Felix's groan was husky and sexy as hell.

"King things," I murmured, dropping a kiss on the tip of his exposed cock.

"Yeah, suc*king*," he joked with a shaky breath as I moved back up to kiss him on the lips.

"Mm, lovema*king*," I said with a nibble to his earlobe.

He moaned. "Too much tal*king*." I could see the light of humor in

Felix's eyes and was secretly thrilled I had the privilege of loving that beautiful, sweet man for the rest of my life.

Seeing him laid out in front of the fire and hard for me was making my head spin. I wanted to make him fly.

"*Your Highness?*" Felix studied me as I stood there staring at him. He loved whipping out the honorific every now and then. He knew it sent all my blood rushing south.

I locked eyes with him and slowly, deliberately, knelt at his feet.

Felix's face softened and he brought his hand up to cup my cheek. "My king," he whispered.

I closed my eyes, leaning into his warm touch.

"And you're mine."

UP NEXT IN the Forever Wilde series: Sheriff Seth Walker and Hobie firefighter Otto Wilde burn up the pages in the childhood friends-to-lovers (turned enemies-to-lovers) story *Wilde Fire*!

# LETTER FROM LUCY

Dear Reader,

Thank you so much for reading *Felix and the Prince*, the second book in the Forever Wilde series!

There will be more Wilde tales to come, so please stay tuned. Up next will be Otto's story as he comes home from the Navy and joins the Hobie firefighting team where he runs into his childhood best friend, Walker, the new sheriff in town. *Wilde Fire* is available now.

Be sure to follow me on Amazon to be notified of new releases, and look for me on Facebook for sneak peeks of upcoming stories.

Please take a moment to write a review of *Felix and the Prince* on Amazon and Goodreads. Reviews can make all the difference in helping a book show up in Amazon searches.

Feel free to sign up for my newsletter, stop by www.LucyLennox.com or visit me on social media to stay in touch. We have a super fun reader group on Facebook that can be found here:

https://www.facebook.com/groups/lucyslair/

To see fun inspiration photos for all of my novels, visit my Pinterest boards.

Finally, all Lucy Lennox titles are available on audio within a month of release and are narrated by the fabulous Michael Pauley.

Happy reading!
Lucy

# ABOUT LUCY LENNOX

Lucy Lennox is the creator of the bestselling Made Marian series, the Forever Wilde series, and co-creator of the Twist of Fate Series with Sloane Kennedy and the After Oscar series with Molly Maddox. Born and raised in the southeast, she is finally putting good use to that English Lit degree.

Lucy enjoys naps, pizza, and procrastinating. She is married to someone who is better at math than romance but who makes her laugh every single day and is the best dancer in the history of ever.

She stays up way too late each night reading M/M romance because that stuff is impossible to put down.

For more information and to stay updated about future releases, please sign up for Lucy's author newsletter on her website.

*Connect with Lucy on social media:*
www.LucyLennox.com
Lucy@LucyLennox.com